Window on
the World

Window on the World

HUGH CORNWELL

QUARTET BOOKS

First published in 2011 by
Quartet Books Limited
A member of the Namara Group
27 Goodge Street, London W1T 2LD

A catalogue record for this book
is available from the British Library

ISBN 978 0 7043 7230 6

Typeset by Antony Gray
Printed and bound in Great Britain by
T J International Ltd, Padstow, Cornwall

I would like to dedicate this book
to the memory of my father
Victor John.

I would like to thank Lola, Antonio, Isabelle, Antonia, Monica and Uncle Antonio at Pajaro Verde, without whose support and excellent cuisine this book would not have been written. Also thanks to all at Chattai in India, especially Charlie de Silva who was there at the beginning.

Preface

You have been given no particular function.
You may give your life whatever form you choose, do whatsoever
you wish.
All other things and creatures are constrained by My laws
But you have no limitations, and can act in accord of your own
free will.
You alone can choose the limits of your nature.
You have been placed at the centre of the world more easily to
observe what is in it.
You have been made neither of heaven nor of earth, neither
mortal nor immortal, so that with freedom of choice and honour,
you can make yourself into whatever you wish.

Pico della Mirandola, *Oration on the Dignity of Man*

Chapter 1

I finally found a word my father didn't know the meaning of. Ever since I can remember, even when we were living in Italy, he'd tried to intimidate me by finding one I didn't know.

'Surely not? You don't know what 'invidious' means? Then look it up in the dictionary. That's what it's there for!' he used to say, making me feel terribly small and ignorant.

At the time I suppose he saw it as a way of increasing my vocabulary but as time passed it had turned into a little sparring match between us, providing him with a bit of fun at my expense whenever I saw him. I tried to pop in and see him as often as I could after my mother died since I had the feeling I was the only person he was having contact with from the outside world. He had refused to move out of the house when she passed away, and pottered around within it incessantly, doing running repairs to the plumbing, the heating and the fabric of the house as it slowly gave up its will to carry on. The small garden at the back had become a jungle and he could hardly pick his way through it to gain access to his tool shed, where he did his running repairs. In fact, in my eyes the house had become an accident waiting to happen, but what can one do when faced with such obstinacy in a parent? I didn't mind his grouchiness and I tolerated his bad humour as I knew that's all he had left in his life. Of course, the inevitable caught up with him in the end. He had an accident and fell down the stairs one day. I had let myself in and found him there, sprawled in a heap in the hallway with the loose piece of stair carpet that had tripped him up lying next to him by way of explanation.

Once I thought I had him with 'ingenuous', but of course he

knew it already. It had done me some good, I suppose, in showing me how useful it was to investigate the roots of words. Most European languages derive from Latin, so making sense of them is easier if you know a bit, and I'd taken it at school in Italy. That's probably why I became so interested in Botany in the first place. As a child I used to love reading the Latin name for some plant, to try to decipher it and guess something about its nature. Combine this with my love of literature and I was bound to write about plants sooner or later.

You can imagine my relief when after all those years I caught him out. I wouldn't have been surprised if he'd come close, but he was way off-beam.

'What?' I said, 'You must know the meaning of 'defenestrate', No? Then look it up! That's what I bought you that Collins for last Christmas.'

He'd looked worried when I first mentioned the word and had struggled before hazarding a guess.

'It must be something to do with being unable to satisfy the requirements for some task, or emotional embodiment.'

'Not even close!' I said triumphantly. 'It means to throw someone, or something, out of a window. From the Latin *'de'* meaning 'out', and *'fenestra'* meaning 'window'.'

He begrudgingly reached for the dictionary and with quivering thumbs flicked through the pages until he'd found it. He closed the book, slowly replaced it on the kitchen table and stared sullenly into space. It was a complete victory for me and I might even describe it as 'pyrrhic'. I'd finally got him.

What's so interesting about 'defenestration' is that the word 'defence' comes from it. You'd have thought the aggressive act of throwing something out of a window would have no connection with defence, which I've always thought of as a reaction, rather than a starting point for something. But when you think about it, it seems logical. If you considered your world as a room, then ejecting a foreign body from it could be interpreted as an act of defence. All you'd be doing is maintaining and defending your space, restoring its equilibrium, and there's nothing wrong with that, now is there?

Even though on the face of it the word seems to be extremely specific in what it describes, the more I've thought about it, the more unspecific it becomes. For a start, there's no distinction between animate and inanimate objects. You could just as easily throw a television, or a person, out of a window and describe it as defenestration. Plus, I feel you should be able to tell whether a person jumped out of the window, or was pushed out by someone else. It would be crucial if you were investigating a death. After all, it would be the difference between murder and suicide. Taking this to the next logical step, shouldn't you be able to tell if the defenestration was fatal? And if the set of circumstances responsible for the death occurred before the defenestration, rather than afterwards, wouldn't that deserve a mention too?

It turns out in history Jezebel is the only person to have been murdered as a direct result of defenestration, and I've yet to hear of someone else.

So, you see, although 'defenestration' appears to describe a very specific action, under close scrutiny it doesn't tell us much about what really happens at all. I only wish I'd taken the trouble to explain all of this to Katherine when I'd had the chance.

Chapter 2

Jehu went with Jezreel. When Jezebel heard about it she painted her eyes, arranged her hair and looked out of the window. As Jehu entered the gate she asked him: 'Have you come in peace, Zimri, you murderer of your master?'

He looked up at the window and called out: 'Who is on my side? Who?'

Two or three eunuchs looked down.

'Throw her down!' Jehu said. So they threw her down, and some of her blood spattered the walls and the horses as they trampled her underfoot. 2 Kings 9:30–33

I could very easily have been given someone else's life instead of my own. You hear those stories about babies being mixed up at birth and ending up being given to the wrong parents at the hospital. It happens all the time and you'd be very unfortunate if you discovered it had happened to you. Or fortunate, depending upon what sort of life the alternative would have been. Well, it sort of happened to me. But in my case, circumstances led to my change in parents, not a random accident.

After my mother died, my father told me I'd been adopted. Apparently my real mother had given birth to me in Whittington Hospital, just off Highgate Hill near Archway. My real father had run off as soon as he'd found out she was pregnant, and left her there penniless in North London a few years after the Second World War ended. She'd worked for as long as she could, selling pots and pans door to door, and then retired exhausted to her bed in a room near the 'Suicide Bridge' on Archway Road. A neighbour had heard her screaming in labour during the night and had taken her in to Casualty at the hospital. She gave birth to me but became the sad casualty herself, leaving me as a newly born orphan. In those days there were plenty of adoptable children, following the heady days of post victory celebrations, and childless couples would quite literally camp-out in local hospitals, waiting to claim any luckless orphan or unwanted baby that appeared. The red tape was kept to a minimum as the country needed every possible addition to rebuild the tired, decimated population left after six years of war. My foster parents had given up the possibility of having any of their own children after years of trying. Apparently in those days it was quite conceivable to be married to someone you weren't sexually compatible with, for no apparent medical reason, and for the union to remain infertile. So, quite a considerable percentage of couples were resigned to living their lives without children, unless they had the chance to adopt. After months of calling in at the hospital on his way home from work as a lecturer in History of Art at Bedford College, my foster father finally heard the news he'd been hoping for. An orphaned boy had been delivered first thing that morning, and provided he and his wife could get the forms filled in correctly by noon the next day, they could adopt the child immediately.

Thus I grew up an only child, and experienced the total love of my two new parents, oblivious to the true nature of my origin. Anything I had need of they provided, if they could afford it. Then, in the late 1950s as Italy began to get back on its feet, amid changes of government as frequent as changes in the spring weather, my father applied for the post of Professor of Art History at Florence University, and the three of us upped and moved there. I was sent to an English School in Florence to continue my studies. My parents were keen for me to attend university in Britain, so I left for Bristol University to study Botany. It was there that I met my dear friend Miles Goodfellow, of whom you'll hear more later. He was studying History of Art and Philosophy, so when our paths crossed rooming next door to each other at a hall of residence, we had a common interest in

Art and I was able to tell him what my father did, which impressed him. Our friendship grew and Miles came and visited my parents with me several times, and we stayed in the beautiful villa that my parents were renting on the outskirts of Florence. It was surrounded by farmland and had a vast flat roof where we would sit and take the sun whilst my father was teaching and my mother would spend long periods confined to her bed.

The years passed, during which I continued to study Botany at Wye College in Kent, and my parents moved back to London in the late 1970s, due to my mother's declining health. Miles dropped out for the best part of a decade and travelled around the world, something he never grew tired of, and my mother's health continued to deteriorate. I tried my hand at writing, about plants of course, initially in journals, mainly to respond to questions I had that I couldn't find the answers to anywhere. In this way I began to carve out a little niche for myself in the world of publishing, and the growing sales of my books meant that I could afford to give up my post at Wye College and finally devote myself full time to writing.

When my mother passed away after years of struggling against her illness my father deemed the time was right to share their little secret with me. Years later, when the time came to clear out the house after my father's accident, I found my adoption papers in one of his dusty folders, but there was no mention of my real father's name on it. This was understandable, but it left me feeling unsubstantiated and I don't think I've ever really come to terms with it.

I was fortunate not to have a strong emotional tie to the house, as I hadn't lived there at all or grown up in it, although I did take pleasure in tidying up the garden when preparing it for sale. The house was at the end of a terrace, and at the front there was a small area bounded by a privet hedge my father had kept scrupulously trimmed. He'd planted a *magnolia grandiflora* in front of the bay window overlooking the street and this had grown well to produce many large white flowers every year that he was proud to show me when I visited. I found an old, rusty lawn mower in the shed and gave the small back lawn a rough cut, and I cut back a winter jasmine growing along a wooden fence. There was a wisteria in need of a good pruning that obviously hadn't flowered for many seasons, and several shrubs that needed freeing from weeds. All in all, there were the makings of a good town garden for a new owner to attend to, although sunken and rather poor in light, so when the house was sold I suffered no regrets and I suppose it helped me draw a line under our lives together.

Katherine told me she too had grown up an only child, in Australia on the outskirts of Sydney. She'd earned the nickname Katherine of Arrogant at her school, PLC Armidale, but holding herself aloof she hadn't taken any notice of the taunts. She'd been a day girl there and walked home for lunch every day, missing out on bonding with the other girls who boarded there, so she hadn't acquired any life-long friends. Apparently her father was a successful corporate lawyer and he'd persuaded her to apply for law school, but after a couple of years she realised she wasn't that interested in it, and dropped out to head for Europe. Her parents hoped she'd come to her senses and return home, but after wandering around the beaches of the Mediterranean for a few months she gravitated to Paris. She persuaded them to pay the high fees to enrol at the Parsons School of Fine Art & Design, and I managed to acquire several early works she'd painted when she was there.

The first is of a young woman – Katherine – riding a bicycle with square wheels. Several people pass her by in the street, paying no attention to her curious bike. The second is quite different and portrays Katherine, but this time she's in a room. On one of the walls is the mounted head of a wild boar and it has its teeth sunk into the back of her neck. I've always found it quite gruesome and disconcerting. The third is my favourite of the three. It's a painting within a painting, a self-portrait hanging in an art gallery, supposedly, as the frames of other works are visible around the edges. But it's as if the self-portrait and the room have exchanged identities, because everything is two-dimensional, except the portrait, which displays remarkable depth. I've always regarded it as one of her best works.

I was quite unaware of any of this when I met her at her debut London show. I'd got an invitation through the post from Miles, my old college friend, who'd become a dealer in London and had introduced me to the joys of collecting art. I'd only ever bought things occasionally, and not always from him. The first purchases were some Dali limited edition prints, but I soon moved on to original paintings. Miles had taught me to only go for things that I genuinely liked, rather than things I thought might make good investments.

Katherine was the new addition to his portfolio, the gallery was packed and it was clear the show was attracting a lot of interest. There were only seven works on display, all of them portraits, which was something completely out of fashion in the contemporary art world of London at the time, but each one was stunning. She'd managed to combine a sense of Renaissance portraiture with modern life. The poses reminded me of those adopted by the Italian masters, like Jacopo da Pontormo, Piero della Francesca and Agnolo Bronzino. I'd become terribly familiar with all of these artists, as my father had dragged me through the rooms of the Uffizi in Florence religiously every weekend when I was a boy. He'd frequently quiz me about the names and dates of the paintings and it all came rushing back to me as I stood there in the gallery. But the contexts in these paintings were totally new. Cars were visible through windows behind some of the subjects, and a TV was on a table in the background of another. Another depicted a fish tank in the foreground. What also struck me as being clever was that no painting was very large, again echoing back to those modest times in the fifteenth century. Overall, I found it completely overpowering. Just then Miles grabbed me by the arm.

'Great to see you, Jamie. Glad you could make it. I thought you'd find it interesting, what with your background. Come and meet the artist.'

He guided me past a couple of animated conversations towards a retiring figure trying to melt into a corner of the room. She was about five foot seven inches tall, of wispy stature and wearing flat shoes, which made her look like she'd just walked out of a ballet class. She was wearing a very elegant long dress, had green eyes and her angelic face was framed within a cascade of curly, light brown hair. I thought she was completely exquisite. Miles introduced us and disappeared into the crowd.

'Your work really is very good,' I told her, 'It's so unusual and refreshing.'

'Thank you. It's very nice of you to say,' she stuttered, 'actually it's all come as a bit of a surprise.'

'How come?' I asked.

'Well, I haven't been in London that long, and to get Miles who has such a good reputation, to represent me, and now a good reception to the work. It's all happened so fast. It's been a bit overwhelming to tell you the truth.'

'That's London for you. I recently met a French artist who's moved here from Paris. It just shows you how important London's becoming.'

'Absolutely. All the time I was studying I knew I had to come here. I knew I'd find something special.'

She told me how she'd ended up studying in Paris before Miles reappeared.

'My God! You two still gassing? Come on, Kath, I've got to drag you away for a moment and introduce you to a couple of bankers. They've shown interest in the one with the fish tank. Number 6, is it?'

He whisked her away and I was drenched in her perfume in the void she'd left behind.

I ended up buying one of the paintings and she was delighted but it seemed a bargain to me. People began to leave and suddenly Katherine, Miles, his wife Ann and I were alone in the gallery with the paintings, which had all been sold. Miles was ecstatic.

'Kath, what a success! Let's go out and celebrate. Ann's mum is baby-sitting, so we can stay up for a bit tonight.'

We waited while Miles locked up and jumped in a cab heading into Soho. He'd obviously noticed Katherine and I had hit it off, and sat us opposite one another at La Capannina's. We ordered a bottle of champagne, had some pasta, and got a bit tipsy. Miles put Katherine in a taxi on Shaftesbury Avenue before finding one for the rest of us to share.

'I get the distinct impression, my lad, that you've got your eyes on her,' Miles interrogated me in the back of the cab, and he nudged me in the ribs.

'Well, you could be on to something,' I mumbled, 'but she is rather special. You obviously thought so, or you wouldn't be representing her.'

'Of course, I knew it the moment she walked into the gallery. There's something really unusual about her, and her work. You'd better not distract her. I'm not letting this one escape in a hurry!'

A few days went by and the impression she'd made upon me completely overshadowed the fact that I'd bought one of the paintings. I was even having difficulty remembering which one it was. It had stirred up a lot of my childhood memories from Florence, and one night I dreamed I was back at the Uffizi with my father again. He was testing me on a painting by Andrea Mantegna, a portrait called 'Cardinal Carlo de Medici'. I had begun to dread the visits there at the weekends, but since my mother was becoming ill at the time, I had been fearful of doing anything that may cause him any further distress.

Early the following week I gave Miles a call. I knew I wouldn't be getting the painting until at least the end of the month when the show was due to finish, but I had no issue with that, I just wanted to see Katherine again.

'Hi, Miles. Shall I put a cheque in the post for the painting?'

'No sweat, mate. Cash flow is good at the moment. Wait till the show ends in a couple of weeks. By the way, did you see the piece on Kath in *Time Out*? Fantastic write up. She's just done an interview for the *The Sunday Times*. Do you want to get in touch with her?'

'Well, yes. I was going to mention it. Could you give her my number?'

'No need to. She's standing about ten feet away. Hold on, chum.'

I heard his footsteps echoing on the gallery floorboards and then some muffled voices as he persuaded her to take the phone.

'Hello?' she said.

'Katherine? Hi, it's me, Jamie – from the opening. How was the interview?'

'Oh, hi there. God, it's so difficult to talk about painting. I hope they got what they wanted.'

'I wondered if you'd like to meet up?' I suggested. 'We could get a bite to eat this week if you've got time.'

'I'd like that. How about lunch tomorrow?'

'Sure, suits me. Where's good for you?'

She wanted to meet at The Whistler Room, downstairs at Tate Britain on Millbank. Miles had taken me there several times and I liked the place. I felt comfortable surrounded by the verdant landscapes by Rex Whistler which were painted on the walls. I thought it was a good choice on her part as there was no reason to doubt that at some point in the future a painting or two of hers might be hanging in the rooms just above the restaurant. She ordered lightly and didn't finish either her starter or her main course, but I was ravenous.

'This is another surprise,' she began, and watched me as I continued eating.

'What do you mean?'

'Having lunch with you today.' But I didn't follow what she meant by this. She could see I looked confused. 'The first surprise was when you rang. I thought you weren't going to get in touch . . . I mean, a week had gone by.'

I was surprised by her frankness so I changed the subject.

'Have you been busy since the opening?'

'Very much so. I do like working with Miles. He's fun. He's having a brainstorm, lining up interviews for me. It's a bit bewildering to tell you the truth. I had no idea being an artist meant you spent so little time painting,' she smirked.

'That depends if you're a success or not,' I offered as an explanation between mouthfuls.

'Don't get me wrong,' she continued, 'I'm over the moon with the attention. I know it sounds like a cliché, but I really feel I'm doing something meaningful with my life for a change.'

'That's good to hear. There's no point doing something you don't enjoy. And you've got the added bonus that you're very talented. And beautiful. In fact, you're very lucky, all in all. Did you ever paint when you were growing up?'

'No, I never got round to it. But I've always been interested in art. I fantasised I might work in a museum or an art gallery one day, when I was at school in Sydney. But you know what happens to childhood daydreams. Have you known Miles long?'

I recounted how I'd met Miles at Bristol and she told me about growing up in Australia, about her parents, and what she thought of Paris. I explained why her paintings had made such an impression upon me and my earlier life in Italy with my father. She was sorry to hear I had become an orphan twice in my life and we found solace in the fact that we were both only children. She told me she painted at her flat in Olympia, as studio space in London was so expensive. I imagined the TV and the fish tank from her paintings would be there, and you'd be able to see the cars she'd depicted in the street through her windows.

We had dinner several times over the next couple of weeks and went to see a film in the West End. Requests for interviews with her were cutting into her painting schedule, but with such interest being generated Miles didn't seem worried, since building her reputation was at the top of his agenda. It was definitely having an effect, as we were in a restaurant one day when a fellow diner came over to our table and asked her for her autograph. She could hardly believe it, but I could see she had enjoyed being recognised. *The Sunday Times* piece came out and reproduced three works from the show. I was pleased because one of them was the painting I'd bought and it meant I'd already made a small profit from the purchase, as her work was going up in value and the publicity was adding to the provenance of the painting.

About a month later I was in Paris arranging the French trans-lation of my latest book about cultivating hydrangeas, as they'd become a fashionable plant for the variable climate found in France. It had sold well in the UK, as well as in Australia and South Africa. Fortuitously, my book had coincided with the increased popularity of the plant and I was looking forward to getting the book out in other territories, including America. One of my earlier books about using cacti in gardens had done exceptionally well in the States, so I was confident this one would do well there too.

One morning I was walking back to my hotel from the

publishers, when by chance I stumbled upon the Parsons School of Art in Rue Letellier, where Katherine had told me she'd studied. It was one of those occurrences we end up accepting as strange quirks of fate. When I realised where I was, I paused for a few seconds in front and found myself wandering in through the large metal doors. I imagined Katherine treading on that same concrete floor less than a year before. The place had that young, exuberant atmosphere you find in places of learning and I started to think about the Student Union at Bristol University where I'd studied for my degree in Botany.

Stepping back outside into the morning sunshine, I continued back to my hotel filled with melancholy. I passed a brasserie with an enticing smell coming from the front door and began to feel hungry and went inside. It was busy, which is always a good sign, and I located an empty table and sat down. The Plat de Jour was the customary Steak Frites, which I ordered with a glass of the house red. I don't normally drink at lunchtime but I had an easy afternoon looking through some of the proofs I'd picked up from the publishers, and I wanted to try to revisit some of the memories uncovered earlier about my time at Bristol. The Steak Frites tasted excellent, the wine had done the trick and my eyes were wandering around the room taking in the appearances of the other diners while I waited for a coffee. I was musing generally when something caught my eye on the wall. It was a painting of what looked like Katherine riding a bicycle with square wheels. She was managing to stay upright whilst clearly not moving, and in the background several people were passing by oblivious to her. I continued to study the painting and when the patron brought my coffee over I asked him about it.

'Oh, that. I bought it from a penniless student a couple of years ago,' he said. 'The girl on the bike, she used to come in here a lot to eat or for a drink, by herself. Nice enough. Very pretty, she was, and foreign. American, I think. She needed money and I thought, why not? A lot of customers ask me about it. Go and take a closer look if you want.'

As I got closer to the painting I could see it was definitely one of Katherine's. Being familiar with her later work I could see the connection. It must have been one of her first paintings and her style was obviously at an embryonic stage. A sudden impulse took hold of me and I went over to the counter and got the patron's attention.

'You wouldn't be interested in selling it, would you?' I asked him, trying not to sound too excited.

'That depends, my friend. How much are you talking about?' he said, with a look suggesting he knew he had the upper hand.

'Name your price,' I said, courageously.

He raised his eyebrows, scratched his chin craftily, and thought for a few seconds.

'Five hundred euros?' he posited.

'That sounds fine,' I accepted, and we shook hands on it.

'Cash, of course,' he added.

He started to look very pleased with himself, and I felt the same. He'd obviously paid Katherine very little for it, perhaps fifty or seventy-five euros plus the price of a meal, so he'd made a killing. I counted out the money and he carefully took the canvas down and asked one of the waiters to get him some newspaper to wrap it up. He went to great trouble tying it securely with some string that he found in the kitchen. A few minutes later I was walking back to my hotel, carrying one of Katherine's first works, picked up for next to nothing. I could hardly contain laughter at my good fortune.

Back in my room I realised I'd created a potentially awkward situation for myself. When I got back to London should I tell Katherine I'd found it? If I did she may take it the wrong way. This painting was very much from her past life in Paris which she might want to dissociate from her new life and success in London. She may also feel embarrassed that I'd discovered about her earlier, penniless state, and that she'd resorted to selling her inferior work to the owner of a brasserie for the price of a meal. But this was hardly a fault. Hadn't Toulouse-Lautrec left drawings on the tablecloth to pay for his supper a century and a half before? And what about Picasso? He'd done the same. But something inside told me it could upset the friendship growing between us. Katherine may feel compromised that I had information that she hadn't volunteered, and this worried me.

Rightly or wrongly, I decided to keep it to myself. I couldn't even risk telling Miles what had happened in case it got back to her. I would also have to be careful about displaying the painting as I could hardly hang it up in my living room for her to discover when she visited me. It was something that was bound to happen in the future if we continued to see one another. I unwrapped it in my hotel room and realised it wasn't even properly framed. I couldn't risk taking it to professional framers in London, in case somebody there recognised her from all the recent publicity she'd had. I picked up the Paris *Yellow Pages* from the bedside table and dialled a few numbers. I spoke to a man who could get it done for me for collection the next day, which luckily was my day of departure, so I jumped in a cab with the canvas and dropped it off that afternoon.

In bed that night, I began to discover that all this subterfuge my panic had induced, however illogical and unnecessary it might turn out to be, was a source of excitement, and I fantasised about seeking out other early works of Katherine's, maybe in other brasseries in the same area of Paris, before I finally dropped off to sleep.

Chapter 3

The First Defenestration of Prague involved the killing of seven members of the city council by a crowd of radical Czech Hussites on July 30, 1419. Jan Zelivsky, a Hussite priest, led his congregation on a procession through the streets of Prague to the Town Hall. The town council had refused to exchange their Hussite prisoners, and an anti-Hussite threw a rock at a protester. Enraged, the crowd stormed the town hall and threw the council members from the windows onto the spears of the armed congregation below.

Katherine began to paint in earnest but we did manage to meet up at least once a week. Miles wanted to compound her success with a show at the Frieze Art Fair later that year, which meant she had over six months to prepare enough work for it. We'd meet for dinner and occasionally go to see a film, and at the weekends I introduced her to the Parks of London. We started with the obvious ones, Hyde Park, Holland Park & Regent's Park, then I showed her Hampstead Heath in the north and Victoria Park in the east. Spring was upon us, and it became an adventure to discover the different plants coming into bloom. She was impressed with what she called my 'vast botanic knowledge' and would point to some flower and be delighted that I could tell her what it was and where it came from.

I'd hung the 'bike' painting up next to the one I'd bought from Miles' show so I was reluctant to invite her over. She never invited me to her place but I didn't mind that as I knew she was working on the new pictures there. Although I was keen to see them, the fact I hadn't invited her to visit me kept a sort of symmetry to the situation. I hadn't made any advance towards her but I had the feeling I was falling in love. It felt as if we were two oppositely charged magnets, and the closer we got to one another, the stronger the attraction became.

I was called to the publishers in Paris to look at the rest of the corrected hydrangea proofs and went to lunch back at the brasserie again. The patron greeted me like an old friend and tried to interest me in two other awful paintings he'd acquired since I'd last been there. I made a show of being interested but didn't buy anything and ordered another Steak Frite. Afterwards I found myself meandering towards the Parsons School of Art.

On one of our dates Katherine had told me she'd had a fling with a fellow student whilst she'd been there and had given him a painting as a birthday present. My ears pricked up at the mention of another early work and I casually asked her what the subject matter was. She dismissed it saying it was boring and immature, but I did find out that the boy was younger than her. She'd said his name was Didier, with rich parents in the French wine trade, but it had fizzled out because she'd found him too juvenile. I thought it was worth visiting the school again to see if I could track him down, and perhaps get to see this other painting.

When I arrived at the school it was busier than the first time. It was the end of the spring term and exam results had just been posted up. Groups of students were sitting around on the floor discussing their results and several others were looking at a list pinned on a noticeboard. When they moved away I had a look for myself and found the name Didier Malherbes was listed. He'd passed, but without distinction and I assumed his life didn't depend upon it if he was from a wealthy wine family, so my sympathy wasn't high for him. Then my eyes moved to another part of the noticeboard, to a hand drawn poster declaring an end of term party that evening at Didier's apartment, and it was an open invitation to the whole school. I recognised the address as being in an expensive part of Paris and guessed Didier had taken over his parents home to throw it, either that or they'd furnished him with his own bachelor pad whilst he was studying at the college.

I was tempted to go to the party. With any luck it would be well attended, and easy to get in as the front door to the street might very well be open. I could take a bottle of wine with me and try to dress inconspicuously. In all probability Didier would be well connected and have friends who weren't students, so there'd be every possibility I could blend in with them. If I got in I could snoop around and see if Katherine's painting was hanging up somewhere and I was intrigued to know what the subject matter could be. Maybe it was a portrait of Didier, or perhaps it was another self-portrait? I decided to go, but to turn up late. The guests would probably all be drunk by then so I thought it may be easier to drift in unnoticed. I began to look forward to it, and I remember I put on an unkempt linen jacket, some denims and a black T-shirt to finish off my outfit. There was a wine shop close by the hotel, so I bought a bottle of Chateauneuf du Pape, and flagged down a passing taxi.

The cab dropped me off outside a large, expensive looking apartment block. There was loud music blaring down the ivy-covered walls from a couple of open windows high above, and although the front door was closed it was immediately buzzed open when I pressed the button labelled 'Malherbes'. There was a well-polished, ornate, brass-grilled lift at the base of the stairwell, but I decided to walk up as I wasn't sure which floor the party was on. As I climbed up the marble stairs the music got louder and on the top floor there were a few student types squatting down and leaning on the corridor walls, smoking a joint. I recognised one pretty girl from the college. The door to the apartment was wide open and I walked in nonchalantly, as if I knew exactly where I was going. I turned left to find myself staring at a broom cupboard, but the party was in full-swing and nobody seemed to notice. Then I was lunged in the back and turned round to be apologised to by a sniggering student who staggered away arm in arm with his Goth girlfriend. After negotiating my way along a crowded corridor to the kitchen I found a corkscrew on a table. I'd just poured a glass from my bottle of wine when it was spotted by a short, drunk, red-headed woman in a stripy blue dress who had materialised in the kitchen doorway. She grabbed the bottle off the table.

'Formidable! Chateauneuf! Merci, monsieur. Tres galant!' she shouted, and disappeared with it down the corridor.

It was relatively easy to make my way through the apartment checking to see what was on the walls, but after about fifteen minutes I was beginning to despair. I hadn't spotted the painting anywhere, although I wasn't sure what I was looking for. Then it occurred to me that perhaps Didier hadn't bothered to hang it up. Katherine had dumped him after all, so he would hardly want that memory staring him in the face every day. I targeted the bedrooms and luckily all the doors were open as people had dumped their coats on the beds and headed for the massive living room where the party was taking place. I looked under the beds thinking that if someone disturbed me I could easily say I was looking for my lighter. There were three bedrooms and the first two revealed nothing. There was only the box room left, which was next to the front door, so I went in and knelt down to search under the bed. My fingers felt the corner of something and I carefully lifted out what seemed to be an unframed canvas in a plastic bag, about two feet long, by one foot wide. I was staggered when I took it out to have a look. There she was again, this time dressed in one of those impeccable signature dresses I'd come to recognise her by. She was in a room warding off a wild boar that had its teeth sunk into her neck. But only the head of the animal was in the room, mounted on the wall behind her. It was a disturbing image and it became clear why Didier hadn't wanted to hang it up. It obviously represented an unpleasant opinion she had of him and, of course, 'boar' does rhyme with 'bore'. I thought it could have been significant. At that moment the strains of *Happy Birthday* came drifting along the corridor and on putting the painting back into the plastic bag, I quickly exited the apartment with it under my arm. The hallway outside was empty, fortunately, as all the guests were celebrating and singing in the living room, so I made my way downstairs with 'Happy Birthday, dear Didier' echoing around the walls, following me down. Out on the street I saw an empty taxi at the corner, so I sprinted up and jumped in the back.

I could hardly believe what I'd done. I was out of breath and my heart was pounding but it wasn't an unpleasant sensation. I'd committed my first burglary. I wondered how long it would be before Didier discovered the painting to be missing. As my pulse slowed, I knew it wouldn't be immediately since he'd hardly be checking on something he'd discarded, an ugly reminder of the angel that had escaped him the year before. He'd probably forgotten all about it and would only discover it was gone when he finally left the apartment and had to clear his things out. It could be years before that happened. By the time I reached my hotel I was exhausted and made my way up to bed.

The next morning I went to a different framers than the one I'd used for the 'bike' painting. I wanted to avoid any suspicions and cover my tracks completely. This time was more serious as I'd stolen the painting, whichever way you looked at it, but I was glad about what I'd done. It had been an unappreciated gift, neglected and hidden away there under a bed, and would provide a lot more pleasure now back at home. I realised it had settled something once and for all in my mind. After discovering the 'bike' painting and saying nothing to Katherine, I'd felt guilty. Now it was clear both episodes had to remain completely unknown to her. It seemed bizarre that I held secrets from a woman I felt love for but had never slept with. It also meant there was another reason I couldn't invite her over to my flat in London.

Chapter 4

Miguel de Vasconcelos (1590–1640) was the last Secretary of State for Portugal during the Iberian Union with Spain. He was probably the most hated collaborator with the Spanish, and considered a traitor. On the morning of December 1, 1640, a group of Portuguese noblemen who supported independence started a revolution. They searched for Miguel de Vasconcelos and found him hiding in a closet. He was stabbed to death and defenestrated, leaving his corpse to the hungry mob.

I couldn't wait to hang up my new treasure at home, and on the plane back debated where to put it. I'd never owned more than two works by any artist before, and now I had three of Katherine's. I wondered if this one would overpower the other two if hung next to them. In the end it looked rather good tucked in on the right, but I was running out of wall space and thought about the possibility of buying a bigger flat to accommodate my growing collection.

I'd been away in Paris for about a week and was excited at the prospect of seeing Katherine again, but when I called her there was no answer. I left a message and phoned Miles to ask if he knew where she was.

'Don't worry. She's off visiting her parents. They've just moved over from Australia. Somewhere down near Canterbury, I think.'

I didn't know what to make of this bit of news. Katherine had briefly told me about her parents but I'd considered them remote and no part of her life in London. I didn't figure them as becoming possible rivals for her time. I sulked for the next few days and didn't perk up until she called me on the Friday afternoon.

'Hi, it's me. My parents just arrived. They've decided to move over here from Sydney. It's been so long since I've seen them I thought I'd go down and help them settle in. When did you get back?'

'A few days ago. When am I going to see you? Are you free later on?'

'Sure. It's too late in the day to start painting now. Besides, I'm exhausted from the train journey back. It's definitely not the 'age of the train' over here like they say it is in the Ad's. There were long delays.'

'The train takes ages, is more like it,' I said. 'Shall we get something to eat at La Capannina's?'

We'd favoured the restaurant ever since our first meal there.

'Why don't you come over here? I make a mean chilli and garlic prawns.'

'You don't have to go to any trouble. Besides, you said you're tired.'

'No, really, I'd like to. It's been a while since I've cooked for someone. Anyway, it's about time I invited you over.'

After I put the phone down I realised an important shift had taken place in our relationship, and she had now put it on a different footing. To eat a meal with somebody in a restaurant is one thing. The venue is neutral and the cooking has been delegated to a third party, but to eat at their house is something else. Sharing food is one of the most trusting experiences in life. We become what we eat and what we put in our mouths represents the difference between life and death. Rulers used to take food tasters with them whenever they were invited somewhere away for a meal. There are plenty of instances of poisonings at diplomatic feasts, and serving certain foods would signify different things. For example, in India one never served peacock to guests. It was the ultimate insult.

I was excited as the evening could possibly be the start of something. We'd probably both drink some wine although I had no intention of stepping over any boundaries with Katherine, I had too much respect for her to do that. But if she decided the time was right I wouldn't be the one to object. In fact, I admitted to myself, it would come as a relief. But it occurred to me there could be a more practical difficulty for the future. After being invited over she'd expect me to return the invitation at some point. And there was the problem. I'd have to take down the two paintings she didn't know about and hide them somewhere, perhaps even remove them from the flat altogether. After considering the prospect of not being able to look at them just when I wanted to, I was filled with panic and a nausea I'd never experienced before.

Katherine's flat was in a quiet backwater not far from Olympia. There was a row of shops: the butcher, the baker and the candle-stick maker, sitting next to a small post office, together with a gastropub on the corner and a small supermarket. It had a village atmosphere you don't find often in big cities these days. She lived on the top floor of a terraced house and when I arrived she buzzed me in from the street. The stairs and communal areas were clean and well maintained, and when I reached the top of the stairs the door to her flat was already open. The stair landing was large and a dormer window had been cleverly fitted in the slanting roof to transform the dark space. A large, healthy peace lily sat in a terracotta pot and welcomed me with its open white flowers. I pushed the door open and wasn't prepared for the immense space that spread out in front of me. It looked like it had originally had two bedrooms and been converted into a vast, one bedroom studio flat. Three large windows were fitted in the exposed pitch roof and together with the existing ones that looked out onto the street they bathed the room in an extraordinary ocean of light. The room was about thirty feet by thirty and there was an open plan kitchen at one end with a dining table. Next to this was a living space with two white sofas facing one another over a glass table. At the far end of the room was a double bed in a quiet, shaded corner. I recall she'd separated this from the rest of the room by cleverly constructing a wall out of bookshelves. There were two other doors at that end of the room, presumably leading to the bathroom and the original second bedroom, which I guessed she used as her studio to paint. She was standing at the stove chopping garlic and I recognised Leonard Cohen's first album playing quietly on a stereo somewhere.

'Come on in!' she shouted across when she saw me.

I walked over and held up a plastic bag.

'Hi! I brought some white wine to go with the seafood, but it's not that cold. Shall I put it in the freezer for a while?'

'That's a good idea,' she said, and offered me her cheek to kiss. 'There's a bottle of Chablis already open in the fridge. Pour yourself a glass.'

'So how are your parents? When did they get here?'

'Last weekend. Couldn't bear me being on the other side of the world from them. They've rented out their house in Sydney and Dad's arranged a consultancy here, but they didn't want to live in London. The English countryside made more sense and Kent's nice. They thought it would make visiting them more appealing to me. He can work anywhere these days. How was Paris?'

'Good. Pretty humdrum, really.'

She prepared the food while we chatted and sipped our wine, and we were onto the second bottle I'd brought by the time she'd cleared the plates away from the table. She suggested we sit down somewhere more comfortable so we moved to one of the sofas. We found ourselves sitting alone for the first time and closer than we'd ever been since we'd met, and when I mentioned this to her she gave a mischievous laugh. It was twilight by now, but I hadn't noticed due to the light provided by all the windows. As we talked I could feel her lips moving closer to my face. We moved into each other's arms in that quite natural way when people are in alignment and pretty soon we'd found our way to her bed.

I returned home late the next day, feigning some outstanding proof reading I had to do before Monday. She was surprised at my decision to leave, perhaps thinking we might have spent the whole weekend together but I needed time to catch up with all that had happened. I thought she was wonderful but the future was problematic. I had to decide what to do with the two paintings if she visited me and I spent most of the Sunday mulling this over. I couldn't entrust them to anyone I knew, and hiding them in the flat really wasn't an option. If she discovered them when she was there – and I really did want to invite her over – the fallout would be catastrophic. I decided to leave them where they were until I knew she was definitely coming over, at which point I could store them in the boot of my car. It did seem like a ridiculous course of action but I could think of nowhere else to put them.

I must say the reality of her living space had disappointed me. It was quite different from what I'd expected. I hadn't noticed a TV set anywhere, or a fish tank, and I reluctantly accepted that she'd manufactured the settings for the paintings, although I hadn't bothered to look out of the windows for any cars. I was also disappointed she hadn't volunteered to show me any of her new work in progress and I used this fact to justify hiding my paintings from her. Quid pro quo.

In the end I was glad I hadn't pressed her to show me her new paintings. It wasn't the basis of our relationship, but had the fact that she'd been an artist influenced me at all? I had to admit my love of her work had influenced my initial attraction to her. If she'd turned out to be an accountant would we still have ended up in bed together? Who knows. The fact remained that I was in love with her and I had enjoyed our lovemaking. Besides, I don't make a habit of sleeping with female artists. I think Miles called them 'art tarts'.

I didn't manage the fallout from the Friday night at Katherine's very well. I did invite her over the following Wednesday evening for supper, and the paintings found their way into the boot of my car. I had to rearrange the other paintings in the flat to compensate for their removal, but I did pretty well. Her canvases weren't that large to begin with and I'd had to accommodate them in the first place by juggling a few pieces around. We had a pleasant enough dinner. I can't remember what I cooked but no matter how hard I tried, I felt distracted the whole evening. In some strange way the paintings had left their presence in the room and at one point Katherine said she thought there was something missing; although how she came to that conclusion I had no idea. Let's call it women's intuition. But when we spoke it felt as if I were deliberately avoiding some topic of conversation. She stayed the night and we made love, but it wasn't like the previous Friday and I just wished we could have been back at her place.

After she left the next day, I waited an hour or so and then went down to rescue the canvases from the car. The weather was still pretty chilly at night so I'd carefully wrapped them up in a blanket to keep them warm. When they were safely re-hung I sat in a chair to enjoy them again. I'd never owned paintings that had been so demanding.

Later on I rang her to apologise for my preoccupied state of mind and she was very understanding but I think I'd disturbed her from painting as she seemed distracted. I agreed to go over and see her the following Saturday, and looked forward to recapturing some lost ground with her.

On the Friday Miles called me.

'Hey! Jaime. Haven't heard from you for a while, I thought I'd give you a call. Did you manage to see Kath before she left?'

'I saw her on Wednesday. Where's she gone?'

'It all came up rather suddenly. She got invited to the Berlin Art Fair to give a talk at the last minute, as someone's fallen ill and dropped out. She's staying the weekend.'

'Why didn't you go with her?' I felt I was interrogating him.

'Hey, don't shoot the messenger! I would have done but I'm preparing for the next show. We're opening on Tuesday and the artist really needs me to hold his hand. He knows nothing about hanging work. I just wanted to ask if you're free on Sunday to come over for lunch with me, Ann and the girls?'

I apologised for being so short with him and said I'd be glad to. After all, I'd be at a loose end now. I wanted to know more about Berlin, and Miles filled me in.

'Oh, it's a huge event. There are exhibitions on all over the city. It's a great opportunity for her to turn on the charm and meet curators. I'm surprised they already know about her over there.'

I have to admit I was upset. Even though it was a last minute trip she could still have found the time to call me to let me know our Saturday date was cancelled. I was crestfallen. I felt as if I was falling down a large hole, rather like Alice when she was chasing after the rabbit. I'd spent the last few months carefully building a relationship with Katherine and it had turned out to be nothing more than a house of cards. The whole thing had been blown down with one strong gust of wind. I'd under-estimated the effect of my behaviour the previous Wednesday evening. How could I have been so stupid?

Back home that night I drank far too much grappa and fell over negotiating my way to bed. I made a half-hearted attempt to undress myself to prove I was in control of what I was doing, but fell into a stupor before finishing. I dreamed I was running after Katherine through a forest and was going as fast as I could, but never caught up with her. The dream ended with her disappearing down a hole with me following into a whirling darkness.

I woke up the next day with the sun streaming through the windows. I was half dressed with my trousers around my ankles and concluded I must have tripped myself up and luckily landed on the bed. After a hot shower and a strong coffee I decided to go for a walk to clear my head of the grappa. Hyde Park was brilliant in the sunshine so I sat by the Round Pond to soak up the sun's rays while the swans preened themselves at the water's edge. It's one of my favourite spots in the park as the wildlife you find there reflects the time of year it is. In the hottest and the coldest weather, the swan population swells and you can always spot the youngsters by their grey plumage.

That particular day the sun was glistening on the surface of the water and the peace and quiet began to make me feel better, but I sensed I was losing control of the situation. My growing feelings for Katherine had made me increasingly dependent upon her and it was hard to think about anything else. This latest development made me fear it was all in jeopardy and I couldn't bear how distraught it was making me feel. I began to resent the control she had over my happiness and had to do something, but I wasn't sure what. My head felt extremely mixed up and I needed the weekend to try to work it all out.

Chapter 5

In 1471 it was discovered that the alum mine outside Volterra in southern Tuscany contained much larger quantities of alum than had at first been estimated. The mining concession that had been granted was withdrawn from a company that had three Medici supporters as major investors. When the Signoria in Florence objected, a riot broke out in Volterra and one of the Medici stockholders was defenestrated.

As the weekend passed my grief changed in character. The liquid dried up leaving a thickening slop and my inner tears evaporated. Vinegar seeped into the exposed cracks, making it hard, preserved and ugly. By the time Sunday came, I could think of Katherine with no more than a wince and I made the effort to go over to Miles' house for lunch. It was good to see him away from his gallery for once which I rarely did, and I perked up enough to retell two funny email jokes I'd been sent during the previous week. One was about a blonde on a plane to Australia, travelling in economy, who refuses to leave first class until she's told that first class isn't going to Melbourne. The other was about two lovers who go to see a psychiatrist, and insist on making love in his office each time they go, saying they need his advice on lovemaking. It turns out they are both married and not only is it cheaper than getting a hotel room, but the man can claim back the cost of the therapy on his tax return. Miles and I even discussed Katherine's artistic merits and I was able to think about her objectively without discomfort. He told me she was due back from Berlin the next day and he couldn't wait to find out how she'd got on. He left after lunch to continue with the hanging for his new show and I started to watch a cartoon with Ann and the girls. We talked about Katherine.

'I've never known you to be so interested in someone,' Ann started, and I assumed she was referring to Katherine.

'Really?' I feigned nonchalance, 'I don't know. It's still early days. We hardly know each other.'

'You can't fool me, Jamie. It was obvious that first evening at the gallery. And at the restaurant.'

I pulled a face and didn't know how to respond. I had known Ann almost as long as Miles, as she had studied at Bristol too. I knew it would be difficult to keep my true feelings a secret from her.

'She's quite a girl, mind you,' she continued. 'Seems very ambitious, though, and that's the worry. But good luck. I'd try to be careful. She looks like she could be high maintenance.'

Then Celia, the elder of the two girls, climbed onto Ann's lap.

'Mummy, what does 'high maintenance' mean?' she asked.

I made an effort to pay attention to what we were watching on the TV screen, but I was finding it difficult after what Ann had said, so after a while I made my excuses, thanked her for the lunch and left.

I decided to go to Miles' new opening on the Tuesday, not because I was particularly interested in the work but because I guessed Katherine would be there. Artists tend to rally round their dealer whenever a new show opens, and I knew for a fact Miles was expecting her. It would be his chance to catch up with what had happened in Berlin. I also wanted to show that I was carrying on with life and hadn't been affected by our cancelled date. She hadn't contacted me? Who cares, so what? I'm too busy to give it a second thought. And my diary's bursting, full up with invitations. I imagined bumping into her and saying some such thing. Just to show she hadn't got to me and to deny her the satisfaction of seeing she'd hurt me.

I could see her now as two separate people. The artist the general public was familiar with and the person I'd got to know.

When we were seeing each other they were one and the same, but now it was clear where the distinction was between them. I found myself wishing I hadn't pursued her and just got to know her as an artist whose work I collected. I had to find some way to reconcile the conflicting emotions wafting around inside my head. I had to otherwise I knew I'd have no peace of mind.

Tuesday evening came and I made my way over to the gallery. It wasn't as full as for Katherine's show but Miles didn't seem worried. He had his coterie of regular buyers there and they were the mainstay of his business. I'd only ever floated on the periphery of his world and Miles would never make a fortune from what I purchased. Since his days of globe-trotting had finished I'd seen him rise through the art world, aware that his eclectic taste and innate business sense would see him becoming successful. If I could make my little contribution occasionally, well, I'd feel the better for it.

The opening was due to run from 6:30 until 8:30, but these things nearly always run late so I thought nothing of timing my arrival for 7:30. I knew the freeloaders would be gone by then heading off for the next free drink at another opening. I spotted Miles coming out of his office at the back so I made my way over. He'd seen me too.

'You've missed her, chum. We had a meeting here at half past five and she left just before seven. Said she had something else planned for the evening. I am sorry.'

I was totally unprepared for this. All I could manage to do was raise my eyebrows at him. I offered a weak smile.

'Oh, and how did Berlin go?' I asked.

He was relieved that I'd changed the subject.

'Fantastic, apparently. She met loads of people and the talk went very well. She's been invited to New York in the autumn. And they want her back in Berlin for a show next year. Sounds like she didn't need me there at all!'

I wanted to say I felt the same but didn't see much point. I helped myself to a glass of wine and made the pretence of looking at the work. I had a brief chat with Ann and thanked her again for the lunch at the weekend. Just before I left she took me aside.

'Remember what I said about high maintenance.'

I spent the next day or so mulling over what a frustrating and disappointing evening it had been. As much as I didn't want to recognise it, Katherine was deliberately trying to cool off our relationship. This wasn't just about the cancelled date on Saturday because, if that were the case, I'd have either heard from her or got a message relayed through Miles. It was the total silence that I found most distressing. I waited until Thursday and then rang her mobile phone. It rang a few times and went through to her voice-mail, so I hung up. On my third attempt I left a message.

'Hi, Katherine. Hope you're well. Haven't heard from you since your trip to Berlin. Sounds like it was a lot of fun. Be good to hear from you. Speak soon.'

The following Sunday I still hadn't heard back from her but I imagined she may have gone to see her parents for the weekend. I realised her parents had now become unsuspecting allies in my pursuit of her. While she was with them there was no possibility of anyone else entering the frame and this was now becoming a logical explanation for the silence.

Let's assume that when she got the invitation to Berlin, on the Thursday, she'd had to dash to the airport. She could have accidentally left her phone at home, or mislaid her charger, and the battery had run out before she could call me. It happens all the time. So she arrived in Berlin to one non-stop merry-go-round. I tried to imagine what it would have been like. She'd probably spent the whole time being introduced to people and being taken around exhibitions. Plus she had the added task of

41

preparing and delivering her talk. So it was possible she'd arrived back in London without having had the chance to contact me at all. It would then make sense for her to locate or charge her phone and make her apologies to me for the broken date, or at least leave a message. But if she'd met someone else in Berlin, and something had happened, the best thing would be to do nothing. That would explain the choreographed early meeting with Miles at the gallery before the opening on Tuesday, which she'd suspected I would be going to. That way she conveniently avoided bumping into me.

Life went on and I busied myself by beginning research on a new book about succulents, to exploit the growing public fear about global warming. I accepted any invitations that came along; work or otherwise, thinking that would occupy me and refresh the claustrophobic atmosphere that had been building up in my mind. A new invite from Miles arrived but I decided not to go as I certainly didn't want to bump into Katherine there. She may be attending with a new boyfriend – at which point I would feel intimidated – but if she were alone I really didn't know what I'd say to her. Miles had been on a couple of trips to Moscow and Shanghai, so I hadn't had a conversation with him in which she could have come up.

About six weeks after my fruitless trip to the gallery, a package arrived one morning by Special Delivery. I was woken up by the postman's bell and when I opened the door I was half asleep. The package was square and it looked like it could be a coffee table book and I looked for the sender's address on the back but there wasn't any. Removing the wrapping was complicated as there was a lot of bubble-wrap and Sellotape involved, and I had to find a pair of scissors to carefully cut through some of it. Inside there was a framed painting together with a hand-written note which said:

First of all, please accept my apologies for my silence . . .
I genuinely couldn't call you until I got back from Berlin
(lost my phone)
Then I went and met someone in Berlin, and I'm in love . . .
Really didn't know how to tell you without bringing you pain
Loved our time together and hope you don't hate me too
much . . .
Am sending you this, it's from my time in Paris, one of the
only ones I didn't destroy
See you soon Katherine x

It was breathtaking. Perfectly square, I can only describe it as a picture within a picture. At the centre was her self-portrait. The technique was flawless and the positioning of it at the centre of the canvas heightened the depth created. I went up close to examine it, to make sure it wasn't carved as a relief. The style of the portrait was redolent of the enigmatic Fra Filippo Lippi, truly magical, and in contrast the rest of the painting seemed two-dimensional. It appeared to be hanging inside an art gallery, as the edges of two other paintings were in the picture, one on each side of the portrait, but you couldn't see any of their canvases, just their frames. This really was the work of Katherine of Arrogant. I was quite overcome. I loved the painting from that first moment and couldn't take my eyes from it. It was mounted in exactly the same frame as the portrait in the centre, which just added to the iconic allure.

For the first time in years I lit up a morning cigarette and propped the painting up on the table in the living room, then sat down in a sofa to drink in its majestic presence. The cigarette made my head swim, so I stubbed it out and picked up the note to read it again. It confirmed all my suspicions, but I felt far from satisfied. One always wants to be let down gently and the extravagance of her gift had sweetened the blow, but I sensed that this was all far from over. I felt I'd been a passive figure in everything that had happened so far between us and I had an overwhelming desire to take a hand in events myself. It could only make me feel better.

I dialled Katherine's number but she didn't answer, and her message service came on, so I said:

'Thank you so much for the present, which arrived this morning. It's absolutely wonderful. I can't believe you sent it. I totally understand. I hope it all goes well for you. See you soon. Lots of love.'

Later that day, I began to appreciate that I'd been weak and conciliatory. It was very nice of her to send me the painting but I felt like the child who's grazed his knee and been given a sweet. The more I thought about it the more belittled I felt, and my anger started to rise. So I took my mind off it by spending the week working on my new book about succulents.

The following week, I was dragged out to Cibo's restaurant in Holland Park by a friend and it was there that I saw them. He had his back to me so it was impossible to see what he looked like, but I noticed her as soon as we sat down. She saw me too and gave a brief smile which I returned with a small wave. Then he made to turn round but stopped after a hurried word from her. We ordered our food and some drinks and later on, on my way to the bathroom, I decided to go over. As I approached their table she got up to give me a kiss on the cheek.

'So nice to see you again. Let me introduce you. This is Lawrence. Lawrence, this is Jamie.'

I shook hands with Lawrence and turned to face her again.

'Thanks so much for the birthday present. It was totally unexpected and has pride of place in my living room. It really was very generous of you,' I said.

She smiled at my complicity and turned to Lawrence to explain.

'I sent Jamie a little picture for his birthday.'

He nodded understandingly from his seat and smiled at us.

'So . . . do you paint yourself, Lawrence?' I asked.

'No,' he chuckled, 'not me, pal. I'm a sculptor. What about yous?'

'No, no talents in that direction, I'm afraid. I write books. About plants.'

I wondered if I should have recognised him. I could see Katherine desperately wanted everything to go smoothly between us.

'Jamie bought one of the paintings in my first show with Miles,' she explained. Then she turned back to me to say pointedly, 'Lawrence and I met at the Berlin Art Fair.'

'Oh, yes, Miles said it went really well over there.' I feigned a smile, but I hoped she hadn't noticed. Then I thought it was time for me to go.

'Well, good to bump into you both. Probably see you at Miles' some time. Bye.'

I went to the bathroom and although I only wanted to pee I took a booth, so I could sit down and study the mental photograph I'd taken of him. He was blonde with straight hair and probably in his late thirties. Judging by his dress and general air, I took him to be an established artist, but his name didn't ring any bells with me. As I sat there I decided to give Miles a call on my mobile, but Ann answered his phone.

'Ann, guess who I just bumped into?'

'Oh, hi Jamie. Don't tell me . . . Katherine and Lawrence.'

'That's right. At Cibo's. What's his last name?'

'My God, that's Lawrence Hardwicke. Haven't you heard of him?'

I wanted to get home and Google him straight away.

I felt a bit of a chump that I hadn't heard of Lawrence. He was an industrial sculptor working in mostly scrap metal that he fashioned ingeniously into all manner of things. I wasn't expecting much from the descriptions of his work, but then I saw some images of them and they were really impressive. They

45

put me in mind of the naïve sculpture you can come across in East Africa, fashioned from old coffee cans and coke tins. Some of them were deliberately meant to look like African masks, but they had a dark undercurrent that I liked. He had a foundry in a large warehouse in the East End, and had been nominated for the Turner Prize two years earlier when his career had taken off, as most nominees do. The size of the pieces meant they were ideal for outdoor public places. He was from Teeside and I thought I'd detected the accent from the little I'd heard him say in the restaurant. It seemed an astute move of Katherine's to shack up with him since he was famous in his own right, so you could say that together they made one of those tailor-made celebrity couples that the press love to write about. Each news article I read on him seemed to put her further away from me, and by the time I drew back satiated from my desk about an hour later, she was as out of reach as she could ever have been.

That night I had a disturbing dream. I was wandering alone around an art gallery and all the pictures were by Katherine. This didn't seem strange to me at the time until it became clear I wasn't in an art gallery at all, but at home. The next day I didn't have much to do so I pottered around doing some odd chores, going over and over the curious dream wondering what it could mean. In the afternoon I got a call from Miles.

'Funny you should bump into Kath and Lawrence last night,' he said. 'How were they?'

I told him what had happened. 'Look, she told me they'd got together in Berlin, but I didn't think it was my place to say anything. I hope you don't mind that I didn't tell you?' When I told him not to worry he was relieved. 'The reason I rang is something has cropped up you may be interested in. One of the buyers from her show has contacted me. He's offered me back one of the two paintings he bought. Apparently his wife doesn't care for it. I thought you might be interested in buying it?'

I was surprised as he'd never called me before with such a proposition but I found myself saying that I was interested. He said I could to go over to the gallery the following afternoon to take a look at it. The painting had sold for £4,000 at the show and the buyer wanted only £5,000 which I agreed was a fair price. Miles confided to me that the minimum price he was setting for her next exhibition at Frieze Art Fair was going to be £8,000 and he'd already sold some, even though they weren't yet finished.

That evening I took stock of my present collection of Katherine's work, only one of which Miles knew about. In fact, no one in the world except me knew I owned four of her paintings, three of which were seminal earlier works. I began to speculate how much they could all be worth. I'd paid £3,000 for the painting from the first show, then 500 euros for the 'bike' painting, and nothing for the other two. That made about £3,350 for four paintings. I was thinking of purchasing a fifth for £5,000, making a total of £8,350 for five of her paintings, and there were only ten known to exist. If her career continued to blossom, in a couple of years what I owned could be worth a lot of money. After all, the note she'd sent me with the self-portrait had said she'd destroyed most of her earlier works.

I began to consider her work just as product, like any other commodity. I went to take a long look at the 'gallery' painting, which I'd put in the bedroom, hanging above the end of my bed. I fantasised about slowly buying up all of Katherine's work. I considered what would happen if she stopped painting for some reason. When supply is plentiful prices go down, but when something becomes scarce, they rocket. It suddenly occurred to me there was meaning in the dream from the night before. All the paintings were in my home, of course, because they belonged to me. But I hadn't been familiar with most of them, suggesting they were paintings I didn't own yet. I knew then that I had to buy the painting Miles had offered me.

Chapter 6

In 1572, French King Charles IX's friend, the Huguenot leader Gaspard de Coligny was killed in accordance with the wishes of Charles' mother, Catherine de Medici. Charles had allegedly said, 'Then kill them all, that no man be left to reproach me'. Thousands of Huguenots were killed in the St Bartholomew's Day massacre after soldiers attacked de Coligny in his house, stabbed him, and threw him out of the window.

I finished reading the proofs for the French edition of the hydrangeas book, sent them back to Paris, and felt it was time to take a break so I decided to revisit Goa. I'd been there several times, first with my foster parents as a child, and had always enjoyed watching the local people make sense of the chaos of their lives. This time I felt it might help me make some sense of my own. However, if I was serious about my plan to own all of Katherine's work, I would have to find out who the other collectors were. So before leaving London, I told Miles I was researching a new book about the art world and asked if he'd let me hang out at his office in the gallery to gain some useful background information. He was pleased to hear I wanted to try writing something that didn't involve plants for a change and I spent a few days watching him getting on with his business. Katherine was away with Lawrence in Morocco so there was no possibility of me running into her there. I sat out of the way, either with a newspaper or with my notepad and pencil, and by the end of the second day Miles had begun to forget I was there. In the evenings we would leave together and if he had time we'd get a drink at the local pub before heading home. I knew sooner or later he'd have to leave me there alone while he popped out to do an errand or attend a meeting, and on the morning of the third day that's exactly what happened. He had to take a mail-out for his forthcoming show down to the post office and asked if I minded being left in the gallery for a while. This was fine by me as I needed as much time as possible to search for the names I wanted.

After he left I waited about ten minutes in case he'd forgotten something and returned to his office at the rear of the gallery. It didn't have a separating door, but once around the corner of the dividing wall it was impossible to be seen from the street. His computer was conveniently switched on and I began to negotiate my way through his files. I typed in 'Katherine Gaunt buyers' and punched 'ENTER'. A page came up with all the details from her first show plus several future buyers for the next batch of works for the Frieze Art Fair. I made a brief visual scan to make sure they were all there – I was expecting at least seven names – but counted ten, including my own. I pressed 'PRINT' and was about to congratulate myself on how easy it had been, when I glanced back at the computer screen to be told: 'PRINTER OUT OF PAPER'. I looked around in some cupboards and found the empty packaging of a ream of paper amongst some other stationary on a shelf. Miles had evidently been printing out his invites all morning for the show and had exhausted his stock of paper. Fortunately, I found a few sheets left in the bottom of the packet and tried to stay calm as I gathered them up with my nervous fingers. At that moment there was a tapping on the glass of the front door and I looked around the corner to see a Fedex van parked up on the pavement outside. The driver was standing in the street with a package. Taking a deep breath, I strode purposefully across the gallery space and unlocked the door.

'Miles Goodfellow? Just sign here,' he said, waving a pad and pen in my direction without even looking up at me.

I signed the delivery note and manhandled the robust package into the gallery. Once I'd relocked the front door and returned to the back, it took a good ten minutes to work out how to load the paper into the printer. My hands were trembling constantly. I made a copy of the list of buyers, stuffed it quickly into my jacket pocket and returned Miles' computer screen to the page it had been on. Just a few minutes later he was outside knocking on the glass door to be let in.

'Why did you lock the front door?' He sounded a little irritated.

'Sorry, I forgot I had. I needed to use the loo.'

'Can't be having that! What if an Arab millionaire happened to be walking past and wanted to part with a few thousand quid of loose change? Tut, tut.'

I looked sorry and offered him an apology.

'Joke!' he laughed 'Look! I got us a couple of toasted pancettas for lunch from the Italian. Dah, dah!'

He triumphantly held up two white paper bags and threw one for me to catch. I showed him the Fedex package and after he'd studied the delivery note we sat down to eat. I made us some coffees and we settled in for the afternoon session. He'd also remembered he was out of paper and had picked up a ream while he was out, but when he opened the printer to fill it up he straightened back up and addressed the room generally.

'That's funny. I could have sworn I was out of paper earlier. Jesus. I'm definitely spending too much bloody time here. One day is merging into the next.'

On my first day in Goa I walked along the beach to the Bliss Travel Computer Café with my buyers list from Miles' computer. I logged onto Yahoo and created an email account in the name of Manish Kumar. I chose the name because there are at least a few hundred thousand men called that in India, making it virtually untraceable. I composed a personalised email from him written to the first name on my list, introducing himself as an English citizen but an Indian resident, interested in purchasing work by Katherine Gaunt. I tried to make the English I used very 'Indian' in style and I'd brought with me a portable DVD player and the films *My Beautiful Launderette* and *Monsoon Wedding*, to study their manner of speech. Rarely would the buyers receive an email from such an exotic collector and for that reason I thought it would grab their attention. If they asked any of their friends in the art world about Manish Kumar, no one would have any information.

I reasoned that art collectors buy art for two reasons. Firstly, because they want to indulge themselves and acquire possessions reflecting their own achievements; by purchasing pieces they actually like they can display an independent side to their personalities, and everyone wants to believe they've got one of those. Secondly, there's an element of risk involved as this is the most genteel form of gambling ever devised. The work has the innate potential to increase in value, and not in line with any of the known indexes by which economic stability is normally measured. When Black Friday happened in London in the late 1980s it was the property market and not the art market, that took the greater fall, and it took longer to recover. The very existence of a Picasso or a Vermeer nowadays proves they can survive the turbulence of human economics and politics. Many works of art survived the despotic priest Savonarola's Bonfire of the Vanities in Florence in 1497.

I was convinced there was a price the buyers would accept for their paintings by Katherine. She was a new artist and it would be very easy for them to get hold of more of her work, since all they had to do was contact Miles and order a painting from the next collection. It would be easy and they probably wouldn't even have to pay for it straight away. I was very fond of Miles but, in the end, he was an art dealer and they've always reminded me of posh second-hand-car salesmen. They wear the suits, they talk the talk, and they're always very amiable, because they have to be. A sale is a sale.

I sent the emails out sporadically, even though I had no reason to believe the people knew one another. And even if they did, they might find themselves rivals at some stage for the same piece so it was very unlikely that they'd discuss the matter. They may mention to Miles they'd been contacted but I doubted it as they wouldn't want to admit to him they were possibly thinking of selling on any of Katherine's work. He may have taken it the wrong way. I only sent out two emails that first day, one to a banker in the City of London and another to a wealthy Northern industrialist in the Macclesfield area. I decided not to approach the 'future' buyers as it would be easy for them to sell on the 'future' painting they'd ordered to Kumar for a healthy profit, and just pick up the phone, call Miles, and order another.

The first email read:

Dear Julian Newton,
It has come to my attention that you are a fan of the work of Katherine Gaunt, and that you are indeed the proud owner of one such of her paintings. I, too, am fully enamored of her work and I would like to propose something to your good self.

I am an Indian art collector based in the industrial heart of India, as I have been for the best part of my life, before which I was lucky enough to have been born in your great country to my esteemed parents. Fortune has smiled on my life, and I am now in the happy position to be able to take an interest in the fascinating world of your Modern British Art Scene. I have substantial funds at my disposal and wondered if you might be interested in selling me your Katherine Gaunt painting? I understand you may find this an improper advance, such as I am making at this moment, but please forgive me for this. I hope very much to be hearing from you at your earliest convenience.
I remain your very humble servant,
Manish Kumar

I hoped that by placing Kumar firmly in India, the distance might make him seem less of a threat to the buyers. By not specifying where, it would also be very difficult for them to find out anything about him. My second mail, to the industrialist, Bernard Merryweather, was similar so I sat back in the blissful Goan heat and waited to see if they replied.

I tried to imagine what might be going through their minds after they read their mails. They'd probably be perplexed as to how Kumar had tracked them down; possibly thinking Miles had passed on their information. They'd lift the phone to ring and ask him, and then think better of it. They'd replace the receiver as it really didn't matter whether he had or hadn't. And they certainly didn't want to alert Miles to a potential customer. They knew he'd pursue Kumar to try to flog some new 'future' work and perhaps scare him off. They would wonder what the painting was worth and how attached they were to it. Then they'd be curious to find out how much this Kumar character was willing to pay and it sounded like a lot, as he had said he had 'substantial funds' available. I tried to guess who would reply first.

It was Merryweather in Macclesfield:

Dear Mr Kumar,
Thank you for your mail regarding Katherine Gaunt. I do indeed share your enthusiasm for her work. Could you give me an idea of what you would be willing to pay for the painting? I paid £4,350 for it at the exhibition in London.
    Kindest regards
    Bernard Merryweather

This was just the reply I was hoping for. He wasn't agreeing to sell but he'd opened the door to negotiate. I replied immediately:

Dear Mr Merryweather,
May I please offer you my worthy thanks for replying to my

enquiry. I would not be thinking to suggest a figure that may beset your good self with disrespect, and so may I ask of you, what would you be happy to accept?

As always,

Your humble servant

Manish Kumar

Merryweather then went quiet on me for two days, during which time I suspected he was getting hold of Miles to find out if he could secure a 'future' work from Katherine's next show at Frieze, and how much that would cost him. Miles told me he was setting an £8,000 minimum price for the next show, so I guessed Merryweather would come back to me with a figure in the region of £8,000, as he would probably want to finance the new purchase from the sale. I thought this might appeal to his logic without him appearing to be too greedy. On the third day I heard from him again:

Dear Mr Kumar,

I must apologise for my delay in getting back to you. My wife has been poorly with her back, and I have been occupied tending to her needs. With regard to the Katherine Gaunt painting, I would be willing to accept £10,500 for it. If that is acceptable to you, please let me know.

Kindest regards

Bernard M

It had worked. I replied accepting his offer, saying the painting could be shipped to a post box in Slough that I'd arranged prior to leaving London. I asked if he'd accept payment using the secure server, PayPal, and I agreed to meet all dispatch charges. I pretended to be unfamiliar with the UK tax setup and asked if I would be required to pay VAT on the painting, which I knew to be unnecessary. He patiently went through the VAT situation with me and I authorised payment.

It was time for me to concentrate on Julian Newton, who hadn't got back to me. This was slightly worrying but I tried to think of various reasons why. Being a successful banker he'd probably be attending all sorts of conferences and meetings and it was a safe bet he just hadn't had the time to get around to dealing with it yet. There was no reason to think he wouldn't reply at some stage because they always do, after all, I may have been a customer at his bank.

It took him ten days to get back to me:

Dear Mr Kumar,
Please accept my apologies for not replying to you sooner. I have been away from my desk in London during the past week and have only now been able to catch up with my personal mail.

I am indeed the owner of one of Katherine Gaunt's paintings, which I bought earlier this year through Miles Goodfellow. I can let you know that I would be willing to sell it to you for £15,000.

Please let me know if this figure is acceptable.
Yours sincerely,
Julian Newton
Corporate Banking
Barclays Bank PLC

I realised Newton was playing hardball with me but it didn't surprise me. He was a tough negotiator otherwise he wouldn't have been successful at what he did. It was clear he was playing the art market for all he could make out of it. The figure of £15,000 was obviously an opening gambit, so I spent the next day or so sunbathing and swimming, contemplating what I'd go back to him with as my counter offer:

Dear Mr Newton,
I am totally understanding of your difficulties in replying to

my earlier mail. May I say that the figure you have suggested for the painting was higher than I imagined you would be finding satisfaction with. Would you allow me to respectfully offer you £11,000?

As always,

Your humble servant,

Manish Kumar

Newton came back wanting £12,500 as a final figure, which I accepted. He knew he was still making a big profit, so he had cut to the chase since he was a busy man. I decided to dispense with the VAT blind, as he was in the money business. I made the payment through PayPal again and picked up the charges for dispatch and another of Katherine's paintings started its journey towards Slough.

Chapter 7

The revolutions of 1848 in France led to a period of unrest in Germany. When an agitated crowd forced their way into the town hall in Cologne on March 3, two city councillors panicked and jumped out of the window; one of them broke both his legs. The event went down in the city's history as the 'Cologne Defenestration'.

A week later I started negotiations to buy the three remaining paintings from Katherine's first show. The next name on the list was Lady Cynthia Hambleton, the surviving wife of Lord Arthur Samuel Hambleton, a long standing Labour peer in the House of Lords. I remembered being introduced to her once or twice at Miles' openings. She was one of his regular clients not in the banking trade and I found her extremely affable and interesting company. She'd kept a motherly eye on Miles and had introduced him to some influential people over the years. She was a petite woman in her late sixties with a lively mind which she enjoyed exercising on anyone who had the time to talk with her. Although she was an upper class English rose, she was surprisingly unpretentious and extremely witty. I sent her an opening gambit email similar to the one I had sent Newton and Merryweather. She replied immediately, which I was surprised at, taking into account the different time zones involved.

My dear Mr Kumar,
What an unexpected pleasure it was to receive your mail.
I am indeed a fan of Katherine Gaunt. I feel she has something new that will give the art scene over here a good kick up the backside. I'm afraid it's been long overdue. She's a marvellous portrait painter of some talent who will finally

get some recognition. Hurrah! I'm fed up with this wave of Conceptualism that has been sweeping across our shores for the last few years.

As far as the painting goes, I never sell anything. Never have done and never will. So I'm sorry I can't be of more help to you. It may be an idea for you to contact Miles Goodfellow, her London dealer? He may be able to point you in the right direction.

Out of interest, whereabouts in India do you live? I spent a lot of my early twenties there, as my husband was involved in the jute trade. That all seems many moons ago . . .

Best wishes

Cynthia Hambleton

Lady Cynthia's mail had put her painting out of reach but it did have one consolation for me. The fact that she never sold any work meant it wouldn't affect any of my plans, but I was wary of entering into a long email conversation with her. I might be forced into divulging details about Manish Kumar and India that I didn't have the knowledge to create. I didn't want her to catch me out on some detail and arouse her suspicions. I waited a day and sent her a quick mail in reply, saying thank you, but without replying to her question about where in India I was based.

I decided to head back to London with two names remaining on my list. Manish Kumar was now well and truly in existence so he could send emails from any Internet point in the world without revealing his true location. London didn't seem to have changed in the slightest in my absence, and it was as if I had temporarily stepped through a time warp in Goa, and I had returned to find that time had stood still.

The first thing I did upon getting home was to drive out to Slough and pick up the two paintings waiting there for me. I went into the freight office and produced the collection slips that had been mailed to me. When the packages were located I signed for them and half an hour later I was driving along the Westway back into London. I was excited to see what they looked like. I unwrapped them, propped them up against my living room wall, and sank back in the sofa to study them. I realised they were the remaining two that had accompanied *The Sunday Times* piece all those months earlier, so I'd come up trumps with my first two Kumar purchases. I now owned all three of the works illustrated in the article and I set about ordering a few more copies of the original edition in which it had appeared. They would be useful later on for provenance purposes.

As I sat there studying the paintings it was obvious my art collection had outgrown the wall space of my flat and I decided to search for a larger one to move to as, like Lady Cynthia, I was loathe to part with any of the work I owned.

I telephoned Miles at the end of the week to try to see if he'd been alerted to Kumar's existence while I'd been away but if he had been he didn't mention it. I asked him if I could sit in at the office for a few more days to continue my book research. I needed access to his files again.

'Be my guest,' he said, 'By the way, did you hear the news about Kath and Lawrence? They're getting engaged. Seems to be the big one for both of them. They're having a party at the end of next week. You've arrived back just in time for it. They said they'd love you to go. I'll fill you in when you come by the gallery.'

It did surprise me. And it made me feel a bit queasy. I could identify with Didier Malherbes, the ex whose painting I'd stolen in Paris, as we now had something in common. Katherine, the beautiful angel, had escaped from both of our clutches.

The invitation arrived for their party. It was to be held at Dick's

Bar at the revamped Atlantic, around the corner from Piccadilly Circus. It was now called The Astor and the party would be a main attraction for the London art scene. I remembered the Atlantic in the early-nineties when Dick Bradshaw was mixing drinks there. At that time it was one of the few late bars in London and there was a marvellous Polish doorman who could remember all the regular's names when they arrived. I spent a while trying to remember his name but it had all been too long ago. It would be the first time I'd seen Katherine since we'd bumped into each other at Cibo's, with Lawrence.

The next day I went to see a few properties with an estate agent and made my way over to the gallery just before noon. I was curious to see if Newton or Merryweather had joined the list of future buyers yet. When I arrived an attractive brunette stepped out from behind the dividing wall.

'Hello, can I help you?' she asked.

'Hi, my name's Jamie. Is Miles here? He's expecting me,' I explained, and she immediately showed some recognition.

'Ah, yes. Miles did say. He's been at the framers all morning, and said to tell you he'll be back at two o'clock.' She smiled and held out her hand to me. 'My name's Jessica, I'm here on a job placement from the Royal College of Art. Would you like a coffee?' She continued to talk whilst making it. 'I'm so pleased Miles agreed to take me on, even though it's only for a few weeks.'

'You never know,' I said, taking the coffee, 'If you do well and impress him he may well take you on permanently after you've graduated. Will that be soon?'

'That would be nice. It's this summer, actually. It's my finals this year. I adore art, but I don't have aspirations to become an artist myself. You need so much self-belief these days to make it. Times have changed since the days when artists could be recluses and have wealthy patrons. David Hockney was the first one to do it.'

'Do you have any favourite artists?' I asked her.

'I really admire female artists, like Katherine Gaunt, of course. I think it's always harder for them. The art world seems to be so male dominated, even in these so called modern times.'

'It's completely different in publishing,' I added, 'It's filled with intelligent, capable women . . . '

At that moment we heard the front door open and who should walk in but Katherine. She was dressed differently from the way I'd come to recognise her, wearing a stylish pair of pastel ski-pants underneath a faded denim jacket, but I could tell it was an expensive outfit nevertheless. The choice of colours suited her perfectly. She was genuinely pleased to see me and gave me a generous hug. I introduced her to Jessica, who had frozen to her chair. Then I remembered the engagement.

'Congratulations! Miles told me the news about you and Lawrence. I'm glad I got back in time for the party. So how's the new work coming on?' I knew the Frieze Art Fair was only a month or so away.

'Good, but slow. I seem to float round working on several simultaneously. It does help. It relieves the monotony of having to concentrate on one at a time.'

Jessica was obviously star-struck and I could tell it was making Katherine feel uncomfortable whilst she was talking to me, a friend. After scribbling a quick note to Miles about missing him, she made a rapid exit, being followed by Jessica who talked excitedly all the way to the door, even holding it open for her, which I thought was rather sweet.

A few minutes later Miles telephoned and was cursing that he'd missed Katherine. More importantly he said he'd been called to a meeting at the National Portrait Gallery at two o'clock and would be going straight there, rather than coming back to the gallery first. Jessica told him she was coping fine without him and after I wished him luck for the meeting, he passed on some instructions to Jessica. I noticed her referring to Miles' computer several times during the call, so the files were available to me if I could just entice her away for a while.

I waited fifteen minutes then suggested to her, 'You know, you can always pop out and get some lunch?' She looked hesitant. 'Miles won't mind. Everyone needs to take a break. Union rules, etcetera.'

'Well . . . ' she said, still not sure if she should, but I persevered.

'Tell you what, you can pick me up something too while you're out. A sandwich from the Italian.'

'Alright then. But I won't be long. What sort of thing do you want?'

This time I was rehearsed for my hacking in. The whole procedure, from locking the gallery door to unlocking it after I had printed out the list, took less than ten minutes. I was determined not to be interrupted this time and didn't even study the list before pocketing it. I settled down to studying some estate agent listings while waiting for Jessica to return.

Miles arrived on a high from his meeting at the National Portrait Gallery, saying they were interested in a major exhibition of Katherine's the following year.

'That's fantastic!' squealed Jessica.

'I know,' Miles affirmed, 'this would elevate her to the big league.'

Later on, when it got close to six o'clock, he suggested I join them for a drink at the local pub, but I told them I was due back to look at some properties and I hurried home to study the new list.

It had expanded since I'd last seen it, and predictably Julian Newton and Bernard Merryweather were new additions. A famous rock musician was down to buy two works and Lawrence had loyally put his name down for another. There were three names at the end with question marks next to them, and one of these was Lady Hambleton. What caught me by surprise was the last name on the list . . . Manish Kumar. He had two question marks next to his name. What with my dealings with the estate agents I'd neglected to keep an eye on Kumar's email account since returning from Goa, and I was angry with myself. Had I policed it, I would have been aware Miles had emailed him. I tried to work out how he'd made contact and came to the conclusion that Lady Cynthia, being protective, must have told him.

I logged on and there it was, a respectful email from Miles saying it had come to his attention that Kumar was interested in Katherine's work. There was an invitation to the forthcoming exhibition at the Frieze Art Fair. He went on to explain it would be possible to buy work prior to the opening. When I weighed up its significance I thought there was nothing wrong with Miles knowing about Kumar. It would compound his confidence in Katherine's career and to some extent legitimise Kumar's existence. After a couple of glasses of wine I came to the conclusion that Kumar could become interested in buying some future work. It would further increase their value.

The next day I found a property matching my criteria, so I put in an offer at the asking price and replied to Miles' mail to Kumar:

Dear Miles Goodfellow,
It was with great honour that I received your friendly email the other day, and I can only say that I offer profound apologies that I was unable to send a speedy response to you at an earlier time than this. I have been engaged in negotiating a major pan-Indian engineering contract for my company (I avoided going into any details), and I am happy to say it has now been successfully completed.
Thank you very much for your kind invitation to the forth-coming display of Katherine Gaunt's new work in London.

Unfortunately, I will be unable to attend as I have to take part in a conference in Malaysia on that very same date. (I'd found no less than five engineering conferences going on in Malaysia on that day by surfing the web).

However I would be interested in buying two of the paintings from the new show. Please to let me know as to how much the prices will be?

Many happy felicitations,

Your humble servant,

Manish Kumar.

I started out thinking he could buy one of the future works but on second thoughts I decided to go for two. Kumar wanted to consider himself a player in the art world and I thought it would carry some authority in Miles' mind. The works already earmarked for sale were nearly up to double figures, which would please Miles no end. At this rate, the show could be sold-out before opening to the public, just what a dealer hopes for. At a minimum price of £8,000, if ten works were sold upfront it would represent at least £80,000 in income, of which Miles would take fifty per cent commission, a whopping £40,000. I estimated the new show must be boasting at least fifteen works, maybe even twenty. If the shows got any bigger Miles would have to move to a larger gallery, or rent a space just to exhibit Katherine. When I went in the next day I asked him about the size of the show.

'It'll probably be about twenty paintings. I toyed with the idea of renting a larger space,' he explained, 'but in the end I decided it'll be more exciting to have Frieze packed to the gills. You know, people clamouring to get in. It helps generate a buzz.'

I admired his canniness and agreed with him.

The following Thursday was Katherine and Lawrence's engagement party, a good choice of day because on Friday most people would be leaving London for the weekend. The venue had been decorated to reflect the heady days of the Twenties, hence the name Astor's. When I arrived it was busy and I saw Miles, Ann and Jessica talking with Katherine and Lawrence, so I made my way over. Miles handed me a glass of champagne from a passing tray.

'Jamie, there you are. Late as usual. Have you met Lawrence?'

I turned to Lawrence offering him a smile.

'Hello again. Congratulations. Set a date for the wedding yet?'

'Not quite, no. Kath's parents wanted us to go over to Sydney but there's no way we can do that till way into next year. So it looks like it'll be down in Kent in the autumn. We both hoped you'll be able to come.'

'I'd love to,' I said.

I had no intention of being disagreeable to him. I glanced over at Katherine who looked uncomfortable at our bonhomie; it had caught her off guard. I was looking forward to getting to know Lawrence and perhaps even inflicting some pain on her for a change. I kissed Katherine on the cheek and moved away from the group, saying to Lawrence that I'd like to catch up with him later.

'Lookin' forward to it,' he said genuinely.

Canapés circulated and they were delicious and plentiful, and the place started to get very crowded. I spotted amongst others Gary Hume, Keith Coventry and Clare de Jong, and even George Melly was there for a while. Gavin Turk, whom Miles represented, was at the bar and I'd met him several times so I had a brief chat with him.

I turned round to find myself standing next to Lawrence.

'Great party, Lawrence,' I said, 'very glad I got back in time for it.' We clinked glasses in celebration.

'You been in Goa, right?' he asked.

'Yes. I suppose Katherine's told you about us?' I was keen to know how we stood.

'Yeah, don't worry, man. I can understand how ye felt. She's a real honey, and super talented.'

It was obvious he was going out of his way to make me feel comfortable. He told me how his career had got started in Newcastle in the early nineties. He'd been inspired by Andy Goldsworthy's 'Angel of The North' after he'd left school and started working close to its beacon-like position outside Newcastle.

'I passed it every fuckin' day on the bus on me way to work, like, and I thought, wouldn't it be cool to be doing something like that for a living? I was working at the car and scrap metal site next to the A1 then. Once I got accepted at Newcastle Polytechnic I was over the fuckin' moon. It didn't take me long to work out what to do. The best way was to make things big scale, like, as that way you're going to get the commissions from the councils, as they're always looking for giant pieces for public spaces and that. And they've got the fuckin' money. Aye, the bigger the better, I say!'

We had a good laugh at the simplistic nature of this plan and the scheme was paying off for him. That year alone he'd had six pieces commissioned, each in excess of a hundred thousand pounds. He was assembling them at his London foundry with a team of helpers. He invited me over to take a look and I agreed to get in touch later in the month after Katherine's show had opened at Frieze. I was relieved to be getting on with Lawrence so well and felt sure we could become good friends. I said goodbye to him, drained my champagne glass which hadn't been empty the whole evening, and made my exit.

Chapter 8

Arthur I, Duke of Brittany (1187–1203), was the originally designated heir to the English throne, to succeed Richard I. When Richard died in 1199, his brother John immediately claimed England, and invaded France in 1202. Whilst besieging Mirabeau, Arthur was surprised by John, captured and imprisoned at Falaise. The following year he was transferred to Rouen, where he mysteriously vanished. The Margam Annals relate: 'In the castle of Rouen, after dinner on the Thursday before Easter, when he was drunk and possessed by the devil, he (King John) slew him with his own hand, and tying a heavy stone to the body cast it from the window into the Seine.'

Katherine's opening at Frieze was the art event of the year. The whole show of twenty works was sold beforehand and there were a couple of hundred unlucky people outside who couldn't get in to take a look. The Press were there in droves and Sky News positioned themselves outside to interview art world celebrities and famous critics on their way in. Miles had sent out far too many invites with the precise intention of creating the melee that had ensued. I arrived early for a change in anticipation of the high turnout but after about an hour I found it was proving difficult to stand still or even hold my glass upright, what with the constant comings and goings. I said goodbye to Miles and Ann, and left just as Katherine and Lawrence were arriving and being interviewed by Sky News.

The following week I put in a call to Lawrence to take him up on his offer of being shown around the foundry. He invited me to come over whenever I liked so I arranged to drive over the next day. The completion for the purchase of the new flat was due at the end of that week and I busied myself with some of the final legal and financial preparations. I wanted to move in as soon as possible and I'd started packing, so the old flat was in a state of flux and disarray. Since returning from India, Kumar had managed to secure the last works from the first show, apart from Lady Hambleton's, which meant I had no fewer than eleven paintings by Katherine. Miles had told me that for the National Portrait Gallery show, pencilled in for the following May, he was fully intent on setting a minimum price of £15,000. He was also excited to tell me that amongst other public galleries showing interest, Tate Britain had contacted him with a view to acquiring a work paid for out of the Trustees Fund.

On arriving at Lawrence's foundry at around eleven thirty, I was impressed when two large, corrugated iron gates opened up, enabling me to drive in and park within the safety of the yard. It was an incredibly large place and a new sculpture close to completion, was being scaled by two shaven-headed men covered in tattoos. Lawrence strode out of the foundry holding a welder's mask.

'Jamie, good to see yous, man. Come on in. I'll show you around.'

We entered the darkness and I struggled to see, but when my eyes grew accustomed to the change I could see that there were piles of twisted and mangled pieces of metal placed at intervals on the floor, and some were in the process of being put together in vaguely familiar shapes. It was as if these were complex geometric puzzles that Lawrence had found ways of solving using an instinct he'd developed over time.

'First, I sift through all the stuff that comes in regularly from the tips, like, and sort of put bits that I think go together into piles. Then I just mess around with a blowtorch and see what happens. If anything takes too long to weld together I get Jake and Dinos to do it for me. They're great. Just two barrow boys who knocked on the door one day, like, asking if I'd take them on. Glad I did too, as work's gone bananas the last couple of year, I can't keep up!'

He then took me outside and introduced them, two solid East End guys obviously totally in awe of him. After showing me some other pieces being made ready for shipment, he suggested taking a break to stroll around the block and get a cup of tea at the local café. I was starving and polished off a full English breakfast with a mug of tea when we got there, while Lawrence told me how he'd met Katherine in Berlin.

'She was standing with a group of people at this show I had there. I just couldn't take my fuckin' eyes off her. I just kept staring at her. So I walked up, bold as brass like, and asked her who she was. The other people were a bit put out and that, when I took her to a bar next door for a drink. But I didn't give a toss, man. It was lust at first sight.'

I got through another cup of tea while we talked and then needed to pee.

'If you can hold on till we get back you're better off using ours, mate. The one in here's disgustin',' he said.

He insisted on paying for the two of us and when we got back the gates were open and a delivery truck was trying to manoeuvre its way in past my car. It had arrived to take away one of the finished pieces, so taking that as a suitable cue to leave, I thanked him for breakfast and agreed to join him and Katherine for dinner later that week with Miles and Ann.

I busied myself packing and by the time Friday came I was ready to move. The completion had gone through without any complications so I was on schedule to start moving in at the weekend.

After the rigmarole of buying the new flat I was looking forward to getting together with the others that evening. Miles had booked a table at the back of the Electric Brasserie and I was the last to arrive. They'd left a place for me between Ann and Jessica who I hadn't realised was going to be there. She was tipsy and began trying to flirt with me but I gave her short change as I wanted to talk to Lawrence who was sitting opposite. He confessed to a love of snooker and I said I'd introduce him to the table upstairs at Groucho's in Soho. We ordered coffees and some brandies, and Miles declared the dinner was on him. Despite our protests, he magnanimously waved his credit card at the waitress when she brought the bill over.

'No, I insist,' he said 'This is to thank you all for making this a fantastic year for me so far . . . and I hope it continues the way it's going, because if it does, you, young lady . . . '

and he waved a finger at Katherine, ' . . . are heading for big things.'

'Let's drink to that!' I threw in and raised my brandy glass, and everyone joined in.

'Which brings me on to another matter,' Miles continued, 'May I ask where you're all intending to spend Christmas this year? Because Ann and me . . . we, and the kids have just rented a house on Lamu – that's in Kenya, if you didn't know. It comes complete with servants, from December 20th for three weeks and I, no, *we*, would like, no, *love*, to invite you all down there. That is, if you'd like to join us?'

Everyone was happy to accept on the spot but I think Jessica felt a bit uncomfortable being unsure if she would still be working for Miles by the end of the year. He noticed immediately of course, and quietly reassured her that to all intents and purposes she was hired once she'd finished at the Royal College. She was overjoyed to hear this and it prompted more cause for celebration.

I'd heard a lot about Lamu. It's an island off the north coast of Kenya where there are no cars and I thought it would be an interesting place to spend Christmas. Miles told us the thing to do there is to hire a house. Apparently there's a trendy hotel called The Peponi, and as the island is so small, everybody renting houses gravitates there in the evenings for a drink. The house Miles was renting came with all mod cons, apparently, including a liveried staff to look after the guests and provide meals cooked in the kitchen. It sounded marvellous and I'd met a few people who'd been there and they'd all come back full of praise.

I spent the weekend at the new flat taking delivery of some furniture. On the Sunday, I ferried over my personal belongings including artwork, apart from Katherine's. There was a large room at the new place that I'd earmarked as my study, with enough wall space to devote completely to her. This way I could surround myself with her aura when I was alone without fear of being disturbed and I could keep the room locked when entertaining. The new place wasn't that far away from the old one, so by the end of the day I'd managed to take everything over and began deciding where to hang the work. It was tricky but the new furniture was in place and that gave me a bit of help, as it's completely different hanging work in an empty room. On the Monday, I was still immersed in all of this, so much so, that I almost didn't hear the downstairs buzzer go. It was Miles outside.

'Hi, mate, hope you don't mind me dropping by like this. I was on my way to the gallery and thought I'd pop in and see how you were getting on. Wasn't sure if I had the right bell. I'm on a meter for about forty minutes.'

I gave him a tour, and he agreed to stay for a quick coffee before heading off. He said he needed my help with something.

'MOMA in New York have contacted me. They're putting a show together called 'Modern Portraits' next spring and they want to include a couple of Kath's. It's a fantastic opportunity. Ideally I wanted to send two of the three featured in *The Sunday Times* article, remember? But the owners of the other two won't agree to lend them to me for some reason, I've no idea why. I've had to rely on good old Lady Cynthia to give me the one she bought, which means I have got to borrow yours as well. I hope you don't mind? You're my last hope.'

I told him I'd be happy to help out and lend the painting and I was relieved he hadn't caught me unpacking the other two he'd been trying to borrow. Thank God I'd left them over at the old place for the time being. But I was relieved at the reaction of the previous owners to Miles' request, as it meant they were loathe to admit that they'd already sold the works to Kumar and I needed their complicity.

By the middle of that week I'd hung up all of the work and Katherine had taken over the study. I calculated there'd be some room left in there but I'd put a temporary curb on my spending and I wanted to get to know Lawrence better. I invited him to meet me at Groucho's on the Thursday, where we could play some snooker on the full size table they have. He said he'd be delighted and we arranged to meet at eight in the bar so we could get a drink first. When I arrived he was already there halfway through a vodka and tonic, and by the time we'd had a couple of drinks together I'd almost forgotten why we'd arranged to meet. He was a pretty good snooker player and it didn't take him long to finish me off. We took on a couple of regulars at doubles and beat them which made me feel better. We decided to have one more drink for the road and we started to talk. We got on to the subject of women and his archaic views surprised me. He said he had great pity for women in general.

'They're pretty pathetic, on the whole, man, I'm sorry to say. Pre-programmed with this crap mission in life to have fuckin' kids. I don't know whether to feel sorry for 'em because they've had kids, or sorry for them because they haven't, if you can sees what I mean, like. You and me, we're the lucky ones. We can't wait to get to work, its fuckin' essential to our lives. For most people having kids is the most creative thing they get to do. No wonder everybody's so keen to have a few before they peg out.'

By the time we left at midnight we were both tipsy and we shared a cab back to West London as he'd recently moved into

Katherine's flat with her in Olympia. He dropped me off and we agreed to play snooker again the following week.

Throughout the summer and autumn we met up nearly every week to play snooker at either Groucho's or the Elbow Room in Westbourne Grove, which was more convenient for both of us and it made a change from going all the way into Soho. We generally made it on a Thursday so it didn't eat into the weekends, as sometimes he'd go down to Canterbury with Katherine to visit her parents. It was clear he looked forward to meeting up with me as he said it provided a window of sanity for him whilst he was shacked up with Katherine. Also, he said it gave him the opportunity to talk, and he did have a lot to say. I'd told him about my recent trip to Goa and he said he'd been there a few times since the eighties and had seen the place go through its changes, like everywhere. I told him why I liked it; the friendly, laid back local people, and the contemplative state of the animals. I told him this time I'd seen a sacred bull by the side of the road, slowly chewing its way through a rolled up copy of the *Times of India*. By way of a reply he launched into the reasons why he didn't like it.

'Ah, it was alright before, like, when nobody used to know about the place. Really fuckin' cool, it was. Nowadays, it's full of Russians with their black market roubles, and would-be photographers taking hundreds of identical fuckin' photos of the perfect sunset. And the restaurants, full of Brummies, all talking about the new exhaust they just fitted on their hot-rod, and whether they'll be able to get hold of a *Daily Mail* before they get back to see's what's been going on. The trouble is - they're spending so much time learning how to cook chips that authentic Indian cuisine is going by the wayside, and that's criminal. Then there's the blokes that just have to buy a fuckin' drum, and bang on it for hours on end, drivin' you fuckin' nuts, as if they think they're gonna master it in the week they got left there. Sounds like they're hittin' pots and pans from the fuckin' kitchen, in reality like.'

He could see he was wearing me down with this tirade, so he unexpectedly added, for my benefit I'm sure:

'But what I did like, amongst other things, was the independent spirit of the wild dogs. I threw a stick for a pack of 'em one day and they just looked at me, as if to say: "What the fuck! Go and get your own bloody stick, ya tosser!"'

This made me think he had a soft spot for it somewhere inside.

He told me they'd started preparations for the wedding and it was scheduled to take place at the end of October. I decided to spend the night down there after the reception rather than come back up to town, and I booked myself into a bed and breakfast a short distance away from Katherine's parent's house.

The day was beautiful but I found myself running late. Being familiar with Kent from my days at Wye College, I thought I knew where Chartham was, but it had been a long time and I had to stop a couple of times to ask for directions. I finally pulled up outside the church and quickly made my way in, dropping off my present on a pile at the back of the rows of pews by the door. An usher passed me a sheet with the wedding service printed on it. I found space on the end of a row and began to sing along with the congregation. Once comfortable with where I was in the hymn in progress, I looked up to find a lot of unfamiliar heads in front of me. I couldn't work out what was wrong until it dawned upon me that I'd stumbled into the wrong wedding by mistake. I made my apologies to the usher and remembered to gather up my wedding present on the way out.

Thankfully I wasn't that far from the right church and as it turned out I got there in plenty of time for the beginning of the service. It was a charming building, obviously lovingly maintained, and the acoustics were wonderful. All around there was evidence of the harvest festival taking place and I have to say that it all felt quite right. It was a great success. Celia and Darcy, Miles' girls, made delightful bridesmaids in matching violet coloured dresses and were on their best behaviour throughout the service. Katherine's wedding dress was in an immaculate white with gold bordered tendrils snaking up the bodice caressing her curves, and I found I couldn't take my eyes off her. Lawrence wore an Oxford grey cutaway with striped trousers and looked particularly dashing, what with his blonde locks.

Afterwards Katherine introduced me to the vicar, who seemed to me extremely young, and it turned out that he was a fan of my books. He was keen to show me around the church grounds which he had personally planted with various shrubs. Luckily he didn't have any books for me to sign otherwise I would have been beside myself with embarrassment. After the service everyone went back to a large marquee set up in her parents' garden.

There was a good turnout from the art world and I could see Miles was itching to get involved in the organisation, as if it were another one of his shows. He was determined to show everyone how things should be done and Ann was trying to rein him in, as it was starting to get on the nerves of Katherine's parents. Miles and Ann hosted a table next to the bride and groom's, which was just for the family of course, and I found myself seated inbetween Jessica and Ann. Celia and Darcy sat in-between their parents, and the table was completed by the best man and his wife. He was a real Geordie who had apparently known Lawrence from their school days and still worked at the scrap metal yard beside the A1. He was effusive in his support for the couple and got completely paralytic on champagne before he had delivered his speech. The result was that no one, except Lawrence and his parents, could understand much of what he said when he stood up. Later on after we had eaten, there was a quite good covers band playing at one end of the marquee. While everyone was milling about socialising, Ann and I found ourselves sitting alone at our table and I thought she looked tearful.

'Everything OK?' I asked her since it was rare to see her looking vulnerable.

'Absolutely fine. It just reminds me of our wedding, that's all. We had a marquee just like this one at my parents' place down in Sussex. Do you remember?'

I did, of course, as I'd been Miles' best man. At the time I'd had a classic old Mercedes and had driven them to and from the service in it. I'd introduced Miles to Ann at Bristol initially, but they hadn't dated while they'd been studying there. It was only when he came back from his travelling that they met up again in London and got together. I remembered their wedding as if it were yesterday, being between two of my oldest friends.

'It's the one day you don't forget in your life, they always say,' she continued, and then, as if to save herself from an outburst of emotion she changed the subject.

'What about you? Must be strange for you, seeing them getting hitched. How do you feel about it? I've seen the way you look at her. Do you wish it was you instead of Lawrence?'

I wished she hadn't asked me that question, but we were old friends and she read me well and I had to think for a moment about what I wanted to say by way of reply.

'I think you were right. You know, when you said she could be high maintenance.'

'But he's a solid guy . . . ' then she paused, thinking she'd insulted me, 'Not that you're not! What I meant was – he'll be able to deal with her. He's much tougher than you are.'

I looked past her and could see Celia, her elder daughter, listening in on our conversation.

Just then Lawrence came up after having been dancing with Katherine, and looked very drunk. He sat down and asked us whether there was any more champagne. Celia got up, ran around the table and climbed up onto his lap.

'Larry. What's high maintenance? No one will tell me. Please tell me. Please.'

But he was far too gone to be concentrating on what she was saying to him.

Jessica and I got drunk and I found myself dancing with her later on at the disco. She'd grabbed my hand and pulled me up from the table before I'd had time to object. Then a ballad came on and we began to slow dance together. Before I knew it, she had started to stick her tongue in my mouth and I decided it was time to make an exit. She wanted to come back with me to my bed and breakfast but when my taxi arrived at around two thirty, I thought better of it and left tired and alone.

Katherine and Lawrence went to Morocco for their honeymoon and while they were away I continued to acquire more of Katherine's work. Through the agency of Manish Kumar I'd opened up negotiations with the rock musician to buy one of the two paintings he'd bought from the Frieze show. I calculated he might be persuaded to part with one for a handsome profit. It looked like I was going to have to pay a hefty £15,000 for it, but this was small money in comparison to what the prices would become later on.

In early November Jessica dropped out of the planned trip to Lamu. It didn't surprise me after the way I had rejected her advances at the wedding and Miles told me she'd got back together with her old boyfriend from the Royal College of Art. But she was instrumental in locating a flight to Lamu for me at the last minute. My new book on succulents was taking up more of my time, and it had completely slipped my mind to book anything for myself. I was due to fly to Amsterdam on December 16th with KLM and change planes for Nairobi, followed by a four hour wait, before an internal flight on to Lamu. There wasn't an airport on the island as it was served by one across the strait on the mainland. The days grew shorter, Lawrence and I played more snooker, and suddenly on December 15th I was packing a suitcase for the trip.

Chapter 9

*Abe 'Kid Twist' Reles was the most feared hit-man in the stable
of Murder Inc., which was the enforcement arm of the National
Crime Syndicate in 1930s America. His weapon of choice was
an ice pick, with which he was so adept that many of his victims
were thought to have died from a cerebral haemorrhage. Reles
turned informant when arrested in 1940 to escape the electric
chair, and was due to testify in a trial against Albert Anastasia,
co-chief of Murder Inc. In the early hours of November 12th
1941, the day of the trial, Reles, guarded by six police officers,
mysteriously plummeted to his death from the window of Room
623 of The Half Moon Hotel on Coney Island. The angle of
trajectory suggests that he was pushed. Reles became known as
'the canary who sang, but couldn't fly.'*

I compared my travel plans with the others and Katherine and
Lawrence were the first to arrive in Nairobi on a direct flight from
London, followed shortly afterwards by me. We then had about
four hours to wait before Miles and Ann arrived with Celia and
Darcy. If Miles' plane were delayed the flight to Lamu would
wait for him. Lawrence and I planned to meet up at Nairobi
airport and take a cab to a restaurant I'd heard about called The
Carnivore. It was famous for serving every possible kind of meat,
including crocodile, wildebeest and lion, and Lawrence agreed it
was too good an opportunity to miss. Katherine wasn't keen on
joining us and wanted to visit The Anthropology Museum in
downtown Nairobi instead. He hoped to talk her into coming
along during the flight but we agreed anything was better than
spending four hours waiting at the airport.

When we touched down in Nairobi I was keen to stretch my

legs. On clearing passport control I headed for the Transit Lounge and spotted Lawrence but there was no sign of Katherine.

'She's decided against the meat place,' he explained, 'she's gone to look around that museum in Nairobi. Told me to say sorry she didn't wait for you's.'

We made sure we were both checked in for our internal flight and headed out of the terminal building into the mid-morning Kenyan sunshine. Our luggage had been checked straight through to Lamu, so we had no bags to carry. We got in a cab and joked about what meat we wanted to try.

'Someone told me crocodile tastes a bit like fishy chicken,' I said.

'Sounds fuckin' disgusting to me,' he replied.

We sat back and enjoyed the scenery from the back of the cab. It was a forty minute drive to the restaurant and after being shown to a table, we were served drinks and given a very large plate each, complete with a steak knife and fork. I remember about a dozen very smartly dressed waiters in chef hats and striped aprons, milling around like a barber's shop choir, politely approaching our table in turn, each armed with a skewer of meat. They all spoke very softly to us.

'Hello, sir, you like to try antelope?' one of them said, while the next offered: 'Good afternoon sir. I have here lion for you, if you wish to try.'

As we got drunk we played at being food tasters for each other, feigning being poisoned and falling off our chairs onto the floor, until the manager came over and respectfully asked us if everything was to our liking, which made us quiet down. We went for a bit of lion, then some crocodile, and after a nibble of zebra, a good plateful of wildebeest, which I must say, smelt mouth wateringly delicious. We both agreed that of them all, the wildebeest was our favourite. We finished up a second bottle of wine and after some strong coffees we paid our bill and stumbled out to find a small zoo next door. We wandered in and caught a docile cheetah snoozing halfway up a tree, but most of the animals were out of sight catching some sleep in the shade, as by now it was the hottest part of the day.

We'd paid the taxi to wait for us and decided to head back to the airport for our rendezvous with Miles and Ann. On the journey back Lawrence told me an outrageous story about a chef he knew of in Teeside.

'This bloke used to love cooking, man. Like, more than anything in the fuckin' world. He used to get his rocks off, you know, completely, I mean, sexually excited. Then he got into the habit of wankin' off into the sauces. God's truth. Funny thing was, all the customers raved about the taste of the food, like. Had no fuckin' idea what they were eatin'!'

I couldn't tell if he was pulling my leg or not, but being drunk, I found it funny and laughed with him.

We found Katherine in the terminal looking worried. She'd seen that Miles' flight had arrived but she couldn't find us, and as Lawrence and I looked like two guilty schoolboys when we arrived, it served to throw us together even more. Lawrence was short with her on account of all the wine we'd drunk at the restaurant, together with the heat, and for the remainder of the journey they said very little to one another.

The internal flight was the highlight of the whole trip for me. It was a very small plane and we flew at low altitude over Kenyan countryside, so it was possible to make out a lot of what was going on down on the ground. I saw villagers driving cattle and the odd elephant within a thicket. The weather was clear and we were served a cup of delicious Kenyan tea. We'd almost filled the plane up with our group alone, but in addition to us there was an aging German couple and an American and his wife, who was wearing a large straw hat. Then suddenly we broke through low coastal cloud and made our descent to land.

All our bags emerged from the plane and the local house agent was there on the tarmac ready to greet Miles and arrange for our transfer across the strait. It was all very exotic and Celia and Darcy were beside themselves with excitement, as was I. They clung to their buckets and spades as we boarded a dhow, and as the sun sank below the horizon we docked at Lamu port and were transferred to our house in a horse-drawn carriage, straight out of a museum.

We were met by two house boys, Lakshmi and Gary, who looked very smart in their identical, liveried uniforms. It was a thick walled, white painted villa made of rough hewn lava stone with a cobbled, central courtyard. The cobble stones had become shiny over the years, as if they'd been painstakingly polished by someone. The house dated back to the Dutch occupation in the early 1800s, although a lot of work had been done to bring it up to date. As I was the only single person in our group I was given a bedroom on the terrace above the ground floor rooms. It was not much bigger than the size of a single bed, but had beautiful, ornately carved, wooden windows through which the moonlight cast a honeycomb of shadows. I unpacked and lay down on the bed looking through the windows at the rising crescent moon. I could hear the sound of Celia and Darcy laughing and then, more quietly, Miles and Ann talking. I stirred when Miles called up to me.

'Hey, Jamie, wakey, wakey. The boys are serving supper in five minutes. It's on the table.'

They'd prepared a vegetarian buffet for us and when we'd eaten Miles and Ann said they were turning in for the night. Katherine retreated into her shell and took the opportunity to excuse herself too. After saying good-night, the girls scampered off with Ann to be tucked up in bed and Lawrence and I were left at the table looking at each other.

We ended up strolling down the road to The Peponi where the bar was still open, populated by aging colonials, together with a smattering of youngsters. I ordered two large vodka tonics and as I waited for them I looked around, I noticed the American couple who were on the flight down from Nairobi with us. The man waved at us and Lawrence and I made our way over to where they were sitting.

Their names were Chas and Robina, and this was their tenth visit to Lamu. They'd bought a plot of land on the beach and were constructing a house but shifting levels of sand during the rainy season had covered the foundations and delayed the building work, so they'd been forced to rent a house again instead. I shared their passion for the movies over another round of drinks and they were excited when Lawrence explained who he was. They lived in Sausolito and were familiar with a sculpture he'd sold to the San Francisco Library the preceding year. After an hour or so, last orders were called at the bar and Lawrence and I decided to finish up and head back to the house.

Lying in bed that night, I found it difficult to sleep because all the vodka and tonics had served to wake me up. My body clock had been thrown through many different time zones on the journey so I just tried to relax. I found myself staring at the slowly moving shadows from the moon on the window frames. I began to think about Katherine and recalled how I'd felt when I'd seen her at the wedding. I tried to run through my collection and pictured them as they now hung on the walls of the new study. I got about halfway through before I finally fell into a deep sleep.

We all had a lie in the next morning and I heard Celia and Darcy running around outside in the courtyard below, familiarising themselves with their new playground. Their voices were light and playful and helped me gradually wake up. The sun was due to come through my wooden windows and bake me within fifteen minutes, presumably leaving an outline of their carved shapes on my skin, so I found a robe and headed downstairs to find a bathroom. After a shower Lakshmi and Gary greeted me with fresh mango juice and a cup of Kenyan coffee and I attacked a plate of home-made toast that was waiting to be buttered and smeared with marmalade. One by one the others surfaced and we decided to explore the beach before the afternoon sun became too fierce for our pale European skins.

The baobab trees made a big impression on me, standing tall and fat on the landscape, looking like they'd been designed by Yves Tanguy. I'd only ever seen pictures of them before and I found myself looking for a valve on their trunks where they could be topped up with air like rubber tyres. We all stood unable to move, including the girls, staring up at these unusual alien looking plants that dominated the landscape.

The heat grew by the second so we decided to take shelter at The Peponi restaurant. We'd missed the first sitting so it was easy to find a table and after a lazy lunch we headed back to the house to rest and agreed to gather at seven o'clock. We'd bumped into the Americans earlier and they'd invited us over to their house for cocktails, as it was just around the corner from our house. Miles was excited to get to know them as he saw them as potential customers, of course. Their house was similar to ours and several boys were running around serving everybody drinks and it didn't take long for us to imagine we hadn't moved from our house at all.

The days drifted by and at the end of our first week we decided to take a trip for lunch to KiWyu, a secluded beach resort located on the mainland about two hours away by boat. It was a collection of luxury cottages gathered round an Italian kitchen backing directly onto jungle, and had been recommended to us by the barman at the Peponi. So at six in the morning we crammed into two fibreglass dinghies powered by outboard motors, with their owners stood at the back steering the rudder. Even though the sea was calm I wondered what it would be like when rough, as the speed with which we hit the passing current lifted the boat high into the air and rendered the water's surface as hard as the tarmac on a road. We all had to hang on tightly to stay aboard. Miles and Ann were with the two girls in one boat, and Lawrence and I sat either side of Katherine in the other. After about forty minutes, I looked around and noticed all traces of land had disappeared from view. I pointed this out to Lawrence above the high noise of the engine and he turned to me with a smile.

'What do we do, Jamie, if we turn round and Captain Pugwash here has gone fuckin' overboard?'

We both laughed nervously but I could see Katherine sitting between us had heard and hadn't found it funny. Both my hands had white knuckles and I felt extremely fragile.

Finally we could see land appearing on the horizon and we cruised up to the KiWyu jetty feeling much worse for wear. Celia and Darcy thought the whole journey was incredible and couldn't wait for the trip back. They ran off together to make sand-castles while the rest of us staggered up to the bar. I needed a drink to calm my nerves and ordered a straight whiskey, as did Miles and Lawrence. We began to feel better and picked a table in the open-sided restaurant while Ann went off to fetch the girls. It felt surreal sitting there on the coast of East Africa eating authentic Italian food and drinking Chianti wine. When the meal was over Lawrence and Katherine went off for a stroll on the beach and Ann took the two girls off to find a loo, leaving me and Miles at the table.

'I've never seen you look so relaxed,' I mentioned to him.

'I feel great,' he said, 'I haven't had a break like this since I took on the lease for the gallery. It's been a hard old slog, matey, but I think things are definitely looking up, at least they seem to be.'

All we could hear was the lazy noise of breaking surf on the beach about a hundred yards away and we enjoyed the moment of peace together and the calm of the place.

'I'm a bit worried about Kath though,' he continued quietly, 'I hope this time away can give her a chance to recharge her batteries too.' Then he surprised me with, 'Between you and me, I don't think they're getting on that well. He likes a few jars, as you know, and of course it serves to encourage her, then they both end up getting pissed as farts, arguing the toss. I've seen it happen a few times, when we've been out together.'

My heart gave a weird flutter when he said this and I wondered if, after all this time shutting off my emotions and managing to turn my love and lust for Katherine into contempt and indifference, I'd really made any progress. I felt unbalanced and wondered if I still held out some vague hope of getting back together with her. The same thought had occurred to me at the wedding.

The boat trip back didn't seem so bad to me, probably because it wasn't so hot in the late afternoon and also because we were heading homeward. It meant I had more time to think about what Miles had told me about Katherine and Lawrence. From what I'd witnessed it came as no surprise and I realised Lawrence would have to leave the picture before there was any chance of me regaining her affections.

'

Chapter 10

In 1383, when Lisbon was besieged by the Castilians, Bishop Dom Martinho was defenestrated by the citizens of Lisbon, having been suspected of conspiring with the enemy.

The call came towards the end of the first week, on Christmas Day in fact. I'd just woken up and made my way downstairs expecting to meet the others as usual for breakfast. I found Lawrence sitting at the kitchen table looking despondent and nursing what looked like a glass of whiskey.

'Merry Christmas. Are you OK?' I asked him.

'I'm fine, mate. It's Katherine's dad. He's gone and fuckin' died back in England. Sudden heart attack. Completely out of the blue, like. She's gone back this morning to look after her mum. I offered to take her to the airport but she wanted to go with Miles. They left about an hour ago.'

I felt like a whiskey myself but I poured some into a cup of black coffee instead. I made one for Lawrence and swapped it for his glass saying it made more sense than drinking it neat first thing. He accepted without a word and just continued to sit there sipping and staring into space. I sat down next to him.

'What was he like?' I asked. 'I only met him the once, at the wedding.'

'Top guy, man. Great bloke. Ya know those Aussies, salt of the earth and that. We got on like a house on fire. Aussies and Geordies are, like . . . simpatico. Got a lot in common, they have. Straight with yous. Down to earth. We went to the pub in Kent, the two of us, when I went down with Katherine to see them, like. He was so funny, man. A fuckin' great bloke.'

I felt a pang of jealousy that he'd got to know Katherine's

parents the way he had. It must have given him great insight into what sort of a person she was. I'd never taken the trouble. It meant he had something else I craved, this knowledge. I found myself asking him more and more questions about her father. What he drank at the pub, what stories he told, where he'd come from in Australia, much more than I'd ever asked Katherine. Stupidly, I'd never seen her parents as a way to discover who she was. I'd been introduced to them briefly at the wedding and had only ever seen them as rivals for the time she could have been spending with me. It seemed obvious to me now and I resolved to get as much as I could out of Lawrence before he got too drunk. It made him feel better talking about it and I managed to lift him out of his sombre mood over the next hour or so.

Ann quietly entered the room with Celia and Darcy. She made a sad face at me and found room for them all to sit down at the table with us. The girls were unusually quiet.

'Merry Christmas, Jaime. I guess you know what's happened,' she said. 'Miles just phoned. He's waiting at the airport till Katherine gets her connection. There's a waiting list for the next flight, but he's making a fuss to get her on it.'

Good old Miles. I had absolute faith he'd manage to get her on the plane. The whiskey got the better of Lawrence and he excused himself to go and lie down. I had a bite to eat with Ann, and agreed to walk into town with her and the girls for something to do. I knew there'd be a lot of local colour to divert our thoughts.

The town was extremely busy, but maybe it just seemed like that after being cocooned away for so long in the quiet of our house. The central square was small and the absence of any cars heightened the human and animal noises that had become audible in their place. It felt like we'd stumbled onto the set of a play, one we weren't familiar with, so we weren't sure where to place ourselves or what our lines were supposed to be. But it wasn't uncomfortable by its very novelty, and of course the girls thought it was heaven on earth.

'Oh, mummy, can we come here every day?' Celia pleaded, 'Please, can we?'

Meanwhile Darcy had spotted something.

'Look at that poor, thin cow! Mummy!'

I was glad to be occupied by keeping an eye on them and I knew Ann felt the same way. It was as if by doing that, we were in some way contributing towards helping Katherine. There were lots of shops to look in with ornate gifts on display. We found a tailor who said he could make us a copy of anything we brought to him at ridiculously low prices. The people had obviously embraced tourism and were making the most of it, and no one paid much attention to us as we ambled along. Smiling faces constantly invited us into emporiums for tea and a look around. One shop had a collection of planes, boats and cars, fashioned from old beer and coke cans, and it reminded me a bit of Lawrence's sculptures, only in miniature. The girls acted as our scouts and Ann and I followed them quite oblivious as to where they were leading us.

Quite suddenly we rounded a corner and came upon a queue of elephantiasis victims. I think they were waiting in line outside some sort of a clinic. Celia and Darcy were spellbound, but luckily didn't scream out and just stared with their mouths wide open. I'd read about the disease beforehand and was expecting to encounter it at some point on the trip. The most grotesque patient in the queue was a man with a right leg about three times its normal size but he didn't have a walking stick and looked perfectly at ease. He was slowly smoking a cigarette and when he noticed he had the girls' attention he started blowing perfect smoke rings. I would guess the man's leg had taken twenty years to reach its size, which would explain why he was so used to it. I'd been told sand ticks carry the disease, and because of this I'd avoided sunbathing on the beach.

I looked at my watch. It was three thirty so I mentioned this to Ann and we decided to make our way back to the house. Ann was hoping Miles had returned from the airport and we were keen to find out how he'd got on. He was back by the time we arrived home.

'Poor Kath,' he said, looking drained, 'she was so close to her father, absolutely idolised him.'

When Miles said this it reminded me of a bizarre conversation I'd had with Katherine soon after we'd met. We were at La Cappanina's having dinner and she'd admitted to me quite candidly that she was aware of how good-looking she was. She said she'd got into the habit of making men fall for her and then dumping them. Now it made sense. Nobody could ever match up to her father. If I'd taken the time and the trouble I might have found this out for myself and maybe taken some action to avoid her dumping me.

Lawrence appeared in a different light now. He'd worked this out and had managed to avoid being dumped. He was smart. At that moment he wandered into the kitchen. He'd slept off the morning whiskey and looked dishevelled. Miles explained that he'd managed to get Katherine on the plane to Nairobi and she would arrive in London the next morning at about 7am. She'd be in Kent with her mother by noon.

That evening the boys prepared food as usual and we ate in silence. We drank some wine, and afterwards Lawrence was keen to continue drinking down at the Peponi. As it was Christmas Day, I agreed to go with him and on the walk over there he told me he was glad to have a break from Katherine.

'Two bloody artists, man. A fuckin' nightmare. We both know what we want to achieve, like, and just seem to get in each other's way the whole fuckin' time. And she's got one hell of an ego on her, man. You would not fuckin' believe it.'

I suspected this but knew she kept it in check most of the time, at least in public. I didn't reply for fear of finding out any more from him, but he presented me with a monologue.

'She's constantly dissatisfied, with her career, like. And with me. And she compares us. She thinks we're in fuckin' competition. How fuckin' stupid is that?'

I could see he was dying to get all this off his chest.

'Another thing that upsets her, like, is that she tries so bloody hard. To make progress. Too fuckin' hard, if you asks me.'

I knew he found making his art easy, as he'd told me so, and I could see how that would be irritating to her.

'And you should hear her swearin', man. When she's had a few, like. Blimey, shocked me, it did. I'm fuckin' telling you. Mouth on her like a trooper.'

We reached the Peponi and were greeted as regulars, with offers of drinks coming from around the bar. One thing I'd noticed whilst being out with Lawrence was that being a celebrity meant he never seemed to have to pay for drinks, and word of who he was had got round the hotel. But he responded in kind, meaning it was never long before he got drunk, and being a Geordie it took a lot. Over the past months I'd got to know which combination of drinks had differing effects on him. If he followed any colour wine with vodka tonics he could keep going for hours, but if he stayed on red wine he'd become comatose and wouldn't be aware of what was going on around him.

That particular evening we hit the vodkas and within half an hour, we were in conversation with two very attractive brunettes who'd just arrived at the Peponi after being on a game reserve. One was a lawyer, and her friend was an ex-Sherborne girl, who seduced me with her beautiful, big, brown eyes. I spotted the Americans on the other side of the room occasionally smiling and glancing over in our direction, curious to see how we were getting on I suppose. As we passed time with the girls, Lawrence made it clear he wanted to be alone with the lawyer, and her friend conveniently sidled up to me. When last orders were called we got a bottle of champagne at the bar and Lawrence invited us both to their room. The suite they had was spacious enough for the party to split in two, so Lawrence and the lawyer disappeared into the bedroom and the last thing I remember was lying on a sofa staring into the brunette's eyes as she switched off the lights.

On waking up, it took me some time to work out where I was. At first I thought I was at home in London, being indoors. But then I remembered Lamu and thought I must be in my wooden bedroom outside on the roof. But it didn't feel right as there was no fresh air circulating round my face. I had a vague memory of the brunette but she'd disappeared. I looked at my watch and it was past midday. Looking around the room, I wondered if I'd dreamed the whole previous evening as there was no sign of any girl having been there. I couldn't even see the champagne bottle we'd brought with us from the bar. There was a scribbled note on the table.

Jamie . . . Great to meet you. Sorry I had to leave . . . Got to catch my plane XXXX Nicola

She'd written a UK mobile number underneath and I was pleased. She could have felt bad sleeping with someone she'd only just met. Thankfully, there are no rules in life, just roles for us.

A door opened and Lawrence came in looking distinctly hung over, scratching himself and yawning.

'Mornin', man. Jesus, what a night! Just goes to show, like. You never knows what's around the corner, do yas?'

He winked at me and started looking for his shoes.

The lawyer had left too. Then I remembered them saying it was their last evening and they were celebrating before heading back to London on Boxing Day. There was a knock at the door and an embarrassed housemaid poked her head in. We took this as our cue to leave and sheepishly exited the hotel through the garden.

I didn't have that bad a hangover but couldn't wait to take a shower and change my clothes. The reality of our sober world returned to my thoughts as we walked back to our house; the death of Katherine's father, her departure, Miles' concern, and more surprisingly, Lawrence's reaction. What he'd said the evening before had made it clear that the marriage hadn't been a success, and the fact Lawrence had fallen into bed with the lawyer added testimony to this. I found myself harbouring a tingling feeling of pleasure and seriously began to wonder how much longer they could stay together, given their tetchiness with each other at Nairobi airport and their silence on the small plane to Lamu. Their distancing from each other during that week all became clear and connected.

When we got back the house was empty. There was a note from Miles saying they'd taken the girls shopping in town, as they hadn't stopped talking about the previous day's expedition. We guessed our houseboys were also in town buying supplies, so we took the opportunity to clean ourselves up. We decided to tell Miles and Ann we'd got blitzed the night before, and we'd decided to take a room at the Peponi. This would save any unnecessary embarrassment with them.

This latest complicity with Lawrence was yet another thing I had no control over. I recalled when Katherine had sent me the self-portrait, and in the restaurant we'd told Lawrence it was a birthday present. My life seemed to consist of a series of haphazard events and these complicities were all invented to protect everybody else's feelings. I had no idea where they were all leading me.

Chapter 11

The Tuscan family Pazzi stemmed from Pazzo 'the madman', who was one of the first over the walls in the siege of Jerusalem during the First Crusade. They became direct rivals with the Medici family as de facto rulers of Tuscany in the fifteenth century. Francesco de Pazzi put together a plan with the Salviati, the Papal bankers in Florence, to assassinate the brothers Lorenzo and Giuliano de Medici. On April 26th, 1478, during High Mass at the Duomo, Giuliano was stabbed nineteen times by a gang including Pazzi and Bernardo Bandini, and he bled to death on the cathedral floor. At the same time Lorenzo was stabbed by two priests at the High Altar, but escaped with serious wounds to the safety of the sacristy. The coup d'etat failed, and a naked de Pazzi was thrown from a window of the Palazzo della Signoria on the end of a noose. Archbishop Francesco Salviati was also thrown from the window on a noose, still in his purple robes.

The rest of our stay was subdued. Miles and Ann took Celia and Darcy into town each morning and returned for a late lunch, either at the house or the Peponi. Lawrence and I lounged around the house during the day reading or playing chess, and in the afternoons we all swam in the house pool as no one wanted to risk the sand ticks on the beach. In the evening, after eating at the house, Lawrence and I would wander down to the bar at the Peponi. No one there had ever mentioned the lawyer and Nicola, and Miles and Ann accepted the explanation we'd given them for our absence that night. A boring routine took hold of our lives, so I proposed to Lawrence we take a day away from the house and just the two of us go over to KiWyu again for lunch. He loved the idea and wanted to arrange it immediately. By the time the others arrived back from town that day, we'd already booked the boat to go the next morning. It meant getting up at five, ready to leave from the jetty at six, and we decided to get an early night.

I found myself on the roof by my bedroom watching the sunset, sitting on the parapet to catch its last dying moments. I heard some noise below in the street and looked down at the precise moment a cat got its head caught up in the wheels of a passing carriage. I saw it being spun around a couple of times before being rudely spat out behind. The driver obviously hadn't seen it, and if he had done he'd made no attempt to stop the horse or divert the wheels from striking it. The vehicle carried on through the darkening streets, becoming a fading cacophony of clattering wheels and hooves and echoing chaos. I watched the cat's body go through its death dance on the cobbles below, its blood pumping up in a dark red arc several times from the severed neck, to fall like passionate black ink strokes on the street. The animal twitched for a few final spasms and lost its connection with life. As silence regained control, all that was left was a bundle of still fur on the ground. I was stunned for a few minutes and my head started to throb, but I found it difficult to tear myself away from the scene. I regained my equilibrium and continued to watch what would happen next. A door opened casting a shaft of light across the cobbles, and two small children came out from the lit doorway to investigate. I recognised them to be Celia and Darcy. They saw the cat's strewn body parts, and began to shout.

'Mummy, mummy! Come quickly! There's a dead cat. Its head's been chopped off!'

Then Ann appeared and took a quick look down at the cat, before grabbing the girls by the hand and marching them back inside the house. The door stayed ajar and a few minutes later one of our houseboys – I couldn't tell which one in the light – came out with a shovel and a plastic bag to collect the cat's body and head. Then he brought out a bucket of water to wash the blood away and by the time the door closed, all that was left of the accident was a dark, damp stain on the cobblestones in the fading light.

Lawrence was up before me and raring to get going when I met him down in the kitchen. The houseboys had cooked up some eggs and coffee for us to eat by candlelight, and the first rays of the dawn were showing as we left the house for the short walk down to the jetty. Our boat was ready with the engine ticking over and our pilot Gabriel was the same one we'd had the last time we went over to KiWyu. All I could see was his bright, white smile as he helped us to climb aboard but I recognised his voice.

'Good morning, boss,' he said to us.

He made sure we were properly positioned on the seat in the middle of the boat, before we pushed off into the open waters, which were emerging from the blanket of the African night. The mercurial water was incredibly still and every sound was crystal clear, as if we were hearing it on some gigantic stereo system. The only unnatural sound was the gentle chugging of the outboard motor behind us. By the time the sun came up enough for us to see more than a few feet ahead, we were almost out of sight of land. I felt Lawrence tugging on my arm and I turned to see him offering me a hip flask. I accepted a nip of whiskey as it was still cold, but to me the water didn't seem that rough, perhaps because it was the third time I'd made the journey. Gabriel suddenly opened up the throttle and we hurtled along, and although we were being bounced up high in the air, I wasn't as frightened as the time before. It's funny how normal things can become as we get used to them. There was a certain sense of inevitability about the journey to me that day.

We arrived at KiWyu and headed up to the bar to say hello to Michel, the owner, who said he was going to join us for lunch.

We both had a quick whiskey shot and I suggested we stretch our legs for a while to work up an appetite. We'd brought our swimming things with us and wandered along the beach to find a suitable spot to go in. The pool at our house was quite small and I guessed you couldn't have a proper swim in it. I saw Lawrence dive through a wave and break out into a strong crawl on the other side but not being very confident myself in the water, I stayed in the shallows watching him. He swam for a good ten minutes before joining me.

'Fucking great idea o' yours, Jamie, to come over here today. I really needed a break from that bloody house. Gettin' like a morgue, it is.'

We made our way out of the water to where we'd put our things and lay on our towels for a while to dry in the sun.

'Have you spoken to Katherine since she got back?' I asked him.

'No, man. Thought I'd leave her to it. She's got the number of the house if she wants to speak to me, like.'

This was probably how he'd managed to maintain her interest, by ignoring her when they were apart. It seemed droll to me, as now they were married they seemed to ignore each other when they were together as well. It was in stark contrast to my behaviour when I was seeing her. I used to ring her every day thinking I was letting her know how much I cared for her, when in reality all I was doing was getting on her nerves.

'Does she still want to sleep with you?' I ventured to ask him and he laughed.

'Not a chance of that, man. Not for months, like. No, it's all gone fuckin' pear-shaped on me. That lawyer the other day was a godsend.'

I suggested it was time for lunch and we gathered up our bits and pieces and headed back to take our table.

Michel had put the red carpet out for us and we started with a glass of the coldest Prosecco I've ever tasted. Plates of antipasti appeared including Parma ham, salamis and the sweetest artichokes. We washed it down with Chianti and were joined by a couple of German girls Michel had taken a shine to at the Peponi the week before. He was hoping to persuade them to stay on for a while as his assistants, as they were enthusiastic about the place and extremely bright. One was a horticulturist that he wanted to landscape the grounds and the other had very good family connections in the publishing world in Munich, and he thought it could be a way of breaking into the wealthy German tourist market. Mountains of home-made pasta arrived; spaghetti with seafood, ravioli stuffed with local mushrooms, and baked cannelloni. Michel was enjoying our company and he kept the Chianti flowing. I was careful to slow my drinking down to a mere trickle and keep my water levels high, but Lawrence saw no need for such restraint and proceeded to flirt outrageously with the horticulturist. It made us all laugh.

Michel told us about a woman who'd come over for lunch once and had run out of petrol on the way back to Lamu. 'Sorry, ma'am. Back in a minute!' her pilot had said to her and had dived off into the open sea, swimming toward the horizon. She'd sat in the boat for hours waiting anxiously while the sun went down, wondering what would happen to her. It had been dark for about an hour when she saw a light coming towards her across the water and there was her pilot in another boat, come to rescue her. Apparently, the whole stretch of sea is infested with sharks that don't worry about sinking a boat, once they've worked out there's something good to eat on board.

Lawrence called for more wine. The lunch must have lasted a good three hours before we noticed the sun going down in the perfect clear sky. Michel tried persuading us to stay the night but I was adamant about getting back. Large black coffees were ordered, plus Armagnacs, "to keep out the cold" as Michel put it. I paid the bill and helped a semi-conscious Lawrence stagger down to where Gabriel, our pilot, was waiting to help me put him in the boat. I said goodbye to Michel and the two German girls, and they waved us off at the jetty.

Lawrence was muttering to himself and occasionally would laugh or try to burst out into song, but it was hard to understand what he was saying above the noise of the engine. Once Gabriel got up to speed it was twilight and I knew he was worried about the time as he'd already come to ask us twice about leaving towards the end of the lunch. Our speed increased and we started hitting small waves with the bow of the boat, each one sending us up into the air and we'd come back down to hit the ocean with a huge thud. I was totally sober by now and I made sure Lawrence stayed on the seat by hanging on to him, as there were no seat belts. This was problematic, and I was getting worried as he wasn't able to sit properly on the seat, and as the waves got bigger we began to actually lose contact with it when the boat hit the waves. He weighed a lot more than I did so I found it increasingly difficult to control his movements. Then he started to vomit, and I felt spots of the warm pungent liquid hit my face as the slipstream caught it up and whipped it into the air. A drop or two went in my eye and I instinctively used a hand to try to wipe it away.

At that moment, we hit a very large wave and as we went up I lost hold of Lawrence and saw him disappear over the side of the boat. He immediately went below the surface and I turned round and yelled at Gabriel. He'd seen Lawrence go in, of course, and slowed the boat to turn it round and go back. Our speed meant we had to backtrack, maybe twenty yards or more, to the spot where he'd gone in. Gabriel throttled the engine down and dived in the water. I began to remember the story Michel had told us about the woman in the boat with no petrol. The only sound I could hear was the gentle throb of the engine behind me and I felt terribly vulnerable and alone. Every second lasted an age and I looked at my watch several times to realise I'd only been alone on the boat for a minute or so. Gabriel broke through the surface and he had what looked like Lawrence with him. I helped to pull them both up onto the boat but Lawrence was a dead weight. He'd been under the water for perhaps four, or maybe five, minutes. Gabriel astonished me by giving him mouth-to-mouth resuscitation and I had no idea he'd have that kind of training, but after about fifteen minutes he stopped.

He slowly turned his face to me in the darkness.

'He's gone, boss. Sorry, boss . . . ' he said, without blinking.

Chapter 12

At Prague Castle on May 23rd, 1618, an assembly of Protestants tried two Imperial governors, Wilhelm Grav Slavata and Jaroslav Borzita Von Martinicz, for violating the Right of Freedom of Religion, the so-called Letter of Majesty. They were found guilty and thrown from the high windows of the Bohemian Chancellery, together with their scribe Phillip Fabricius. They landed on a high pile of manure and all survived unharmed. This event was central to the initiation of the Thirty Years War in 1618.

It was dark by the time Gabriel got the boat back but it didn't take long for a crowd of locals to gather where we'd placed Lawrence's body on the jetty. Gabriel said he'd go and fetch the police and I sent someone up to the house to tell Miles what had happened. I took off my jacket and covered the body with it, and kept all the onlookers at bay. They were all keen to get a glimpse with their torches and I started chain smoking as I stood guard. It was something I hadn't done in years, but I felt helpless standing there waiting for the police to arrive. I started to think back to what had happened. I'd felt powerless as I'd watched Lawrence go over the side of the boat. Gabriel would say the same as me; people are always getting drunk and falling out of boats.

Within fifteen minutes the police came, followed by an ambulance which was the only motorised vehicle on the island. The body was taken away and Gabriel and I were asked to go and give statements. We were on the point of walking off with the police when Miles arrived, out of breath, after running down from the house.

'I can't believe what's happened. Jamie, are you all right? God. What a tragedy.'

It was all he could think to say. I explained to him how drunk Lawrence had been at lunch and that I needed to go with Gabriel and the police. I asked him to make sure Lawrence's body was being looked after properly, as I assumed that at some point we would be organising its return to the UK. He was relieved to be able to do something useful and we agreed to meet later at the police station.

Gabriel and I made statements separately but as it turned out, he totally agreed with my account of what had happened on the boat. A hearing was arranged for the next day and Michel came over from KiWyu with the two German girls to add their testimony as to how drunk Lawrence had been. The coroner reached a verdict of death by misadventure and the case was closed. The chief of police told me afterwards that it wasn't the first time this had happened on the island, and Miles and I were left to pick up the pieces. We made the necessary arrangements to have the body flown back to London, and then on to Newcastle for Lawrence's parents to arrange the funeral. Miles had the unenviable task of phoning Katherine and she asked him to collect up Lawrence's things and take them back for her. There seemed no point in changing our travel plans as we were due to leave in two days anyway. There was very little conversation for the rest of the time, and we left each other alone in our private thoughts.

It gave me a chance to take stock. I did feel very sad about Lawrence. I'd originally befriended him to provide a source of irritation for Katherine, but I'd genuinely grown fond of him and found myself remembering the fun we'd had together in London. In essence, he was a decent bloke and I realised he'd become a good friend to me. What did surprise me was how easily the local police had accepted his death as an accident. Naturally they'd had to rely entirely upon what Gabriel and I had said, but we could quite easily have conspired together and invented a story which they would have been forced to accept as the truth.

It struck me that the world could be quite a different place to that which most people believe. Just take a sunset, for example. It's universally accepted as being beautiful and a wonder to behold, but I had experienced the decapitation of a cat during a sunset a few days earlier and that had changed my view of them entirely. I'd never look at another one again without remembering that cat, and I'm sure the woman in that boat off of KiWYu, without any petrol, had a personalised opinion of them too.

Thanks to Lawrence I'd also gained a rare insight into Katherine, especially that whole thing about her father. All in all, it was strange behaviour on her part. My chats with Lawrence had revealed how I could maintain her interest in me. If I was to ever get another chance I wouldn't make the same mistakes next time. I'd need to show a more forceful side to my character if she wasn't going to lose interest in me a second time. After losing Lawrence she was going to need a good friend to lean on, someone to help her through all of this, and I thought it could be me.

I was packing up my belongings on that last day, when I found the note from the beautiful, brown eyed girl I'd met at the Peponi on Christmas night, and I remembered how good it had felt when we'd been together. I'd lost my libido of late and didn't know when I was going to rediscover it. "You never know what's around the corner" as Lawrence had so aptly said. I could feel a lust for Katherine returning too.

On the flight back from Nairobi to Amsterdam I tried to imagine myself in my new flat. Closing my eyes, I opened the front door and walked into each room familiarising myself with the paintings. I found I could remember where I'd put every-one. I got more excited heading down the hallway. I opened the door to the study and found myself getting an erection, just sitting there on the plane. It was time to close the curtain on the study for the time being, but I was slightly concerned as I hadn't had to use the key to unlock the door. I tried to remember locking it before leaving, but then fell asleep.

As I put the key in my front door the next morning, it felt like I'd been away for years. I left my bags in the hallway and went to the kitchen to make a cup of tea, then headed to the study and was relieved to find that I had locked the door after all. Once inside and sat down in the swivel chair I'd bought, I slowly pivoted round to look at the paintings. I remember the moment distinctly. It was precisely eleven o'clock in the morning and my cleaner was due in any second as it was a Monday. I closed the door so she wouldn't have the opportunity to peer in and catch me in there. It took me a good hour to check them, although I could have taken longer, but I wanted instant gratification. I drank in their characters thirstily, reacquainting myself with the faces I'd become so familiar with.

I wasn't sure which one was my favourite. I didn't want to be influenced by the fact the 'bike' and 'boar' paintings were early works, and the self-portrait I had special personal connections with, so I tried to exclude those three from my appraisal. It was a close call between the painting I'd originally bought at Katherine's first show, when we'd first met, and the one I'd got from Newton, the banker, through Manish Kumar. It made me think of Goa, where I'd met him, in fact, where he'd literally been conceived and it highlighted something I hadn't looked at for some time.

Miles knew of Kumar's existence but I still wasn't sure whether this was a good or a bad thing. Here was Miles, Katherine's dealer, in control of her flow of work and my personal good friend. Kumar, on the other hand, was a collector I knew of unknown wealth – in fact, he could be as wealthy as I wanted him to be. I started to see a way forward. Miles would never have to meet Kumar, in much the same way that identities of auction bidders are sometimes undisclosed. Who was it who said "privacy prevails when wealth watches?" If I was careful I could employ Miles to achieve Kumar's aim, which was to acquire as much of her work as possible. Miles was keen to make a living from dealing in art and as long as he could retain his integrity there seemed no reason why Kumar couldn't engage his services to seek out works that were beyond his reach. At that moment I owned around seventy-five per cent of Katherine's entire output, but with Kumar and Miles' help, I thought I might be able to boost that to somewhere above ninety.

The phone rang in the living room so I carefully locked the door to the study and went to answer it, lost in these thoughts.

'Hi, Jamie, is that you? Sorry to disturb you after the long flight. Did I wake you?'

It took me a moment to place the female voice on the line. It was Katherine's.

'Oh, no, not at all. I don't know what to say to you. I'm so sorry. It's terrible what happened. Lawrence was a fantastic guy. How are you? How's your mum? Is there anything I can do?'

She was subdued, of course, but being level-headed and precise, it was probably a defence mechanism to deal with the shock of losing both Lawrence and her father.

'Oh, Mother is bearing up, sort of. I have to come into town to pick up Lawrence's things from Miles tomorrow afternoon. I'd like to meet up, if that's ok? How about if we met first? Say for coffee in the morning?'

I said that was fine and we arranged to meet at Liverpool Street Station, on the concourse of the Royal Exchange, at 11 o'clock. She would then only be a few minutes walk away from the gallery in Farringdon.

It was a good place to meet being always busy, and had a high ceiling which meant one could have an intense conversation without fear of being overheard. As it turned out, I was late as there had been a problem with the tube trains, but she wasn't angry with me when I spotted her sitting alone at a table outside one of the cafés. We ordered two cappuccinos and I got up and walked around the table to give her a hug. I became intoxicated with the mix of her body and the scent that she always used. It had been such a long time since I'd held her that I'd completely forgot what it was like. It felt exciting to have her locks of hair brushing the side of my face again. The months we'd been apart, the advent of Lawrence into her life, and my anger and jealousy, all slipped away. I made to let her go but she held on to me for a few, extra special seconds.

After we sat down I told her what had happened on the boat. She stared at me the whole time without blinking, which was pretty unnerving. There was silence as the cappuccinos arrived and I broke open the top of a packet of sugar and poured some into my cup. It gathered on the top in a heap and then fell through the foam, disappearing rather like Lawrence had done that day. As I stirred it I could feel her green eyes boring into me, even though mine were looking down at the swirling coffee.

'God, it must have been awful for you,' she finally said.

'I felt helpless. The poor bloke. I can't even swim properly. I was amazed when Gabriel jumped in to get him.' There was a pause after which I offered, 'Look, if there's anything I can do, anything at all, to help – Just say . . . OK?'

She continued to stare at me for a while. I had no way of telling what she felt as she was always so inscrutable.

'I'd better be going,' she said abruptly, 'I'm going to be late for my meeting with Miles. I'll be at my mum's till Dad's cremation next week. It's just a small gathering down in Kent with Mum and a few relatives who live in the UK.'

'Why don't we travel up together on the train to Newcastle? For Lawrence's service?'

'Yes, I'd like that,' she said, and a smile broke through her solemn face.

'Let's speak once the date's been fixed.'

I noticed her brow furrowing.

'There's a lot of things to attend to, concerning the foundry. Some of his sculptures are sitting there still unfinished. I'll have to put my painting on hold for a while. I must go.'

She got up and I got up too, to hold her again, and she lingered there in my arms as the echoes of people's footsteps enveloped us.

Chapter 13

Czech politician Jan Masaryk was found dead in the courtyard of the Foreign Ministry in Prague on March 10th, 1948. In 2004, a police investigation into his death concluded that, contrary to the initial ruling, he did not commit suicide, but was defenestrated by his Communist opponents. He was wearing his pyjamas.

For the rest of the day I was walking on air. I hadn't realised just how down I was and how much self-restraint I'd been exercising since Lawrence's accident. With one whiff of Katherine's perfume, my grey London world had been transformed into a garden of earthly delights. On my way back from our meeting, I started to notice all manner of things, the complete zoo of individuals you see on the London Underground for one. I counted twelve back-packers, five Muslim women in veils, fourteen uniformed schoolboys on a school outing, an albino West Indian girl with dreadlocks, two Goths, three women with prams, any number of shoppers laden with bags from the New Year sales as we went through Oxford Circus, and an Eastern European woman asking me for change when I hopped off the train at Queensway. I was in such a good mood that I gave her a pound.

I walked past Whiteley's Shopping Centre and decided on a whim to go in and see what was showing at the cinema upstairs, and walking towards the ticket hall I bumped into Nicola, the brunette from Christmas night at the Peponi.

'Oh, my God, it's you . . . Jamie!' she cried out at me.

I remembered her saying she lived near me in Bayswater when we'd met. It was good to see her again and we agreed to speak on the phone later to arrange meeting up. My new home situation meant I could entertain without my secret art collection being discovered. I attended to the mountain of mail that had arrived whilst I'd been away and amongst all the junk mail there were the customary credit card invitations, bank statements, bills and the like, plus an invitation to the posthumous launch of a book about Lawrence. I'd forgotten it was due for publication that spring by Booth Clibborn, the Rolls Royce of art publishing, and Lawrence had let me have a look at his proof copy in the autumn. It was magnificent, but far beyond the pockets of most book buyers, although the limited edition at £200 would undoubtedly be snapped up by collectors of fine art literature in the light of Lawrence's death. The invitation said the launch was due to be held at the foundry but I suspected there would be a change of venue under the circumstances. I supposed this to be one of the things Katherine had been referring to earlier that day. It was only a few hours ago but it seemed like a lifetime to me. Much as I wanted to pick up the phone and call her, I resisted the temptation and instead called Nicola to leave a message. A few minutes later Miles rang me.

'I wanted to ask you. How was Kath when you saw her today?'

'Well, she seemed to be holding herself together. I don't know how she's managing, to tell you the truth. She wanted to know everything about that day on the boat, understandably. I thought she'd break down after I told her. But surprisingly she didn't.'

'I agree,' he confirmed, 'She's showing amazing courage coping with it all. And there's her mother to look after as well.'

'She said she wouldn't be doing much painting for a while. I thought you should know she'd mentioned it,' I added.

'Oh, dear. I suppose I should have expected that. Ah well, it's totally understandable.'

This was something he didn't want to hear as she was a big part of his business now and he didn't want to delay her next exhibition. His discussions with the National Portrait Gallery – of the initial plan to have her as a resident artist over the coming summer – had burgeoned into the idea of a full exhibition to coincide with the start of her tenure there. If he pulled it off it would be a first for the institution.

'I'm going down to Kent tomorrow for her father's cremation,' he continued, 'I expect Lawrence's service won't be held too long after that. I guess I'll see you next up in Newcastle. She said you'll be bringing her up, right?'

Just after his call Nicola rang me back and her voice brought back the gaiety that had first attracted me to her. At the time Lawrence and I were smarting from Katherine's news about her father's death and her mischievous sense of humour had lifted both our spirits. She wanted to apologise to me immediately.

'I'm sorry for leaving the Peponi so suddenly that morning. But you were sleeping like a baby and there didn't seem any good reason to wake you up. You looked so sweet. Penny can't stop talking about your friend Lawrence.'

I briefly explained what had happened to him and we agreed to get something to eat the following evening at Ping Pong, a dim sum restaurant close to both of us on Westbourne Grove. I was glad I'd bumped into her as she was someone I could have fun with and she was frivolous, in stark contrast to Katherine's sobriety.

I walked over to Ping Pong the following evening in high spirits and eager to see her again. Nicola had put a smile on my face but I knew next to nothing about her. I had no idea what she did for a living, but I guessed she was from a wealthy family and she'd probably inherit substantial money at some stage in her life. I'd met people like that before and most of them were pretty miserable, with aimless lives, but if that was her story then she was an exception to the rule.

When I reached the restaurant she was already sitting at the bar in cowboy boots, downing a tumbler of warm sake. I told her it was considered rude in Japan to pour your own, so we got another tumbler and spent the next half hour filling up each other's, and exchanging news. This was only the second time we'd met, not counting at Whiteley's, but it felt like we'd known each other far longer. I loved the way she put her head back and laughed unrestrained. She told me she was in PR and spent her day showing TV producers around expensive editing suites in the West End. We ordered a selection of dim sum dishes and more sake.

'Since Lawrence died I've been without a drinking partner,' I admitted.

'And it sounds like you're in need of one at the moment,' she observed cannily.

'I've never had a female one before, so this whole situation's a novelty,' I joked, adding, 'Presumably, you can drink enough to keep me company till I fall over?'

'And get you home. Or take you home,' she bantered.

I was starting to relax and after we'd eaten I went into the details of Lawrence's death and began telling her things about him. I must say I enjoyed describing him to someone new, and someone who didn't know him at all. She'd been on one of those fibreglass boats herself when she was in Kenya, and confirmed how dangerous they were. When she passed on her friend Penny's condolences, I realised that to the outside world I'd become Lawrence's best friend, and at that thought I fell silent.

Nicola leaned across the table and took my face in her hands to give me a sensuous kiss. I smiled at her and thought we should ask for the bill. We left the restaurant and I instinctively turned as if to head for home, and Nicola came with me.

Chapter 14

On September 24th, 1483, a violent overthrow of the municipal governments of the Old and New Towns of Prague ended with the throwing of the Old Town portreeve and the bodies of seven killed aldermen out of the windows of the respective town halls.

Several weeks passed, and I experienced a calm that had eluded me for some time. My work on the book about succulents progressed rather well and I made a few trips down to Kew to immerse myself in the humidity of the large hothouses they have there. Succulents smell differently from all other plants even when they're not in flower, and I felt comfortable surrounding myself with their intoxicating aromas.

Nicola and I met up several times a week and occasionally she'd come straight over from working late and stay the night with me. We made no demands upon each other and we laughed a lot. It was a delight to be with someone happy to take things as they came, with no plans or preconceived ideas, and she wasn't looking to start a family. She didn't say much about her relatives and gave the impression she didn't want to talk about them but I discovered they lived abroad. If she were with me at the weekends we'd drive over to Kenwood House and have a walk around, and sit and read the papers at the cafe in the open air, enjoying the spring weather. A year earlier I'd taken Katherine there once but we hadn't gone back again. The woods have the most remarkable gnarled tree trunks resembling all sorts of animals and imaginary creatures, and we animatedly pointed these out to one another. We both loved the cinema, so we'd go and see a movie on Saturday afternoons then spend the evening discussing its merits and weaknesses over a meal.

But I digress . . .

Katherine and I travelled up by train to Lawrence's funeral and rather than stay in Newcastle for the night, I said I had to leave for a meeting in London the next morning. In earlier times I would've been all too keen to spend more time with her but my new attitude was having an effect. As I was saying goodbye to Lawrence's parents at the wake she said:

'Can I speak to you before you go?' She walked outside with me to the waiting taxi. 'I need your advice. The publishers of Lawrence's book have moved the launch away from the foundry. But I really need to decide what to do with it. Jake and Dinos have said they want to take it over and continue with the commissions in some way. I'd like to know what you think.'

I carried on with my new attitude.

'Why don't you ask Miles what he thinks? He is your dealer, after all.'

'I'd prefer to hear what you think.'

'All right. I'd be glad to help if I can,' I offered, 'why don't you call me when you get back to London?'

She hugged me and the concoction of her body smell and perfume, once again, stayed with me in the taxi and on the four hour train journey back down to London.

She called me early the following evening and asked if we could go over to the foundry together and take a meeting with Jake and Dinos, so I suggested she come by the next morning for coffee and I could drive us both over afterwards. She arrived soon after twelve and I showed her around the new flat passing by the study door without even referring to it. It could have been the door to a closet and the fact I'd ignored it, I reasoned, would lead her to assume some such thing anyway. I made some coffee and when she sat down at the kitchen table she promptly burst into tears. This took me by surprise, never having seen her cry before, and I saw for the first time how her pretty face could become ugly with lines of torment and pain. I gave her a paper handkerchief and stood behind her with my hands holding her shoulders. I gently stroked her, saying soft words, while she continued to sob into the hankie. She seemed to regain her composure and blew her nose. I gave her a fresh hankie, and she meekly looked over the top of it at me.

I thought some music might help, so I found *Wave* by Antonio Carlos Jobim and put it on quietly in the background. By the time it had got to *The Red Blouse* she'd stopped crying. I remember I mutely offered her a warm pecan twirl from the oven to have with her coffee. I broke it in half and offered her one of the pieces. I comically dunked mine in my coffee and it made her laugh. I'd overcome another hurdle with her.

'I'm so sorry. It's the first time I've broken down. While I've been with Mum I thought it would be best not to cry in front of her. I thought it would be of help. But there's no way of telling. She's so quiet these days. I just can't reach her.'

'But grief has to come out at some stage,' I said firmly, then more tenderly, 'I'm sure she appreciates your support. Just by being there for her.'

I was secretly overjoyed she felt relaxed enough to show some vulnerability to me. By the time the CD had finished she was feeling better, so I suggested we make our way down to the car. I'd only been to the foundry once before but I vaguely remembered which route to take there, so I concentrated on the driving and didn't try to speak. We'd got to Old Street and were heading north east through Hackney when she asked me, 'So, who's this new girl in your life?'

I was surprised at her question coming out of the blue and it probably showed on my face.

'A friend of mine saw you together, on Westbourne Grove recently. They said you looked pretty much, well . . . together.'

'Oh, it was just an old girlfriend I was catching up with,' I threw at her nonchalantly. I could tell without looking that she was studying my face, no doubt looking for me to betray some more information. I didn't want to explain, partly because I was concentrating on the driving and partly because I saw no reason to tell her. My new attitude involved keeping her guessing as to where my ambitions lay as far as she was concerned. I thought she might find the energy to try a little harder with me. She fell silent at my reply and a few minutes later we arrived at the foundry.

The place didn't look that different from the last time. Sculptures were awaiting collection near the entrance and two others were nearing completion. I could tell this was the case as Jake and Dinos were scrambling over them like ants with oxyacetylene torches. They climbed down when they saw us drive in, and led the way into the darkness of the foundry to a lit area with some makeshift seating around a table. Jake went off to make some tea while Dinos made it clear how indebted they were to Lawrence for taking them on. He explained they'd been spying on him for months, trying to work out how best to approach him. Then Jake reappeared with the tea and picked up the story.

'Of course, in the end we just knocked on the door and came out with it. We didn't want no money or nothing; we were just in it for the crack. Nights, we was working down Smithfields, then having a line of speed and helping him out during the days. When he saw how much enthusiasm we had, that's when he asked us to do it full time. We had to give up the drugs though, that was the condition.'

'Yeah, and we ain't looked back, have we, son?' chirped in Dinos.

'Too right, bro, too right,' affirmed Jake.

'Nah, it's been fantastic, it really has. So, what we thought was, we learned so much from the guv'nor when we was with him, we wanted to have a go on our own, like. We've finished a couple of pieces since he's been . . . well, gone, and they've been accepted.'

'Yeah, the clients, they all know us. We wanted to start a website of our own, with a link to the guv'nor's . . . If that would be cool?'

They both looked over at Katherine for her agreement, and she looked at me.

'There are ten years left on the lease,' I said. 'We'll have to go into that side of things first and get back to you. But it shouldn't take very long.'

They seemed happy enough with this suggestion and it was obvious Katherine was relying upon me to take control for her. We got up to leave, and I said I couldn't foresee any major objections to them taking over and some agreement could probably be reached by the time Lawrence's book was launched at the end of that month.

We drove back across London and my autopilot guided the car back to Bayswater, as I couldn't think of anywhere else to go. As we pulled up outside my flat I asked her if she wanted to come up for a while, and she did.

'I think the sooner you get rid of the lease on the foundry the better. It will probably become a financial burden at some point, unless you've got any plans to work there yourself?' I told her.

'I definitely don't intend to do that,' she confirmed.

'Then I suggest you write to the landlord, and put Jake and Dinos forward as the new tenants. You can leave it between them to work out the details of taking it over. Do you think they can afford it? That's probably what the landlord will want to know.'

'Lawrence paid them a good wage as his income increased, so they can probably give themselves a few months financial cushion to get started.'

By now it was after five and I was very hungry, so instead of making tea I offered to cook something up for the two of us. She said she hadn't eaten anything all day and immediately accepted, and I noticed her visibly relaxing as she took off her coat.

'Thank you for dealing with Jake and Dinos today. And for being so understanding . . . you know, when I cried.'

She watched me prepare the ingredients for an omelette.

'God, you do that so neatly!' she exclaimed.

'Virgo. My parents always wanted me to be a surgeon,' I explained to her.

After we'd eaten and drank some coffee, I felt it was time for her to leave and told her so. She looked a little put out at first, but then seemed to understand.

'I know what you mean. You're right. I should go.'

Five minutes later, alone, intoxicated and out of breath, I felt I had to see her paintings and hurriedly unlocked the door to the study and tiptoed in. I sat in the swivel chair and drank in what was up on the walls. I went back to the kitchen and picked up the paper handkerchiefs she had discarded that morning. I took them into the study and sat down again, touched the hankies to my face, and masturbated.

Chapter 15

One of the greatest myths about the Wall Street Crash of October 29, 1929 is that traders and bankers were jumping out of buildings and committing suicide in droves. A story often told, probably apocryphal, is that clerks in downtown hotels were asking guests when they checked in if they wanted the room for sleeping in, or for jumping. Divya Watal

The book launch was moved to the lobby of the chic Sanderson Hotel on Berners Street, and the publishers made sure it would be noteworthy. They'd invited not only dignitaries of the art world and journalists, but also gossip columnists from papers and magazines. Lawrence's death, as I'd predicted, had elevated him to iconic status and in anticipation of increased demand for the book they bumped up the first edition run to 25,000, with the first 5,000 in hardback at £200, and then 20,000 in paperback at £50. If it sold out in hardback Katherine, as his spouse, would be looking at picking up a large royalty cheque.

She arrived accompanied by Miles but I decided to go there alone. It was clear the interest of the media had been aroused and I found out that Luke Johnson, Chairman of Channel Four at the time, and Nick Powell and Eric Fellner, apparently both successful film producers, were among the guests. Perhaps they were thinking of making a biopic of Lawrence's life? I was introduced to a gossip columnist with a devastating figure called Zoe something, and a Polish model who shared my passion for jazz. At a table by the entrance, paperback copies were being given to the five hundred guests as they were leaving and there were hardbacks on sale as well.

I spotted Jake and Dinos holding court so I went over to say hello. They thanked me for helping out with the takeover of the foundry although I really hadn't done that much and I told them so. Jake disagreed.

'No, Jamie mate, fair play to yous. Katherine really respects you, and what you said really made a difference. And it looks like it's all cool with the landlord.'

I left them in conversation with a curator from the Tate Modern, and you can't get a better start to your career than that.

I stayed longer and drank more than I'd originally intended to but I hardly saw Katherine and Miles, apart from a few minutes when we found ourselves standing next to each other, getting our glasses refilled by a waitress. It was like the enormous ball at the end of the film *The Leopard*, at which dancing couples glide past one another, recognise friends, exchange a greeting, then float away into the throng. Katherine touched me tenderly and I found myself putting my arm around her waist. She responded by drawing herself closer to me but I was aware of how it could have looked, so I drew myself away before Miles had noticed. A second later they were gone into the crowd and I was talking to someone else. In a similar fashion I found myself standing next to Jessica from the gallery. I hadn't seen her for a couple of months and her face had grown thinner to show off a superb bone structure.

'But, Jessica, you look absolutely stunning!' I could tell she was pleased to hear this.

'Why, thank you, Jamie. I must tell you . . . I was so sorry to hear about Lawrence. How are you coping? I know you two were very close.' She stroked the arm of my jacket.

I wasn't sure how to respond and thought for a second.

'I do miss him . . . It's just one day at a time at the moment. It's much worse for Katherine, of course. Are you still at the gallery with Miles?'

'Yes. Full time now. I really love working for him. I've split up with my boyfriend again . . . ' and on saying that she smiled at me, waiting for me to comment.

'Oh . . . Well, I have to say, he's the unlucky one. We should meet up one evening . . . for a drink?'

'I'd love to,' she said, 'You live in Bayswater, don't you? Now the weather's improved, I'm cycling in to the gallery from Chiswick every day, so I could drop by on the way home one day. That would be perfect.'

On my way home in a cab I was finding it hard to remember who I'd agreed to have drinks with, and my pockets seemed to be full of business cards and bits of paper with numbers written on them.

March and April passed, and Nicola and I continued to see one another but the more I crossed paths with Katherine the more I realised I was falling in love with her all over again. This time it seemed to have some purpose whereas before it had lacked one. I could see Nicola was the antithesis of Katherine and no sooner had I said goodbye to one, I felt compelled to seek out the company of the other. I was finding it hard to maintain a balanced view on life in general and other women only reminded me of my yearning for the two of them.

I decided to take a break from working on the succulent book for a week and thought of inviting Katherine to come away with me. I'd just received a royalty cheque from sales of the hydrangeas UK edition and wanted to celebrate. She had immersed herself in painting for the past two months, but we'd met up regularly when she wanted advice concerning Lawrence's estate. She was beginning to rely heavily upon me which was what I'd been hoping for. We'd shown affection for one another but hadn't shared a bed again. There was no hurry for that as far as I was concerned. I was content with the way things stood between us.

I called her to ask if she wanted to come to Spain with me as I knew some out of the way places by the Atlantic where we could slow down for a bit. I'd spent time down there several years before when I'd been working on a book about the flora of Andalusia, which is plentiful and delightfully varied due to the balmy climate. She showed no hesitation in accepting my invitation and we agreed to leave on the Sunday afternoon, giving us a week by the beaches south of Cadiz. After our plane landed at Seville we picked up a hire car and drove an hour or so down motorway. They still hadn't closed the bar at the hostel I knew of, and within five minutes of arriving we were standing on the roof terrace looking at the azure ocean enjoying a glass of chilled manzanilla.

'Mmmm, this feels good,' she said, 'you are clever, Jamie. What a great idea it was of yours to get away.'

She pecked me on the cheek and strolled over to the edge of the terrace. It was out of season and we were the only people staying at the hostel. I looked around and saw the tall flowering heads of the yuccas, looking like telegraph poles, dotted along the side of the beach road we'd driven down. Some were still growing ever upwards, some had just flowered and others were tipping over, past their peak and signifying the death knell of the plant, as it only flowers the once in its lifetime. It always served to represent the pathos of Spain to me. We took a refill before the bar closed up and went back up to watch the black dots of the surfers as they appeared and disappeared in the waves below. We tried to count how many we could see, but it was impossible to keep track of those we had and hadn't counted.

'It's like trying to count your blessings,' Katherine said, and it reminded me of a joke I'd heard once in Spain.

'Did you hear about the short man, who was asked what he wanted his son to be when he grew up?' I asked her.

'Can't say I have. What did he say?'

'Tall,' I said, and it was nice to hear her laughing again.

The weekend was winding down and there were very few people about. When we'd finished our drink we took a walk to stretch our legs. There was a fresh wind blowing and the tide was on its way out. As I pressed my shoes into the pristine yellow sand, the pressure squeezed the water away from my footprint and it began to look like concrete. We found odd bits of coral and a million tiny, coloured shells that the surf was washing up, and I was reminded of the beach paintings by the 1930s surrealist Yves Tanguy. I mentioned this to Katherine.

'Who's he?' she asked. I was surprised she didn't know of him.

'You know. The surrealist who ate live spiders.'

'Oh, him,' she tossed back and I could tell by her tone of voice that she was none the wiser.

After a while we turned and headed back in silence, and her hand searched for mine.

By the time we'd unpacked it was dark and I suggested going over to eat in the local town, twenty minutes away by car. As I drove we didn't speak, and it seemed we were finally getting to a place together that I'd been waiting a long time to reach. At that moment I wanted to be with Nicola but hid this desire away in my head to concentrate on remembering the right roads that would take us to the restaurant. We skirted the town centre on a newly built ring road lined with abandoned half-finished apartment blocks, and came down from the northeast, past the Eroski supermarket on the corner of C. Chiclana and Ave. Bajada del Chorillo. We decided to sit inside as a spell of bad weather was just starting and the famous Levante wind was coming in directly from the Sahara across the ocean.

The vast covered area outside was understandably empty of diners that night and the multitude of blue and yellow painted chairs were pleasing to look at from the warmth of the room. We took a table next to the fish tank holding the live lobsters, with their claws closed with rubber bands, and I felt rather sorry for them manacled like that on death row. I ordered two manzanillas and we looked at the menu to see what else there was apart from lobster. I felt the trip with her was an achievement, some sort of a landmark, and I told her how happy I was that she'd decided to come along with me. As there were two beds to a room, she'd suggested that we just take one, so there was no question mark over where she'd be sleeping that night. With no more to prove to myself that day, I made sure we got through a second bottle of wine with our food.

That night a terrific thunderstorm came over and the drama of forked lightning and flashes of daylight penetrated the darkness of the bedroom. It woke me up and I watched it for a while from our balcony, before it receded into the Atlantic. The next day was clear and we headed down the road to have breakfast in the garden of a bar directly across the road from the ocean. The sun was warm, although it was only ten o'clock in the morning, and we sat out to soak up the heat like two storage heaters. Katherine had slept through the storm so I described it to her as being like a Turner painting, needing only a couple of man o' war from the 1800s to complete it in 3D. We walked back along the beach and then it seemed perfectly natural to make love with the balcony doors open wide and the sounds drifting up from the bar below, with the odd car passing by. The road out front marked the boundary of protected land that sat between the hostel and the beach and it was ablaze with wild spring flowers. There was a scruffy haystack right in front of our window and the luckiest mule in the world lived in this beautiful spot.

The week drifted by and the sun shone every day in clear, exquisite light blue skies. We ventured into the ocean a few times, but only briefly and at the hottest times of day. We'd get breakfast and then go back to our room to make love. There were several places along the road to have lunch, all within a hundred yards of the sea and we took turns deciding where to try next. When the evening came, we sat on the roof to watch the sunset and it reminded me of the accidental beheading of the cat on Lamu and Lawrence's death, but I didn't mind so much. It seemed part of another world to me now, a period when Katherine wasn't in my life. But I missed Nicola's laughter and her sense of fun as it always seemed such an effort with Katherine, so I sent a few texts to her.

After four days I suggested going for a drive to break the tedium that was gradually seeping into our time together. We visited Tarifa and looked across the straits at Morocco. I showed her Bolonia, from where you can see the minarets of Tangier on a clear day, and the vast wind farms set high above Gibraltar before the road sweeps dramatically down to Algeciras. One day we headed inland and got as far as Grazalema and Zahara de la Sierra, perched above El Gastor reservoir, where we bathed in the cool, still waters and allowed the silence to smother us.

Suddenly it was Sunday, and before we left I went up to the roof and took one last look at the sea and there were more surfers out than I'd ever seen before, bobbing up and down, in and out of sight in the water. I didn't even try to count them this time. I was glad we'd come away but also relieved to be heading back to London.

On the drive back to Seville Katherine revealed something of the nature of the new work she was eager to return to. Apparently the mood of the paintings was darker, using the chiaroscuro technique of strong side-lighting, and there were to be portraits of her mother and father, and Lawrence too. This excited me, and I felt like pulling the car over to the side of the road and having her right there and then, savagely, but I thought better of it and just said it sounded interesting.

Chapter 16

On November 7th 2003, John J. Kokal, a fifty-eight year old senior analyst at the State Department Intelligence Unit (INR) was found dead in the late afternoon at the bottom of a 20 ft window well, eight floors below the roof of State Department Headquarters. A colleague of Kokal's told this writer that the Iraq analyst was despondent over problems with his security clearance. Kokal reportedly climbed out of a window and then threw himself out in such a manner that he would 'land on his head'. INR occupies a Sensitive Compartmented Information Facility (SCIF) on the sixth floor that has no windows, and a windowless structure on the roof. The other windows at the State Department have been engineered to be shatterproof and cannot be opened. A former INR employee revealed it would have been impossible for Kokal to have gained entry to the roof on his own. He was not wearing a jacket or shoes when his body was found.

For the duration of the flight back, I was preoccupied with what Katherine had told me about her new work and there was no doubt her grief had contributed to its darker mood. The fact that her parents and Lawrence were figuring as her subject matter intrigued me, as it meant her work was beginning to become autobiographical, which was crucial for any serious artist. I wondered if she were using any other people from her life as subjects, such as Miles, and Jake and Dinos, maybe even myself. I was dying to question her more about this but knew it would all be revealed to me in the fullness of time. Besides, my new attitude of leaving her alone was paying huge dividends as she was now seeking me out for anything she had need for: be it sex, advice, or just a person to listen to her. She'd taken to calling me at least once a day during the week before we'd left for Spain about all manners of things, and if I were to be honest it was beginning to irritate me. At least when we were in Spain together there was no way she could call to pester me the whole time and I was grateful for that small mercy. But I knew that as soon as we got back to London and went our separate ways the scenario would start up all over again. What new things would she discover to ask me? Should she recycle, or not recycle? Was there a public library within walking distance of her flat? Would it be a good idea to get an entry phone installed so she could find out who it was at the front door? These were the things she'd come up with the week prior to our trip. Once she'd called when Nicola was visiting and I didn't like that one bit, but I had to be patient as little by little, she was beginning to lose the immense arrogance that had initially intimidated me. Just then I turned to look at her sitting beside me on the plane and at that moment she looked quite vulnerable. I took her hand in mine and sat holding it for a while, and looked out of the window pitying her.

By the time we'd reached Victoria Station I couldn't wait to put her in a cab to have some time to myself again. I was relieved to open my front door and empty my mailbox. When the lift doors opened at my floor, I pulled out my keys and noticed that my front door was ajar, so I checked for any signs of damage to see if it had been forced. I put down my bags and entered the flat as silently as I could, in case there was someone still inside. All my furniture seemed undisturbed and nothing had been touched as far as I could see. The key to the study was on the swab I always travelled with, and my heart quickened as I tried the doorknob and found it still to be locked. There didn't seem to be any sign of a burglary so I concluded that in my rush to catch the plane the week before I hadn't shut the door properly. I made a cup of tea and phoned Nicola to see if she could come over, as I was desperate to see her again.

Katherine's show was due to open in the middle of June at the National Portrait Gallery, and I secured several of the paintings beforehand from Miles, both as myself and as Manish Kumar, serving to legitimise his identity to the art world. I also made another sortie to Miles' gallery for my book research and managed to entice Jessica to go out again, leaving me to print out an updated copy of the buyers list. It had noticeably grown, and I was pleased to see Kumar's name wasn't at the bottom any more with a question mark next to it, but was near the top close to my own.

Between us we had bought six, and Miles had been offering them up-front at the knockdown price of £12,000 each, as opposed to £15,000 at the show, making a whopping saving of £18,000 for me in total. He was only asking for fifty per cent in advance, so I used some of the royalties that had just come in from the UK hydrangeas book. If he pre-sold the whole show he would gross a total of about £250,000, of which he would take home £125,000. Luckily he had no costs as the National Portrait Gallery was staging the show for him in return for Katherine's summer residency there. While I was at the gallery Jessica reminded me we'd agreed to have a drink sometime, so before I left I gave her the address of my flat.

As I'd predicted, Katherine started calling me again and it got to the stage where I was ignoring her. I started to enjoy this, but sometimes felt sorry for her and answered to listen to her latest life threatening problem. She also began turning up unannounced at my front door, probably as a result of my not taking her calls. There was no pattern to the visits and I thought that perhaps she was trying to surprise me if I was with another woman. She would come up with some excuse like she was in the area, or she couldn't ring first as she'd mislaid her phone. I would have to sit there feigning interest in the immense burden of being Katherine Gaunt and I began to think she was fabricating most of it as a bizarre way to make contact with me. I stopped answering the buzzer if I had any suspicion it could be her standing outside.

One evening I was enjoying a glass of Prosecco and listening to the Sonny Rollins Prestige Studio Sessions 1949-1951, when I heard someone was at the front door. I suspected it to be Katherine, so paid no attention and turned up the volume of the music. It rang three or four times before falling silent and a wry smile found its way onto my face. I'd just started to feel sorry for her, when my cell phone beeped – a text message had arrived:

JAMIE! R U IN? I'M OUTSIDE ON MY
BIKE! JESSICA XX

I cursed Katherine and released the front door lock. A few seconds later Jessica stepped out from the lift and stood in front of me looking flushed from her cycling. I led her inside, poured her a glass of Prosecco, and let her have a quick sip before taking her glass and placing it next to mine. Her clothes were loose and I began to kiss her neck and shoulders, and in no time at all she was letting me fuck her on my sofa.

My life was becoming complicated. Nicola was happy to meet up every week and Katherine expected me to make love to her whenever I picked up the phone. Now Jessica began calling by on her way home. I barely had enough time to devote to my writing and after sex all I wanted to do was to spend time alone in my study. At first when I'd met Katherine it had been hard to distinguish between the artist and the person, but now Katherine Gaunt, the artist, was confined within the four walls of my study and Katherine Gaunt, the person, had become a crashing bore. I'd even begun to pretend I was making love to Nicola or Jessica when we were together to make sure I could maintain an erection.

It was at around this time that I discovered Country and Western music through Jessica, of all people. She arrived one evening, and after fucking her, I saw her iPod and asked what she was listening to. I put on the headphones and Frankie Laine started singing *Jezebel* in my ears, I sat down and let his voice creep into my head, when that finished Patsy Cline began to sing *A Stranger in My Arms*. I'd never paid much attention to country and western music before but began to hear it differently from then on. It seemed to embody a lot of the things that I was going through at the time. The lyrics were about sadness brought on by love, or the lack of it, and ordinary day-to-day events were chronicled in interesting, clever ways. The musicianship was consistently excellent and some of the musical changes really were brilliant. I guess you could draw comparisons with the blues, but country has a certain happy-go-lucky quality to it, missing from the blues. Jessica began to get impatient so I finally gave her back the iPod and sent her away on her bicycle.

The next day I went to HMV in Whiteley's and found a six-volume collection of country and western greats. I hurried home and started to devour them, listening to them in the study and looking at the paintings. There was scarcely a bad track in there with Waylon Jennings, Willie Nelson, Merle Haggard and Burl Ives, all singing about things happening to me in my life. But I was particularly taken with Frankie Laine singing *Jezebel*, maybe because it was the first thing I'd heard. I did some research into his life and was astonished at his story.

He was born in Sicily and had emigrated to Chicago with his parents, where his father had become Al Capone's barber. He had to wait until he was in his mid-thirties to gain recognition as a singer and was discovered in a Los Angeles club at an open mike session by the great Hoagy Carmichael. Amongst other things he was known as Old Leather Lungs, and his voice became a distinctive trademark. Apparently he triggered a general change in direction from the smooth, lounge music of Frank Sinatra to a more character driven vocal style, which can only be described as the forerunner to rock and roll. As soon as he started making records he had huge success and he still holds the record in the UK for the number of weeks at Number One, and the number of weeks in a single year at Number One. He had twenty-three gold discs and sold a mind boggling, quarter of a billion records. At various times he'd been a bouncer, a dance teacher, a second-hand car salesman, an agent, a leatherette-factory worker, and a machinist at a defence plant. On top of all of this he had time to be a social activist, becoming a prime force in the American Civil Rights movement, as well as Meals on Wheels, The Salvation Army and Shoes for the Homeless. I bought a CD player to keep in the study, where *Jezebel* was on continuous play.

On the latest future buyers list was a name I hadn't seen before, a Luis Dean Reyes, with an address near Baton Rouge in Louisiana. What particularly interested me was that he'd agreed to buy no less than five of Katherine's new paintings and that was nearly as many as Kumar and myself put together. I was immediately suspicious and curious about him, and began to consider if he could be an invented character rather like Manish Kumar was, whose sole purpose was to conceal the identity of someone else. As I turned his name over and over in my mind, I even entertained the possibility that I'd invented him at some stage. I decided to Google him and found out that he was indeed a real, living person.

Luis Dean Reyes was born in Austin, Texas in 1938 and had won the Grand Lottery prize of $50,000,000 in 1996. He was a veteran of the Korean War and had been married four times, but there were no children. He was known to be an eccentric art collector who lived alone in a sprawling mansion outside Baton Rouge in Louisiana. He was a self-educated homosexual, a reclusive pederast who travelled the world searching for what he took a liking to, and I got the impression it didn't just apply to art objects. The more I read about him the more intriguing he became. There were no pictures of him but I conjured up one of my own which was a cross between Donald Trump, Phil Spector and the villain Blofeld from the James Bond movies, all rolled into one. As it turned out my image wasn't that different from the reality.

Chapter 17

On September 11th, 2001, an estimated two hundred people jumped to their deaths from the burning towers of the World Trade Centre in New York, landing on the streets and rooftops of adjacent buildings hundreds of feet below. To witnesses watching, a few of the people falling from the towers seemed to have stumbled out of broken windows. Nearly all of those who jumped were from the North tower. They struck the ground at just less than 150 mph, fast enough to ensure instant death on impact. They jumped alone, in pairs, and in groups. Ultimately, they were choosing not whether to die, but how to die. One falling body killed a firefighter.

London was enjoying a hot summer that year, probably the result of global warming, but I heard few people complain. Most were grateful for small mercies and took whatever opportunity they had to escape from their offices into the warmth and the sun, preferably in the comfort of some green space somewhere. The downside was that every park was littered with ugly, pink, burnt shoulders and white strap lines and it led me to the conclusion that the British aren't very good dealing with hot weather. I found the heat an even greater spur to my libido but however many times I made love it seldom brought me satisfaction.

I saw less and less of Katherine as the National Portrait Gallery show drew closer which I wasn't unhappy about, as it meant she was preoccupied with finishing the work and had no time to bother me with inconsequential things. She had warned me that I figured as one of the subjects in the new collection and I wasn't sure whether to be flattered or insulted by this bit of news. I don't like the spotlight on myself at the best of times, and the thought of my name being bandied around on the lips of people I didn't know confused me. I decided not to dwell on it and instead to concentrate on the other things she'd told me about the new work. The paintings were to be smaller which was pleasing to hear as it meant my six could easily be accommodated in the study. It put me in mind of Raphael who had also started to paint smaller pictures once he'd got into the big league. I suppose once you're up there you feel you have less to prove to the world. I hadn't seen any of them yet as Katherine was guarding them like the crown jewels, even from me, her erstwhile lover, and on the two occasions she'd invited me round to her flat, I'd seen no half-finished canvases anywhere. I'd tried the door to her studio a couple of times on the way to the bathroom, hoping to sneak a quick look, but it was always locked and she never offered to take me in there. I even toyed with the idea of breaking into her flat when I knew she would be out of town visiting her mother. It was hard to sleep properly as the date of the opening approached, but my dream of the art gallery did return, only this time a man that I'd identified as the American collector Reyes appeared whenever I turned a corner. He seemed to be always smiling at me, but not in a malevolent way, and that was a relief.

I went over to Miles and Ann's for Sunday lunch the weekend before the show and Miles was beside himself with feverish excitement.

'You know,' he confided, 'I never thought I'd have one of my artists' work going up in that dreary bloody place. Never in a million years. I always thought my future would be in Conceptualism, but it looks like that bubble's burst, big time.'

It was funny to think of the National Portrait Gallery representing the future of British Art for a change, especially so soon after the explosion of Conceptualism. It just goes to show that the taste of the public and the media always fluctuates between one thing and the other, if only to relieve monotony, rather like hemlines going up and down in the fashion world, and the pace of change is forever getting faster.

'I reckon that more than a thousand invitations have been sent out,' he said with a note of pride in his voice, 'What with my list and the gallery's combined. And I'm expecting a lot of people to come in from out of town.'

I took 'out of town' to be a veiled reference to Reyes, as he would be keen to take a look at what he'd bought on speculation. This I kept to myself, of course, as Miles couldn't be aware that I knew of the connection between him and Reyes without admitting I'd been through his computer. I sensed he was warming to his subject as he continued to say:

'She's let me have a look at most of it, and it's fantastic stuff. It's been so easy to sell as none of the works are too big. I wouldn't be surprised if it's all gone before Thursday.'

As I was leaving on the doorstep Ann quietly said to me:

'He can't stop going on about this next show of Katherine's. It's doing my head in. I'm looking forward to taking a break after the opening is over with. I've persuaded him to take me and the girls to Spain for a month in July. Will you be around to come by and feed the cats?'

As I walked down the road I was glad he hadn't brought up Jessica's name as it probably meant he didn't know about the little thing going on between us. Besides, our attraction to each other would probably evaporate as soon as he did get wind of it.

When I got home, a note had been put under my door from my neighbour saying he intended to move, and did I know of anyone who might be interested in buying his flat to save on estate agents fees? This was fortuitous news for me. When I took delivery of the new work, the study would be nearly full with seventeen paintings and if I was to secure any more, I was going to run out of space. I scribbled a note back saying I would be more than interested in buying it myself and slipped it back under his door. It was a studio flat, about twenty-five feet square, with plenty of light and generously high ceilings. I knew this as I'd been in there once when he'd invited me round for a drink. I made myself a cup of tea and considered how I was going to pay for the purchase. I headed for the study where I sank into the swivel chair and put on *Jezebel*.

What with the mounting expectations for the forthcoming show, I wanted to make sure I slept well so I started a routine that involved lots of exercise. I went for extended walks on Hampstead Heath to tire myself out and my sleep patterns seem to improve. By the time the Thursday arrived, I felt calm enough to meet Reyes in person.

In comparison to the last two openings of Katherine's, the National Portrait Gallery was a very sober affair and not at all what I'd been expecting. It was an austere setting for such a cutting edge show, and the plain, formal décor did nothing to create any excitement but, with all credit to Katherine and her talent, the work transcended the location and in some way served to lend legitimacy to her new found status. For another thing, there were no canapés, just ordinary white wine being served at a tad above room temperature. I remembered Miles telling me the gallery had insisted on organising the catering themselves to save money and it showed. But it was packed, and Katherine looked radiant in a flowing, sequin-festooned gown that looked like she'd been whisked straight out of Renaissance Italy. The gold sequins were set in black velvet and as she floated around she made a constant connection with the paintings. I kept stopping to look at the people I recognised in the canvases. The work was hung rather like the table placements at a banquet, with her parents at the centre and Lawrence on one side, Miles on the other, and Jake and Dinos on Lawrence's side, followed by the others, including me, at one end where I'd requested to be positioned to avoid drawing attention to myself. It worked very well but the reference to the seating at a banquet was making me feel hungry. I recognised Reyes immediately as he came drifting towards me, a little under five feet tall, wearing jeans and a Levi jacket over a black DEVO T-shirt with a pair of shiny, brown loafers. He had a silver pendant cross and chain around his neck and several large, silver rings on his short, podgy fingers. I remember one of them was a silver skull with deep hollowed eye sockets. As I'd guessed his hair was blonde and coiffured across his forehead, a la Donald Trump. He was tanned, with leathery skin like a lizard, and had some large, dark freckles on one side of his neck. He smiled and offered a hand out to me.

'You must be Miles' old college friend . . . Jamie? He pointed you out to me. Do let me introduce myself, Luis Dean Reyes, at your service. I'm so pleased to be here, so pleased. I find you do things in a whole different way over here in London.'

He held up his glass of tepid white wine and gave me a smile of complacent resignation. We shook hands and I was surprised to find myself warming to him. He seemed genuine enough, and turned out to be one of the most erudite and learned Americans I'd ever met. He was obviously a raving deviant but an interesting one at that, and his take on Katherine was refreshing.

'I own one of Lawrence's sculptures, you know, which sits majestically in my pasture land at home. I first read about her in *The New Yorker*. They printed a piece on their wedding last autumn, with a picture of them together. It aroused my curiosity. What was Lawrence doing with such a cutie pie? It was a relief to discover she's not just a pretty face.'

As we talked more I could see elements of, oddly, both Quilty and Humbert Humbert, the two protagonists from Nabokov's *Lolita*, added to the image I'd created for him beforehand. Miles came over and interrupted us.

'Glad to see you two have met each other. Don't know about you but I'm starving. I've just booked a large table for us all upstairs at Groucho's for later. I did say there'd be nothing to eat at this do.'

Reyes and I agreed to continue our conversation later over dinner and we went off in different directions to talk to other guests.

As I walked towards the Groucho with Miles he told me a bit more about Reyes. We were at the front of the group and Reyes was talking to Katherine further behind, so there was no fear of them overhearing us but he still kept his voice down as he spoke.

'He's absolutely loaded – won the lottery or something in America. He's bought five bleeding paintings and says he'd have bought more if they'd not all been sold. I'll have to chase up the buyers who haven't coughed up yet, just in case any of them want to change their minds and back out. As of now it's past the start date for the show so I'd be able to get him to pay full price, that is, if I can source any for him.'

We turned into Dean Street and Miles led the way into the entrance of Groucho's and up to the first floor dining room. There was room at the table for about twenty, and Miles busied himself getting everyone seated. I saw Reyes shuffling awkwardly at the back of the group near the door, so I went over and steered him around to the other end of the table and we sat down next to one another. I told him I'd been buying Katherine's work since her first London show.

'Oh, yes,' he said, 'Miles told me you owned one of the celebrated *Sunday Times* paintings. You wouldn't want to part company with that, now would you? I guarantee it would go to a careful and loving owner. In other words, myself. Please say yes.'

We both laughed, as he knew damn well I'd never agree to sell. But I liked his sense of humour. Now that he was sitting up close, I could see he was wearing make-up which is an unusual thing for a man to do, but it had been applied very discretely.

'So what else are you interested in, Luis?' I asked him, genuinely interested.

'Oh, a multitude of things, Mr Jamie. Human sacrifice . . . Mayan culture, the origins of all cultures, in fact. Animals . . . Gods, Idols . . . Love. The elements, in general. May I ask you a blunt question? Do you like women?'

'Yes. Most definitely,' I replied and I liked the way he'd gotten straight to the point.

'Now I am disappointed to hear that, truly. But that doesn't surprise me, not at all. I've been married four times myself, and believe me, every one of them was a delightful nightmare. Don't they just flash their Jezebel eyes at you? Turn us men into zombies, pure zombies. Yes, sir.'

I wasn't sure if he was referring to his own four wives, or all women, but I suppose it didn't really make that much difference either way.

'I do believe, Mr Jamie, women are the source of all the evil in the world. If men were left to their own devices, why, they'd sleep, work, eat, drink, smoke . . . fight sometimes, even fuck one another, but cause no real harm. You see, it's because they understand the nature of logic.'

I was keen to discover what his ambitions were, towards Katherine and her work.

'Miles tells me you've secured several paintings in the show . . . ?' I said.

He laughed and sat upright as if he were making a press statement and being interviewed.

'I will be looking to increase my collection in the future, God willing. Yes, sir.' At this he closed his eyes and put his hands together in mock prayer.

Other people began to sit down next to us and we started to talk with them. I noticed Jessica a few places along and caught her winking at me. Katherine was deep in conversation with the art critic Waldemar Janusak at the far end of the table, where Miles entertained Katherine's mother with Ann. The wine flowed and everyone got quite drunk. The food was served although no one seemed to be paying much attention to it. Luis drank a lot which served to loosen his tongue and he told me about where he lived.

'I have a wonderful home in Louisiana, Mr Jamie, truly wonderful. And I've been collecting ever since I got my money. I find it a satisfying way to express my personality. You know you can tell all about somebody by looking at the art they collect. You sure can. Think about it. You know it makes sense.'

I could see he had a point and considered my own collection and what it betrayed about me. Just recently I'd begun to think about getting some insurance in place, so as a fellow collector I asked him if security was an issue at his house.

'Why? Are you thinking of coming by and booglarising me, dear boy? At some point in the middle of the night? Now that would be interesting. If that's the case you'd better take my card.' He passed his business card to me and winked. 'Every work is protected by a system of laser beams, so if anything is touched a security firm will immediately arrive at the scene. I'm real sorry to disappoint you.' Then he became serious for a moment. 'I may have plenty of money, Mr Jamie, but deep down I'm a simple man at heart. I do not abide by the paranoia associated with wealth. Not at all. Not at all.'

He told me he lived alone in his vast house outside Baton Rouge and had a list of different skilled people whom he could call out at any time of the day or night. I began to imagine a house rather like the one Betty Davis occupied in the film *Hush, Hush, Sweet Charlotte*, with a sweeping central staircase and very large, floor to ceiling windows. I asked him if that was a fair comparison to make and he agreed it was.

'Oh, God, yes. How did you know that? I adore that film. I'm just like Betty Davis in that movie!' And he laughed at this comparison.

The evening drew to a close. He told me he was due to fly out early via Paris the next day for Louisiana, so he had to go, adding that he'd been thoroughly entertained meeting me. He invited me to visit him at some stage and view his collection, and he got up to say good-night to Katherine and Miles.

Jessica sidled up to me on my way back from the loo and asked if we should leave separately and meet up back at mine, but there was a lot to think about so I told her it wasn't a good idea. She went off in a huff and I guess the drink was responsible for that. I took her exit to the ladies as my cue to leave, so I said goodbye to Katherine, Ann and Miles and left in search of a taxi.

On the drive home I mulled over what I'd learned about Luis Dean Reyes. He was a fascinating man and one side of me was glad he'd taken an interest in Katherine's career. It was just the tonic she needed after the horrendous start to that year. But there was a growing desire inside of me to punish him. How dare he think he could buy my *Sunday Times* painting? He'd obviously seen it at the MOMA show in New York that spring. As if I would ever sell it. He probably believed I could be persuaded if he dangled enough of his stupid lottery money in front of me. I mean, he hadn't even earned it by working at a decent job. The effrontery of the little man!

I'd been drinking steadily since eight o'clock that evening so at the time I didn't pay much attention to these thoughts and tried to think about other things to calm myself down. Mainly that I'd made a mistake with Jessica, as by then I was just getting in the mood for her. I tried to text her but in my drunken state my fingers refused to pick the proper keys on the phone pad, and what with the sudden movement of the cab around corners, I gave up.

Chapter 18

On February 3rd, 1997, Bohumil Hrabal, popular author of 'I Served the King of England' and 'Closely Observed Trains' fell from the fifth floor window of his hospital and died in his pyjamas aged eighty-two. Two of his books describe people choosing to fall out of fifth floor windows.

The next day was spent nursing a terrible hangover and pieces of the evening began coming back to me in a disjointed fashion. I distinctly remembered Miles ordering several rounds of Armagnac after dinner, and I vaguely recalled Lemoncello being passed round the table before leaving. In light of this, it was surprising I'd made it all the way home, got myself undressed and into bed successfully. I drank several glasses of water and seeing as it was a bright day, I headed out to get some fresh air. It wasn't until I sat down at the Round Pond that I looked at my watch and saw it was only eleven o'clock in the morning. Then my mobile beeped with a message from Miles:

> GREAT NIGHT! YOU WERE
> ON GOOD FORM, LUIS
> REALLY LIKED YOU . . .
> JANUSAK FEATURE
> CONFIRMED FOR BBC2 . . .
> GOD WHAT A HANGOVER
> FROM HELL MXX

I was glad he hadn't called me as I wasn't in a fit state to talk to anyone. The news about the TV exposure for Katherine was a coup and I felt better in the knowledge that my collection was bound to go up in value as a result. Reyes began to drift back into my mind along with some of what had been going through my head in the taxi on the way home. His sudden appearance had presented me with a problem, since he'd said he was looking to increase his stock of Katherine's work which would put him in direct competition with me. This could force the prices up, something I didn't want to happen while I was still buying. But we'd got on extremely well, so well in fact, that he'd invited me to visit him at his home in Baton Rouge. Over breakfast I thought I might take him up on his offer at some point and I could feel my spirits lifting again.

My neighbour got back in touch and was pleased about my desire to buy his flat from him. I sensed I could negotiate a very good price as he said he'd found somewhere else and wanted to be out by the end of September.

I realised it was Friday which meant the incomplete chapter about yuccas that was still on my desk could remain there until the following week, and I could while away the day recovering, doing some chores, and thinking about what to do over the weekend. The forecast was good so I got an early night, and took a train down to visit a friend in Wivenhoe in Essex where I was able to take a break from Nicola, Jessica, Katherine and all of the paintings.

I spent the beautiful weather lounging on my friend's veranda, looking at the boats coming and going on the water, and watching two men pounding wooden posts into the muddy shoreline underneath a jetty next door. It was unsafe and in danger of collapsing, so they were strengthening the supports. It took a good fifteen minutes to get each new post three-quarters of the way down into the mud, and they used an ingenious weighted jackhammer to force the rest of it in. It was difficult to maintain a vertical trajectory and I could see some of the posts were off kilter, but it was satisfying to watch their progress over the three days of my visit. My friend came by frequently with cups of tea for me asking for updates on how they were getting on. As I sat in the sunshine watching them I sifted through all the information I had about Reyes. I felt an urge to visit him in Baton Rouge and take a look at his intriguing art collection, and discuss Katherine's work with him as a fellow enthusiast. It was certainly tempting but I wasn't sure I could justify such a trip as I was behind schedule with my book on the succulents. On the Sunday night, laying in bed with the image of that jackhammer in my mind, pounding the posts rhythmically into the mud, I came up with an idea. The jackhammer had reminded me of an oil derrick and it all just fell into place.

At the end of June I decided to leave London and head for the countryside for the summer. I saw a cottage outside Bath advertised in a Sunday supplement, complete with a fresh water swimming pool in the garden. On an impulse, I picked up the phone and rented it for two months. I decided not to take my computer with me and instead stay email free down there. My plan was to drive up in the late evening, once a week, and stay at my flat to write for maybe two or three days at a time, catch up on my mail and indulge myself in my study listening to Frankie Laine. I liked the fact that no one would know I was there, and it would be different to what most people do, which is to leave London at the weekends.

I didn't pack too many things as I'm always caught out on trips by taking far too much along. In the week before leaving, Nicola visited me and Jessica dropped by one day after work. Katherine insisted that I see her but I left her place at two in the morning, despite her protests, not being able to get to sleep. I headed for Bath on the Saturday morning listening to the Country and Western collection but I deliberately left the CD including *Jezebel* in the player in the study. The cottage was just the trick, and that weekend I pottered around familiarising myself with my new surroundings, listening to radio commentary on a Test match against Pakistan that was taking place somewhere in the Midlands, I forget where exactly.

By the time Tuesday arrived I was dying to get home. Amongst the post back in town, there was an invite from Jake and Dinos who'd taken over the foundry in the spring and now looked set to make a mark for themselves with a grand opening. On the front was a photo of one of their own sculptures and the dimensions printed on the reverse told me it was bigger than anything Lawrence had ever made. The show was called 'FOUND', playing, I presumed, on the word 'foundry' and the fact that all the elements they were using had, quite literally, been found. Their opening was in the middle of September which was in two months time, and I fully expected to be back from my trip visiting Reyes by then. On the Wednesday, I drove over to Miles' house to feed their cats as I'd promised to Ann. I considered coming back the following day to lie in wait and pounce on Jessica, who had volunteered to look after them the rest of the time, but I desperately wanted to get back to the cottage, so thought better of it.

When I arrived in London the following week I discovered Reyes had been in touch with Manish Kumar by email:

My dear Mr Kumar,

Allow me to introduce myself.

We have a mutual friend in the personage of Miles Good-fellow, the London dealer, and he has told me you are an avid collector of Katherine Gaunt, the celebrated Australian portrait painter. I, too, find myself under the spell of her talent and am at this moment in the process of trying to secure some of her earlier work. If at any time in the future you find yourself wanting to dispose of, or want to find a secure alternative home for, any of her paintings, would you please consider me as a most worthy prospective owner?

May I add that I have considerable funds at my immediate disposal.

Yours most truly,   Luis D. Reyes

It was becoming clear just how fast he was moving and it was worrying me. It seemed he'd got Miles wrapped completely around his finger and I wondered what other email addresses he'd acquired. Reyes could now be party to the details of all the current owners of Katherine's work and this possibility really annoyed me. His wealth had got him information that I'd carefully and painstakingly stolen – at great risk – from Miles' office, also jeopardising my longstanding friendship with Miles. I was beside myself with rage and felt strangely violated by this interloper, and I could see how Miles had unwittingly become embroiled in his plans. Miles had told me on the way to Groucho's for dinner that if he could retrieve some of the work earmarked for other buyers from the National Portrait Gallery show; he would stand to make more money by selling it to Reyes instead. He would also be entitled to a finder's fee for any other work of Katherine's he could help him buy.

I found a calendar and started to make some plans. It was now approaching the end of July which meant I had five weeks left at the cottage. First of all, I sent Reyes a reply from Kumar thanking him for his email. I worked out that it was around six in the evening in Louisiana, so I drove over to Miles' house to feed the cats and thought about what to say to Reyes when I called him later that evening.

At midnight I dialled his number through an intermediary service provider. It rang a few times before he answered.

'Hello? Luis Dean Reyes speaking.'

'Hi, Luis, it's Jamie here, calling from London. We met at Katherine's show, do you remember? I thought I'd give you a call. How are things?'

'Mr Jamie, what a pleasure to hear your voice again. I'm just fine and dandy, fine and dandy. We're having the most humid weather here at the moment. My clothes are sticking to me like a French whore. And how is dear old London town? God, I do miss that place.'

'Good. It's good. I just wanted to tell you, I'll be down your way soon, visiting some friends in Texas. I wondered if it might be a good time to accept your invitation, and drop by and see you?'

'Well, that is good news, real good news. Sure, I'll be here. I've no plans to go anywhere until I go to Thailand in the fall.'

I told him I was due to be in Texas in about four weeks, so we agreed that I could visit him on August 28th for lunch.

'You're more than welcome to stay over for a few days if you want to. There's plenty of room. You'll be perfectly safe alone with me.'

I thanked him for the offer but didn't commit myself either way, before saying goodbye.

I studied a map of the States to check distances between the various cities involved. He was located outside Weiss, a small town to the north east of Baton Rouge, off of Highway 16. I knew people in both Houston and Austin that I hadn't seen for a few years. One was an old school friend from Italy who was in the oil business and the other was my publishing agent in America, who had just moved down to Austin from New York, so it made perfect sense to use visiting them as my legitimate excuse for the trip. I rang them to say when I was coming through, and they were both more than happy for me to visit whenever I wanted. I booked a flight arriving in Houston on August 24th, leaving from Austin back to London via New York on September 1st. I booked a hire car at Houston airport to drop off at Austin, something that happens all the time in the States. Feeling as if I'd made some progress I went to the study to tell Katherine and the others about my planned trip.

August turned out to be a very hot month and I enjoyed dipping into the cold of the fresh water pool at the cottage. The garden was surrounded by fields containing grazing cows and the two lawns were mostly on a slant but there was one level spot where you could sit at a table, and I took to having breakfast there each day. The flower borders overlooked small, dry stone walls around the lawns and the garden on the whole had a pleasant and unassuming flavour to it. There were tall conifers on either side of two short, stone flights of stairs, taking you from one level to the next, and they added a hint of Italianate design which I particularly liked. Two stone-carved elephants sat beneath the conifers at the top of the first flight of steps, to greet you as you entered the garden from the house.

Katherine had gone to Australia with her mother for a while to visit relatives, and I was making the most of her time away by inviting Nicola down to stay with me at weekends. Jessica was busy with Miles for the whole month. He'd returned from Spain and was moving to a larger gallery and she was helping him to organise a group show to kick off the new space at the beginning of September. The rest of the time I was on my own. I spent the time planning my trip to the States and acquainting myself with Bath and the surrounding countryside. There were two mountain bikes at the cottage so Nicola and I did some exploring of the area. We found country pubs to stop at and enjoy a pint of real ale during rides in the early evenings. Most of the lanes had tall hedges giving the impression you were hurtling down a green tunnel with little idea of where you were heading, which I likened to my own life in many ways. I saw no need to mention my intended American trip to Nicola and to all intents and purposes I was at the cottage until September 4th, the day before the private view of Miles' group show. The cottage was in a secluded location accessed down its own track, which was convenient as there was no fear of anyone dropping by to see me uninvited. Even if they did try and I wasn't there, they'd probably leave me a note to say they'd called by. There was no telephone line installed, and the cell phone reception was so bad that I'd warned people beforehand they might not get hold of me. On the evening before my flight I did a final check of everything for the trip:

e-ticket for the flights
voucher for the hire car
driving license
passport
American currency
credit cards
Emma by Jane Austin
A small carry on suitcase

Everything seemed to be in order so I went to bed.

Chapter 19

If you would be so kind as to help me find my mind
I want to thank you in advance
Know this before you start my soul's been torn apart
I lost my mind in a wild romance.
My future is my past this memory will last
I live to love the days gone by
Each day that comes and goes is like the one before
My mind's lost till the day I die.
Words would fail me if I tried to describe her
Although I know she's not all she should have been
She was the devil with the face of an angel
She was sweet and cruel, cruel and sweet, as home-made sin.
If you would be so kind as to help me find my mind
I want to thank you in advance
Know this before you start my soul's been torn apart
I lost my mind in a wild romance.

P. Mayfield

My alarm clock didn't go off but everything was ready so I was in my car and away after a quick shower. I listened to some Country and Western as I drove up the M4, to put me in the right mood for the States. I hadn't been for several years and it occurred to me just how far away and removed life was over there. I got something to eat at the airport before the flight and wasn't in the mood for lunch when it was served, so I settled back to begin reading *Emma* by Jane Austin. The flight wasn't busy and after a few hours of reading, I drifted off into a deep sleep.

At US immigration I gave my friend's contact address in Houston, but when I stated that my flight home was leaving from Austin, the official was curious as to why, until I explained

I was visiting my book agent there. I made my way through the vast air-conditioned terminal to the Alamo hire desk to pick up my rental car, and was led into the blistering, humid heat outside. I was blinded until I managed to locate my sunglasses, and narrowly missed being run over by a limousine. It sped by honking its horn angrily at me. I stumbled across the road trying to keep up with the Alamo rep who had the car keys.

Fifteen minutes later, I was on my way to a dull suburb of Houston where my school friend and his American wife had recently moved, as their two growing children required more space than he'd previously had downtown. I remember the houses on their street were detached, low-lying affairs and there were few trees or vegetation to brighten it up, but once inside the house I'd forgotten its drab location. The downstairs area was a sprawling, open plan kitchen-diner and living room, kids' paraphernalia and toys were strewn everywhere. In one corner was an ornately carved, wooden bedchamber from India reminding me of the one I'd slept in on Lamu, and I was pleased to find out it was where I would be sleeping during my stay. The next morning the home help arrived and talked to me as I was getting up.

'I tidy up twice a week, only to find it looking exactly the same the next time I comes in. It's my groundhog day, yes siree, I'll tell ya that. Where did ya says y'all from?'

I spent the time there lounging around, catching up with my friend, drinking beer and watching movies, whilst he and his wife looked after their hyperactive children. I left late on the afternoon of the 27th, making sure to get directions from them for the right road to take to Austin, which was Highway 10, heading west. But I headed east at Highway 10 as I was going to Baton Rouge, Louisiana, to keep my lunch appointment with Luis Dean Reyes.

The sun was setting in my rear view mirror as I left the outline of

Houston behind me in the clear, deeply reddening sky. There was a wide choice of radio stations to browse through and when I'd tired of Country and Western I punched the automatic redial button and found some jazz to while away more time. I periodically looked at a map to check my progress towards Baton Rouge. I'd told Reyes I would arrive in time for lunch the next day, so as the sun was setting I pulled off at a La Quinta Inn with a Waffle House next door.

Checking into a room at the motel, I went to get something to eat next door, and sat at a window booth. I ordered a blue cheeseburger, fries and coffee from a waitress called Delilah and opened my copy of *Emma*, to pick up where I left off. At that moment, the headlights of a car pulling up, flashed brightly, and I was startled to see it was a police patrol car. Two uniformed troopers got out, joking with one another as they headed towards the front door. The place was empty apart from me and an elderly couple sitting at the counter. I could hear most of what the troopers said as they placed their order with Delilah and chatted with her. I couldn't wait for them to leave as they were making me feel uncomfortable and I was finding it impossible to concentrate on my book. I had to keep re-reading the same page over and over again. Finally their order was ready, and they made their way back past me to the door which shut automatically behind me. They got back in their patrol car and the headlamps lit up again, full in my face, which made me look up. The driver looked over his shoulder as he was backing the patrol car out and I wondered why the other trooper was staring at me for so long. Then they were gone and I was able to finish the page with Miss Woodhouse and her father.

The next day, the 28th, was my birthday. I still had a hundred miles to drive and ambled along Highway 10 after a hearty breakfast back at the Waffle House. The countryside was now becoming more and more lush and I'd felt the humidity rising as I'd crossed over from Texas to Louisiana the night before. The highway rose on stilts above the mangrove swamps as I headed east and I reached Baton Rouge at around noon. Taking the ring road to the north I followed signs for Weiss on Highway 16. There was a sign for the Weiss Road turning on the right and within a minute or two, the sign for Connie Clarinda Lane came up on the left and I turned into it. Around two miles down the road I spotted his house off to the right, set back and as elegant as I'd imagined. It looked away from the road and faced meandering pastures which extended into grove upon grove of magnolia, as far as the eye could see. I followed the long gravelled driveway around the house and pulled up on the far side, away from the road.

Stepping out of the car, I closed my eyes and drank in the strong smell of magnolia and the other plants surrounding me. I could smell eucalyptus, lilac and maybe a hint of petunia in the air. I heard crickets in the pasture and a large, winged, beetle flew noisily past my nose. Looking up, I saw him standing in front of two open, French windows on a balcony that extended around the entire first floor of the house. He was furiously waving his arms at me.

'Whoa, Mr Jamie! I do declare! Up here! Up here.'

He disappeared through the windows for a few minutes and then I spotted him again, downstairs this time, framed in the large, open, front door. He was wearing a pair of knee length frayed shorts and an old Grateful Dead T-shirt, in front of which hung the pendant I recognised from London. He greeted me as an old friend and led me into the house, and I was struck at how lacking in grandeur the interior was. A marvellous, sweeping staircase dominated the ground floor but there was very little opulence surrounding it. I realised Reyes was just an old hippie doing as he pleased, going where he wanted in the world, and I couldn't think of a better person to have won the $50,000,000. I noticed there were paintings everywhere. It was like being on a beach thinking you're alone when you see a hermit crab crawling along, and suddenly you see there are hundreds of them everywhere and you know you're not alone at all, but a solitary stranger alone in an alien community.

'I'm so glad you made it, you're just in time for lunch. I do hope you're hungry? I'm about to prepare us a tomato, garlic and St Agur cheese omelette, you will never in your life have tasted the likes of it before. This way please,' he declared proudly with an extravagant gesture.

I followed him behind the staircase and through a door disguised in wood paneling, into a vast kitchen equipped with every possible culinary gadget, and I smelt the aroma of home-made bread in the room. On the way through, I was sure I recognised a Dorothea Tanning painting hanging next to what I thought was a very familiar Max Ernst frottage.

We made small talk while I watched him prepare lunch and we sat down at an elegant dining table he'd laid out for the two of us. We had some buttered asparagus to start with and then the omelette with fresh baked foccia bread. He drank Chablis continuously, whereas I stuck to San Pellegrino, and we finished the meal off with a berry pannacotta. Everything tasted exquisite. We talked of many things; modern America, the English obsession with football, the currency of time, our hopes for the future of the planet, and our shared love of Katherine's work.

'Do you believe in God?' I asked him.

'Indeed I do, Mr Jamie. I sincerely do. Always have done. But does God believe in me? Now that's what I'd like to know.' He winked at me.

He made us both strong black expressos, and I was surprised to see him doing the dishes by hand. He offered to show me around the house and after pouring himself a fresh glass of Chablis to bring along, we started downstairs and worked our way up. I was astonished at the scope of his taste. It was as if the entire history of art from the last few hundred years had been distilled into the house. I recall there was an old master hanging next to a small, blue period Picasso, and a Constable etching lurked in the shadows underneath the stairs opposite an Alan Jones. I noticed a Calder mobile turning lazily above the stairwell as we went up the staircase and a soft plastic typewriter by Lichtenstein sitting on the first floor landing, seemingly groaning like a well-worn sofa. He led me into the grand drawing room towards the open windows from where he'd greeted me earlier and as we stood outside on the balcony, I looked down over the balustrade and noticed a sunken, ornamental pond containing koi carp directly below us. I could see the water was green and murky when large gold fish periodically appeared and disappeared from view, not quite surfacing, but just giving a vague hint of their dark existence below.

He came and leaned on the balustrade with his wine, and looked down at the pond next to me.

'I often wonder what it would be like to be a fish, Mr Jamie. Their silent world must be full of intrigue, so many mixed emotions, so silent. They have no idea that they are so beautiful. And no memory, unlike us. You know, they drafted me into the Army for the war in Korea. But they didn't even ask me if I could swim. Saw a lot of action while I was there. I was in the field kitchen on the front line. Burgers mostly, that's what they get, the American marines. Thousands and thousands of burgers. The beef came all the way from Texas. I cooked 'em all day long. Meatloaf sometimes, as a special treat. You think they'd have got hold of some fish down there, being so close to the China Sea. A lot closer than Texas. But I never saw the sea the whole time I was there. Flew in, flew out. I love water, you know. But it frightens me being so helpless in it. When I was a baba, I used to holler and cry when my momma took me into her bath with her.'

He turned and looked up at me with a tired, worn out expression on his face and held out his free hand towards me. I wasn't sure what he wanted, if it was to touch me or if he was offering himself up to God, ready to be taken. I felt trapped with this strange, drunken, little multi-millionaire, an ex-army cook, standing far too close to me, and I started to panic, feeling powerless to do anything. It was as if he'd been expecting me to come into his life and now I'd arrived he wasn't going to try to resist. I took hold of his outstretched hand and with the tips of my fingers I felt the deep grooves that covered his palm.

Suddenly, he went up through the air and down into the pond like a stone with a loud splash and disappeared beneath the surface. Some drops of water reached me up on the balcony and they made spots on my linen jacket. I could see him feverishly coming up for breath, making gurgling noises like a pitiful, frightened baby. He was still holding his wine glass as he failed to stay upright in the water. I didn't know what to do.

I went back inside and sat down on a large divan, waiting for him to stop. I saw some of the paintings were looking down at me from the walls, perhaps in judgement. It took a good few minutes for the noises to die down and then all I could hear was the peaceful sound of insects in the pasture outside, beyond the windows.

I made my way downstairs and had to literally push myself through the humid atmosphere that hung like a heavy curtain across the front door. I walked down the steps to the edge of the pond where his still body was floating face down. Some of the carp were trying to peck at his clothes thinking it could be something good to eat. On the ground was a rake for gathering leaves and I carefully lowered it in to see how deep the water was. I felt the bottom and pulled it out. It was only about five feet deep. If Reyes had been just a few inches taller he may have survived the fall. But he was drunk and water panicked him, he'd said, so maybe it wouldn't have made a difference. I heard something above my head and looked up to see a pair of eyes looking down at me from the balcony. One was green and the other was grey.

A cat was looking down at me from the open windows and I wondered if it had been there the whole time, as I hadn't noticed it before. I went back inside and upstairs to the drawing room, and as I came through the door the cat gave a lazy 'meow' and padded over the polished wooden floors to walk in and out of my legs, purring.

Now I was alone I felt conspicuous in the vast, silent house and it occurred to me that my presence there would seem suspicious to anyone arriving. I was the only witness to Reyes' fall, apart, perhaps, for the cat with the odd coloured eyes. I began to seriously doubt the police – or anyone – would believe what I had to say. I'm never that good under scrutiny and I was sure my demeanor would be interpreted badly and held against me.

I decided to get away from there as soon as possible. His collection of art watched me as I went through the house with a duster from a kitchen cupboard, removing my fingerprints with trembling hands. The cat followed me around, presumably glad of the company. I also made sure to put away all signs of two people having dined together. All this was extremely time con-suming and by the time I'd finished the house was full of lengthening shadows. It was lucky no one had happened by and found me there. I took one last look from the balcony down at Reyes' body floating in the pond and went outside to the car. I opened the driver's door and the cat tried to get in but I shooed it away with my foot, and it sat angrily in the porch with an arched tail watching me drive back slowly around the house. I looked to my left and suddenly recognised one of Lawrence's large sculptures way off in the pastures. I'd never seen one in a rural setting before and thought it looked out of place, but to be fair I was probably in the wrong state of mind to appreciate it properly. Within ten minutes I was back on Highway 16 heading west towards Baton Rouge. I made good time back into Texas and by nine o'clock I was about fifty miles east of Houston, so I decided to stop for the night.

I almost missed the signs for the Best Western, being so engrossed in re-enacting the day's events in my mind. I checked in, took a shower and got something to eat in their diner with a beer. I headed up exhausted, and lay in bed with a picture of Luis' cat in my mind with its strange odd coloured eyes, staring unnervingly at me. I couldn't get to sleep as someone in the room next door had the TV on very loud. The front desk said they couldn't get any answer from the room. I'd heard the phone ringing through the paper thin walls after I'd complained, to no avail. I got up and thumped on the wall heavily for a full minute and used such force that I thought it would give way, but it seemed to do the trick as the TV went off and I was finally able to get to sleep.

Early the next morning someone knocked at my door. I got out of bed and tiptoed over to see who it was through the spyhole. There was a large man outside with a moustache and goatee beard, dressed in a Western shirt and holding a gun. I supposed it to be my noisy neighbour wanting to confront me so I pretended I wasn't at home. After several more knocks he gave up and slowly walked off down the corridor in his noisy cowboy boots. I quickly dressed and packed, and within ten minutes was checked out and on Highway 10, this time heading west towards Austin.

Chapter 20

Francesco Bassamo (1549–92) was an Italian renaissance painter who studied under his father. He moved to Venice to run the Venetian branch of the family's workshop, and committed suicide by throwing himself out of a window a few months after his father's death.

The next morning I arrived at my agent's house in Austin as I'd planned and later that day we caught the news about Reyes being found dead in his pool on a local television channel. He was an unknown recluse that my friend and his wife hadn't heard of before so they didn't pay much attention to the story. Apparently he had fallen from his balcony whilst drunk and it was being described as a tragic accident. We went to an Italian restaurant in Austin on 8th Street, and had a belated birthday dinner, and they had a barbecue in their backyard the night before I left. On the flight back I thought it might be possible to get hold of the work Reyes had secured from the National Portrait Gallery show, so I tried to remember which ones Miles had said he'd bought, but I gave up and finished reading *Emma* instead.

I was exhausted pulling up outside the cottage after the overnight flight as I hadn't been able to sleep at all. After stumbling in with my bag, I craved a fresh juice so I lined up some ginger, beetroot, apple, carrot and cucumber and cut them up to feed into the juicer. I was so tired I lost control of the glass and the juice spilled out over the worktop and then onto the floor around my shoes. Very soon I was standing in a pool of deep burgundy liquid and in my jet lagged state it resembled blood, so I quickly checked my hands to see if I'd accidentally cut myself. I mopped it up clumsily with some paper towels and made another juice, and carefully sat down in an armchair to drink it, as the sight of the 'blood' on the floor had made my head swim.

I was due to leave the cottage the next day, and decided to get a few hours sleep before trying to pack my things. I immediately slept deeply, and the images were confused and concerned with size. Items that were normally small had become gigantic and larger things had shrunk. At one stage I was running down a narrow street under a hot blue sky and every time I looked round there was nothing to be seen except the odd coloured eyes of Reyes' cat behind me. Then the wall close to me turned into one of Katherine's paintings and in my desperation to escape the cat, I sliced through it with my hands and stepped into darkness. I woke up more jet lagged than before and saw I'd been asleep for over three hours. I thought about taking a shower but there was no hot water as I'd forgotten to turn on the immersion heater on arrival. I waited for the water to heat up, making myself some coffee and opening some redirected mail from London. The invite to Miles' group show was at the top of the pile. Curiously the address of the new space, Good-fellows 2, was almost identical to that of Goodfellows 1, the original gallery, so I gave him a call. It was a relief to hear his familiar voice, providing some normality to my disorientated morning.

'Hi, matey. Good to hear from you. Hope you're coming tomorrow night? Kath phoned from Sydney the other day, she was desperate to get hold of you. No idea what about. Have you been away?'

'I've deliberately been out of touch to concentrate on some writing down here at the cottage,' I explained, and wondered why Katherine had been trying to reach me.

'Ah, I guess it's that art book you've been researching. Hope you're painting me in a good light? I'll make it worth your while. You do accept bribes, I trust?'

This made me laugh and it felt good. I'd sorely missed Miles' sense of humour.

'You don't need to worry about that,' I said, 'I'll be there tomorrow. But let me ask you something . . . how come the addresses are so similar between the old and new galleries?'

'Easy. I was offered the lease on that Italian restaurant across the road. Rather than relocate to some other part of London, I thought I'd be better off staying put. I'm going to use the old space as an office and storage area. Please, try not to be late tomorrow.'

Over the summer months I'd come to associate the cottage with some feelings of home, and I thought I'd look into renting the place over Christmas and invite a few friends down. Reading *Emma* had brought to mind the pleasures of a traditional English Christmas, something I'd missed for several years, what with my lack of a family.

By the time my packing was finished and I'd made something to eat it was past midnight, so I went to bed knowing that the next day I'd be able to drink in the paintings back in London. I was also excited at the prospect of expanding across the hallway into my neighbour's flat, rather like Miles was doing with his new gallery, and it wasn't until the first rays of daylight appeared that I was able to rest properly.

I tidied the cottage up before the local agent arrived and she penciled me in for a two week rental over Christmas. I drove off up the track and felt my enthusiasm for London returning as I approached the M4, and several times I had to slow down for fear of being caught on speed cameras. Once home, I dumped my bags and headed straight for the study. It was exciting to hear the familiar sound of the key turning in the lock and feel the slow depression of the handle to open the door. My heart-beat quickened as I circled the room, passing ever so closely in front of each one, absorbing their different characters.

I reached the swivel chair and was about to sit down and put on *Jezebel* when I heard the noise. I stood still hoping not to hear it again but there it was; that irritating, irritated, alien sound of a fly's wings buzzing in short angry stabs, trespassing in the silence. I looked around to find a cloth or a newspaper to attack the creature with and eject it, but there was nothing vaguely adequate in sight and I was forced to leave in search of some weapons. At the door I toyed with the idea of leaving it open in the hope that the fly may decide to exit the room into the larger space of the flat. But then that may encourage others like him, so I closed the door and headed towards the kitchen.

I sourced a tea towel, a paper towel, a newspaper and a can of air freshener, which I'd only use in desperation, if perhaps I caught the fly in mid-flight away from any of the walls. I sat back down in the swivel chair and waited, listening. It was such an unfortunate creature unable to move silently in the world, therefore continuously revealing its location to anything that may want to kill it. After five minutes it moved again and this time it seemed to be to my left, in the direction of the door. Perhaps it knew that there might lay the road to freedom. It seemed to be staying close to the walls, somehow sensing that proximity to the paintings held the key to survival. I stood up and moved slowly towards the noise which stopped again. Searching the surfaces of the walls and the paintings, I spotted it sitting on Katherine's nose. I had no intention of swatting it there, not wanting to risk any damage to her or to the frame, so I tried wafting the air in front of it with the newspaper. If I dislodged it I could use my other hand with the tea towel. As I focused on the fly I could see it rubbing its front legs together as they do in that malevolent, dirty mannerism of theirs, and I'm sure I saw Katherine twitch her nose. I approached and slowly raised my left hand with the newspaper and started to slowly waft the air in front of it. The fly stopped rubbing its legs together and prepared to take off.

Surprisingly it didn't budge, sensing a trap, and I became concerned that the force with which I was fanning the air might disturb the painting from the wall, rather than the fly from her nose. Then it moved quickly and to my right, up above my shoulder, leaving me no time to hit out with the tea towel. But it was in the air and angry, because as I turned to gain position it swooped down very close to my face, as if in counter-attack. Then it was off again to settle on the other side of the room. I returned to the swivel chair to start the hunt again and wondered what on earth the fly had been surviving on in the study. Perhaps the oil in the paint was supplying it with nourishment and the idea that it was gorging itself on the very flesh of the paintings filled me with horror. I needed to get rid of it as soon as possible and before the effects of its feeding became obvious to the naked eye. It struck me that some effect may already be noticeable and I experienced a panic attack at that thought. But it was up again, this time making a short flight, landing on a clear space of wall above two of the canvases, Jake and Dinos.

'Go on! Get him!' they cried, 'Over here. Above us!'

I moved in with the paper towel and on tiptoe at arm's length, smothered the creature, making sure to squeeze my fingers together and there was a mild release of pressure as its body split open. I slowly brought the towel down to check inside and seeing the squashed corpse lying on it, I showed it to Jake. The whole episode had taken up an hour of my time and I cursed the fly. I had to prevent any more of these invasions happening and thought to get some insectivorous plants such as pitchers, which attract insects into their vases and dissolve them. It was five thirty, and I'd promised Miles that I'd be on time for the opening, so reluctantly I gathered up the dead fly in the paper towel, plus my other weapons, and relocked the study door behind me. I needed a shower as I was feeling desperately sticky.

Chapter 21

On the night of August 29th, 2005, at around 10pm, a fire broke out in the Marais quarter in central Paris engulfing an entire five storey building. The residents were mainly African immigrants waiting for permanent allocation and the authorisation of their residence permits. Several people remained trapped in the flames and were unable to be saved. Four of them were children and one died in a desperate attempt to save his life by throwing himself out of the window on the fifth floor.

The shower revived me but I'd left very little time to get over to Miles' opening, what with the business with the fly. The tube took me to within a few minutes walk of the gallery and being back in the streets helped me readjust to the London air. There was still an atmosphere redolent of summer and it was evident people were loathe to accept autumn had arrived. People were making their way home from their offices in the City and every pub I passed was more than full with drinkers exchanging news about how they'd spent their holidays. It was mild but still a far cry from the heat of Texas I'd just endured so I had to walk briskly in order to keep myself warm. I spent the time thinking about the drawbacks of growing pitcher plants in the same environment as oil paintings. It would mean supplying a con-tinuous diet of insects just to keep them alive, unless there was something in a bottle that I could feed them on. Perhaps there was another way to protect them from being eaten alive.

At the gallery people were spilling onto the pavement and even before I had turned the corner, I could hear the growing rumble of activity. There were guests leaning up against the front windows of Goodfellows1 which was closed, so I crossed the road to the new gallery. I was impressed with what Miles had done in such a short space of time. I'd been there with him earlier in the year when it was still the family run Italian restaurant, but it hadn't occurred to me there was an upper floor to the building. I had a quick look around the crowd on the ground floor but couldn't spot him, so I took the stairs and found him holding court with Ann and a brunette.

'Jamie! Not bad, only half an hour late. This is Katy Lynton, my new find. Katy, meet Jamie.'

Miles had dedicated two of the upstairs walls to Katy, whose two large canvases were back-lit. The subject matter was oriental and I liked the look of them. Katy and I chatted for a while and found we had a lot of friends in common. We'd attended the same parties, the same weddings, been to the same places on holiday, even been staying on the same beach at the same time in Goa the year before, and yet had never met one another. We pointed this out to Miles and Ann who were equally mystified. Katy was the latest addition to Miles' stable of artists and he had high hopes for her. Ann and Katy left to get some more drinks and Miles reminisced.

'Do you realise it's been eighteen months to the day since my first show with Kath?'

I hadn't, of course. To me it just seemed like a few weeks ago. Then something occurred to him; 'Oh, did you hear about Reyes, that Yank with all the lottery dosh? He was found dead in his fishpond last week. At his mansion. Fell off the balcony apparently, pissed as a newt. In Louisiana. Tragic, really. Must have been what she wanted to tell you. You know, when she phoned from Sydney.'

I showed surprise to hear about Reyes and that it could have been the reason Katherine was trying to get hold of me. Ann and Katy returned and passed us glasses of wine. We drank a toast to Katy's future success and she took me over to tell me about her work.

'I was in my studio one day when I accidentally slashed a painting,' she pointed at the relevant canvas, 'At first I was mortified. But then I thought, why not, perhaps it was meant to happen anyway. So now I accommodate accidents when I'm working.'

'But doesn't that mean they cease to be accidents any longer?' I asked.

'Hmm . . . ' she considered for a moment before replying, 'I think you're being a bit pedantic.'

I decided to tell her about my recent dream.

'It's funny what you say. The other day I dreamed I stepped through a slashed painting . . . '

She turned to look at me suspiciously.

'Are you making this up?'

I could tell she didn't believe me when I said no, and we both stood there not knowing what to say next to one another. Then I spotted Jessica downstairs and excused myself to go and say hello.

I recognised several of the works displayed on the ground floor, including the painting I'd loaned Miles for the New York exhibition earlier that year at MOMA. It would probably become the first to grace the walls of my new space in my neighbour's flat. Miles caught me admiring it.

'You know, it's becoming increasingly difficult to get hold of any of her work these days. Nobody wants to part with anything. It wouldn't surprise me at all if something turned up at auction soon.'

At about nine o'clock the gallery began to clear and Miles gathered some people together for a meal around the corner at The Rivington. All his artists were there except for Katherine. Katy and I sat next to each other and discovered a few more coincidences in our lives. I joined her in suspecting we were both making them up for one another. I asked Miles about Reyes, but he didn't seem to know too much about it.

'All I can tell you is that his four ex-wives are fighting tooth and nail over the estate.

It's going to take years to resolve, bound to. These things always do.'

Reyes' estate now included the five works he'd bought from the National Portrait Gallery show, but Miles wasn't sure if they'd ever reach the shores of America.

'One thing's for sure. They'll all want to get rid of his collection for some cash at some point. Now that'll be one hell of an auction for sure.'

I thought back to what I'd seen in Louisiana and silently agreed with him.

Miles had been in touch with the National Portrait Gallery already and arranged for the paintings Reyes had bought to remain there on display until his estate had been sorted out, which would further enhance Katherine's reputation.

I thought it was time for me to leave, and despite Miles' protesting, I forced him to take a contribution towards the meal. My taxi appeared outside and once settled in the back, I considered what he had said about something of Katherine's coming up for auction. The time was right to gauge the value of Katherine's work on the open market for myself. As Miles had said, Reyes' vast collection – including the five NPG paintings – would probably end up at auction at some stage, setting a benchmark for the price of her work. But that could take years to happen, so I decided to put one of my paintings up in the meantime. I could influence the value, being a known collector of her work, and take part in the bidding and maybe even force the price up. If I did end up securing the painting it would be of no financial consequence to me. All I would be paying would be the auctioneer's commission, a small outlay for such a valuable piece of information. The simplicity of the idea appealed to me. When I got home, instead of going straight to bed, I listened to the Mose Allison *Sings and Plays* CD and opened a bottle of Pinot Grigio that had been sitting lonely in my fridge all summer, and poured myself a glass.

Chapter 22

Jean Michel Frank (1895–1941) was born into a prosperous Jewish family, but his life was marked by tragedy. He lost his two brothers in World War I in 1915, as a result of which his father committed suicide the same year. His mother was confined to a sanatorium where she died in 1919. The hefty inheritance he received enabled him to travel the world and establish a name for himself as a designer. He befriended the Surrealists and eventually fell to his death by throwing himself from the window of a New York building in 1941.

I had to decide which painting should go to auction. It was going to be difficult as none of them were keen on the idea of leaving the study. It couldn't be the 'gallery' painting, as Katherine would know that it had come from me. It couldn't be the 'boar' painting because Didier, her ex, in Paris might find out about it and expose the fact that I'd stolen it from him. It could possibly be the 'bike' painting, as only the brasserie owner knew I'd bought it and he would hardly be checking auction houses regularly, but then again, I had to be sure the identity of the owner was totally untraceable, so I thought that Manish Kumar could come to my rescue and provide a work. Miles could suspect him of being the seller but he had no way of being sure unless it was one of the paintings he'd directly supplied to him, which meant that my choice was narrowing. It had to be one of the other two *Sunday Times* works that I'd secured for Kumar, from Merryweather and Newton, the previous year. I opted for Newton's. It would also supply a logical reason as to why I'd be so keen to bid for it, as I already owned one of the three. I could arrange for it to be collected by the auctioneers from the Slough delivery office that I'd used on behalf of Kumar before. There was no necessity to show it had ever come from India and its origin could remain concealed. Kumar would contact an art curator from Christie's in London by email and request inclusion of the painting in an upcoming sale. I would then take it to Slough, from where they could collect it, value it, and take a photograph for the catalogue. All I had to do then was sit back and wait until the date of the auction.

That night Kumar wrote an email to Pilar Ordovas, a curator of contemporary art at Christie's in London, asking her the date of the next contemporary sale. It turned out to be in late November, so Kumar said he had a Katherine Gaunt painting to sell and described it in detail. After she'd done her research she replied to say, predictably, it would become a sought after lot and sent him the documentation to be completed by email. I printed it, filled it out, and signed it as Kumar, and then waited a few days before sending it back by registered post. Kumar explained that the painting was already in London with his business associates, and they would be arranging for the painting to be ready for collection by Christie's from the Slough address within a few days. I carefully wrapped up the painting and delivered it to Slough ready for collection. And that was that. It couldn't have been any easier.

Katherine returned from Sydney with her mother, desperate to see me. They went straight down to Chartham Hatch and invited me for the weekend. It was a delightful place, famous for a charming sweet shop that had been there for many years. We took her mother out to The Chapter Arms for a pub supper and I made a fuss over her whenever I could. Katherine was pained that I was inattentive to her, which I enjoyed, so I paid even more attention to her mother.

She was a tough and pragmatic woman, I discovered, and from what she told me, had been through the mill in her early years of marriage. This was after the Second World War, when there was a small population in Australia and migrants clung to their original nationalities as if their lives depended upon it. As a result Australia had developed a complex multi-faceted personality to go with the extreme climate there. But it was a land of opportunity and her husband had worked hard, so the idea of a child had come later on in their lives. She was now approaching her late sixties and was in robust health. She told me she'd feared for a long time that her husband's heart wouldn't last long if he continued to work, but like most men he feared retirement. She seemed to be surviving well enough without him, as long as Katherine wasn't too far away from her, she said.

There was no opportunity for Katherine and I to make love whilst staying at her mother's house and to tell you the truth, I was glad of the chance of a couple of early nights.

I accepted their invitation to stay on with them over the Sunday night and travel back to London on Monday after lunch. Katherine decided to stay on a few more days. The two of us went for a walk on Monday morning.

'I'm actually thinking of spending more time down here. Mum appreciates having me close and she's offered me a room where I can paint. What do you think?'

I thought it was a good idea as it would remove her from London and leave me more time, although I still expected her to be bothering me on the phone with things. But I knew it wasn't what she wanted to hear me say.

'It sounds like it could work. Would you like me to help you move your painting things down in the car?'

She said she'd order a whole new setup, but then she suspected the motives for my enthusiasm.

'Sounds like you can't wait to get rid of me!'

I took her in my arms saying it wasn't true, and she wasn't being fair to me. She calmed down as I held her and apologised for the accusation.

'Sorry, I know you meant well. It's just that, when I was in

Aus, I started to really miss you. Did Miles tell you I was looking for you? I tried your mobile. I wanted to hear your voice again, in my ear. Like now.' She gave me a long hug, and then said, 'I want to start on a whole new series of portraits – of Mum.'

When I got back to London I found an email from Pilar Ordovas to Kumar suggesting a reserve price of £25,000, considering the provenance of the piece and the timing of the auction, which would apparently be taking place the week after the screening of the Waldemar Janusak programme on BBC2. I couldn't believe my luck. Katherine had told me about the intense interview she'd filmed before leaving for Australia, saying it had left her completely drained. Christie's attached a photograph they'd taken of the painting for my approval and it was magnificent. Kumar immediately responded in approval, as he didn't want to hold up publication of the catalogue. It would be mailed around the world to prospective bidders and I wanted it out as soon as possible. I'd be receiving one myself in due course, as I was on Christie's mailing list.

I spent the following ten days finalising the purchase of the flat next door. What with my art acquisitions over the summer, I'd have to take out a mortgage on my place to afford it. Before I'd realised it the date for Jake and Dinos' opening at the foundry arrived. I thought I'd drive over there and take an old friend along, knowing his presence meant I would be unavailable for Katherine. She intended to go and would be eager for us to spend the night together whilst she was up in London. I was thoroughly enjoying our game of cat and mouse and it seemed the more I became unavailable to her, the more she wanted me.

The foundry looked surprisingly different since Jake and Dinos had taken it over. They'd stamped their character on the place and although they were still in awe of Lawrence, it hadn't inhibited a desire to make it their own. I found somewhere to park in the street outside, and my friend and I wandered through the large, open gates. A full-scale party was in progress, complete with barbecue and a house DJ, pumping out acid house and garage music. We got a couple of cold beers and a girl dressed in war paint, pigtails, nose piercings, Doc Martens and wearing a big smile offered us veggie burgers. Jake and Dinos had arranged three of their new pieces under floodlights in the foundry building, highlighted like alien spacecraft in the darkness and the quiet strains of an organ playing a Bach cantata reached us from within. The rest of the floor was now clear and we both stood at the entrance feeling we were on the threshold of some special space like a cathedral, and my friend said he could smell incense burning. Just then I felt warmth behind me and smelt the familiar perfume of Katherine close by. I turned round to find she'd crept up on me, which I found a bit scary. I hugged her, although the veggie burger in one hand, and the beer in the other, made this quite a complicated manoeuvre. She laughed at my awkwardness.

'Hey, you. Did I scare you? Good!'

I introduced my friend to her and asked what she thought of it all. She was effusive in her praise.

'I'm so pleased for them! They've transformed the place, really made it their own. Have you seen their monument to Lawrence?'

They'd assembled a sculpture resembling a human figure, which stood in the middle of the yard and I'm surprised I hadn't noticed it earlier. It had subdued lighting on it so as not to detract from their own pieces on display, but it was a nice gesture nevertheless. The three of us wandered over and gazed up at it. There was a plaque at its base saying:

'THE GUV'NOR'

Miles put in a brief appearance accompanied by Katy, his new protégée, and I detected a coolness about Katherine. No doubt she felt a twinge of jealousy and panic that Miles had found some other artist's career to work on, possibly instead of her own. She also wasn't very happy when she realised that I'd met Katy before.

Meanwhile, Jake and Dinos were triumphant at how everything was turning out for them. When they spotted us, they told me how much they'd appreciated my initial help. They had the curator from the Tate in tow. I'd seen them with him at Lawrence's book launch and I assumed that sooner or later their work would be on display at Tate Modern. There were a few more people I recognised to say hello to, and then conveniently my friend suggested that we leave. On the way out I looked for Miles to ask him if he fancied lunch soon and we agreed to arrange it that week. Katherine tried to persuade me to stay longer and we exchanged a few kisses under the cover of darkness, but I made my excuses and promised I'd spend the following evening with her.

Autumn took hold of London and I got down to writing again as the leaves started to fall about my ears. Katherine began spending long weekends painting in Chartham Hatch. She was fired up with the new set of portraits of her mother and had already taken a large series of sketches for them to the Berlin Art Fair. One morning the catalogue for the Christie's Contemporary Art Sale arrived in my post, so I tore open the envelope and nervously flicked through the pages. I studied the photograph of Lot #236 and it really looked breathtaking. At that moment Miles rang me excited.

'Morning. Guess what I've just seen coming up at Christie's next month. One of the other two *Sunday Times* paintings! You see, didn't I tell you we'd be seeing something up for auction soon?'

'Yes,' I said, 'I've seen it myself, this morning in the catalogue. It's a great photo . . . '

'Will you be going for it?' he asked, almost interrupting me.

'Well, I'd be a fool not to,' I said. 'Don't you think the reserve is a bit high?'

I was keen to find out if he agreed with my estimate of her worth but secretly I was very confident. He'd noticed that the date of the show coincided with the screening of the BBC2 film and suggested it had influenced the reserve price.

'I guess we'll find out soon enough, mate. How's about that lunch you promised me?'

I'd completely forgotten to ring him about it, so I asked him to give me a time and a place.

I met him over in Farringdon at the gallery, and relaxed in one of the Corbusier chairs he'd installed in Goodfellows1 while I waited for him to finish a call to Japan. A few large, extravagant potted palms stood in the corners of the room, and on the walls there was a selection of work representing his stable of artists. There were also several framed, choice press pieces hanging discreetly on one narrow wall. The room was obviously dressed to show the degree of success he was enjoying, and I marvelled at the change in his fortunes in the couple of years since he'd discovered Katherine. As his voice echoed through from the office, it amused me to consider the small part I'd played in it all. Jessica's head appeared round the corner of the dividing wall and she winked at me before disappearing. We'd continued our haphazard liaison which seemed to suit us both but my libido had slowed down of late. I found myself shunning Katherine's advances, which would infuriate her, but occasionally I would relent and let her have her way with me. Miles suddenly appeared from his office.

'Sorry, chum. Had to take that call, it's close of business out there. I'm trying to put a package together of Katherine, Katy and a few other artists, for a group show next spring in Tokyo. That was a potential sponsor. Let's go. I've booked a table at Eyre Brothers round the corner. Hope you can afford it?'

We left the gallery and strolled down the street together.

'I haven't spoken to you since Jake and Dinos' opening at the foundry,' I remarked. He was equally amazed.

'I know. I've been so bloody busy. Been to Tokyo, New York and Basel this month already. Hardly seen the family. Still, you can't let up for a second, now can you? Make hay, as they say.'

We arrived at the restaurant and he asked for our table. He was obviously frequenting the place a lot as he knew several of the waiters by name. I let him order for me and sat back to enjoy his company. We used the time waiting for our food to exchange bits of news and I guided him onto my favourite topic.

'Got anything in the pipeline for Katherine?'

He immediately leaned forward conspiratorially.

'Well, funny you should ask. I'm going to the Australian High Commission tomorrow to discuss her showing at the Venice Biennale next spring. They're very interested in her. I assume they'll be watching what happens at the auction next month. You know, how high the price goes. Not a word to her, by the way. I'd hate to build up her hopes, just in case nothing comes of it. She'd be distraught, as you can guess.'

Knowing her the way we both did, I assured him that my lips were sealed and I would keep the news to myself. He'd become aware of my seeing her again but hadn't voiced an opinion one way or the other, so I assumed he was content. I'd made sure I was totally supportive of her, so he had no axe to grind with me regarding disturbing her work schedule.

On the way home I couldn't stop thinking about what he'd told me about the Venice Biennale. It was one of the most prestigious art events in the world and to be asked to represent your country there was, well, a golden seal of approval. It virtually guaranteed your status as an artist for life, if not longer. The fact that one of Katherine's paintings was in the catalogue alone, could have brought her to the attention of the Venice selection committee in Australia. I could see the auction coming up at Christie's could go a long way to becoming Katherine's ticket to Venice.

Chapter 23

The artist Nicholas de Staël (1914–55) committed suicide by jumping from his studio window in Antibes.

I was a little disappointed that Miles hadn't brought up the identity of the seller of Lot #236 over our lunch. I was sure he suspected it to be Kumar but from his point of view it was of no consequence who it happened to be. There she was next to Damien Hirst and Tracey Emin, bastions of Contemporary British Art, and a portrait painter at that, harkening back to the glories of the Renaissance. I wondered if Brian Sewell knew of her existence because if he did he would be overjoyed. Now Reyes was gone, I felt had a clear run at securing the work, but then I already owned it so there was nothing to worry about on that score. Perhaps there were other private collectors, who'd realised a serious artist had been discovered, and they would remain in the shadows until the very last moment before revealing themselves at the auction.

After Katherine returned from Berlin she insisted we spend some time together besides, she said she could do with a break away from her mother. I couldn't summon the energy to refuse her so we drove up to The Kings Arms in Masham, in the Yorkshire Dales, for a long weekend. We missed the exodus from London by leaving on Thursday afternoon and arrived in time for supper in front of a comforting log fire. We took the best room they had and ordered breakfast to be delivered to our room late on the Friday.

It turned out to be a crisp and refreshing morning so we put on our walking shoes and went for a hike across the dales until

173

mid-afternoon. We were famished on our return and decided to take an early supper in the room, but first Katherine insisted on making love and I could hardly summon up the strength, but after applying myself to the task – and a task it had indeed become – I managed to satisfy her. The outcome for me was a ravenous appetite, so I added some smoked salmon to our supper order and tucked into that before taking on the local pheasant that was on the menu. After that I still had some room in my stomach and ordered a helping of their warm apple pie and ice cream. That seemed to do the trick, and while Katherine deposited the remains of the meal out in the corridor, I settled back to finish off the bottle of Chateauneuf du Pape we'd ordered. I was tempted to get some cheese and crackers sent up to go with the remains of the wine when Katherine turned to me.

'By the way, darling. I'm pregnant,' she pronounced.

'Sorry?' I thought I'd misheard her.

'I said I'm pregnant. And before you ask me who's it is, it's yours of course,' she said it a bit louder this time, and with a rueful smile.

I drank the last of the wine, put my glass down on the table and started to feel the full effects of it. I realised I'd drunk the whole bottle when I saw Katherine's unblemished wine glass standing next to mine, and it added some validity to what she'd just said. I wasn't sure how to react, so I considered the options that were open to her.

'I thought that's what you said. So what are you going to do? Are you ready to be a mother?' I was feeling bullish from all the wine and quite frankly, didn't really think she was ready for the responsibility.

She drifted over to where I was sitting and sat down on the arm of my chair. She draped her arms around my shoulders and lolled her head next to mine.

'I want it, I really do. But you have to as well, darling.' Then she whispered in my ear,

'Aren't you pleased? Do say something.'

Yes . . . of course I'm pleased,' I managed to say. 'It's great news.'

Her revelation had started a train of thought in my head. It raised all sorts of complications and unanswered questions. How on earth had this happened? Ultimately I'd had no control over whether Katherine took birth control or not, and I hadn't been bothering to use contraceptives myself. She must have stopped taking her pill at least a couple of months previously to have conceived. I felt more than a little compromised in light of this and began to suspect that she'd engineered the pregnancy.

'But why didn't you tell me you'd gone off the pill?' I asked her, trying not to make it sound too accusatorial.

'I did, when I got back from Sydney,' she said, matter of factly, but I was sure she was mistaken in this. I was certain she hadn't told me. Perhaps that was the real reason she was trying to get hold of me when she was in Australia with her mother. To tell me she was pregnant. It made no real difference, but I still wanted to find out how it had happened.

Surprisingly, the more I thought about it, the more I wanted her to go through with the pregnancy. The Venice Biennale was happening the following May and there would be just enough time for her to give birth and still take part. So, on our journey back to London I told her I wanted to have the child, and had trouble keeping control of the car as she flung her arms around me. I narrowly missed hitting the back end of a tanker as we swerved in the heavy rain that had started to fall. I dropped her off at Waterloo as she wanted to go straight to Kent to tell her mother the news. Driving to Bayswater, I wondered if this development was likely to alter anything. I would have to make changes to my will of course, so that the child was provided for, and I'd have to include Katherine too, as it would raise suspicions if I didn't. But I had no intention of marrying her and my head wasn't filled with any vague, unrealistic notions of undying love for her.

The rain continued to fall over the coming weeks and the skies stayed grey, whilst the Sunday papers filled with inviting offers to spend the coming winter somewhere bright and cheerful instead of London. The final countdown to the auction began. There had been a public viewing the Sunday afternoon beforehand where the painting looked fabulous, totally at home among the other illustrious names. There seemed to be a continuous stream of people dallying in front of it which I thought could only be a good sign. I didn't stay long, opting to return home to spend time with the others in private.

Since the news of Katherine's pregnancy the study had begun to look different to me. I began to draw comparisons between the paintings and the baby, after all, weren't the paintings Katherine's babies too, conceived, formed, grown and produced from within her? The room had taken on a womb-like intensity recently, and in my mind I'd started to refer to it as the 'room', rather than as the study. I was due to take possession of the flat next door, the following week, and wondered which paintings to transfer over.

As I began to dress on the appointed day, I was aware of how significant it could become, so I put on a smart suit with a new shirt and tie. I wanted to commit to memory as much as I could of my feelings at that moment. It would be wonderful to be aware of times like that when they occur in life, to fully appreciate them, but, so often, we don't recognise them until it's too late.

The BBC2 feature had screened the weekend before and Katherine couldn't have come across in a better light. She proved to be a natural in front of the camera and Janusak's questioning, although probing, had brought out the gravitas in her character perfectly. Although critical at times, any artist would have given anything for such exposure. Fortunately the weather had cleared, and it was crisp when I stepped outside my front door and hailed a cab. When I arrived at the auction it had already started so I registered and secured myself a paddle. They'd only reached Lot #185 and on leaving the room to compose myself I bumped into Miles outside the door. I was glad to see his familiar face and told him what the state of play was. He suggested we go and get a coffee somewhere, so we left the building and crossed King Street to order cappuccinos in a cafe opposite. We sat on stools in the windows facing Christie's and the light paled as the sky darkened ominously.

'So, chum, feeling nervous, are we?' he joked. But I couldn't answer him as my eyes were focused on the entrance across the street. 'Don't worry,' he continued, and I could see he was noticeably on edge. 'I am too. Bleeding petrified. First time one of my artists has had a work up for auction. It's in the lap of the gods from now on.'

I wanted to tell him it wasn't at all and everything was under control but he wouldn't have understood what I meant by that. I wasn't sure if he knew of Katherine's pregnancy but I decided it wasn't the right time to find out. He told me his trip to the Australian High Commission had been promising but very serious, rather like being interviewed for a job, but he felt it had gone rather well. He said a lot depended upon the outcome of the auction.

'Of course, they would never admit they're influenced by the commercial market. But you can be damn sure if it doesn't make the reserve they'll withdraw their interest, for sure.'

We judged it was time to head back so we sprinted across the street just as the heavens opened up. Back in the room they'd got to Lot #228 and we searched around for a couple of seats we could reach easily and without disturbing too many people. Miles nudged me and pointed at someone who was seated and whom he'd recognised.

'There's Bernard, one of my clients. I hear he's just retired and sold his business for a few bob.'

Merryweather was sitting near the end of a row and had several empty chairs next to him, and Miles pushed me in that direction so we could sit down. I'd been keeping track of Merryweather's purchases from Miles in my regular hackings at his gallery, and Kumar had gotten hold of two more of Katherine's works from him since I'd introduced them in Goa. I knew he was there primarily as an observer and he confirmed this by whispering to Miles across me, that he was seeing his lawyers that morning about the sale of his business, and had thought it too good an opportunity not to drop in before jumping on the train home. I'd never actually met him before so we briefly introduced ourselves and shook hands.

We settled back and watched the lots go under the hammer and then the moment arrived:

'Lot #263. A work in oil by Katherine Gaunt, entitled 'Portrait Number III'. In a gilt frame, featured in *The Sunday Times Magazine* article on the artist, dated last year. We have a copy of the said article as part of the lot. Shall we start the bidding at, say, £10,000?'

I saw a hand go up towards the front of the room and then several others joined in. Once it got started it reminded me of a car gaining speed as the engine warms up. We reached the reserve in less than five minutes, and then the auctioneer cleverly increased the increments that he was inviting bids for. In eight minutes we'd reached £50,000, and the leading bid was with a young man standing towards the back holding a mobile phone to his ear. I entered the fray at £57,500 and stayed in until the price had entered the high seventies, at which point the young man holding the mobile went straight to £90,000, obviously to clear the floor of rival bidders. Merryweather let out a breath of air from his pursed lips and I could see that Miles was biting his nails feverishly.

'£90,000 . . . Do I hear £95,000 . . . ?' On saying this, the auctioneer looked towards us for a second or two before continuing, '£90,000. Going once, going twice . . . sold to paddle number eighty-four at the back. Thank you, sir.'

The hammer came down and it was all over. As one, the three of us got up from our chairs and made for the door. Once outside, Merryweather started mopping his brow with a handkerchief.

'Unbelievable. Absolutely incredible,' he said putting all our thoughts into words.

Miles patted me on the back in consolation.

'Never mind, matey. It was a brave try. It would have been nice to have kept it in the family, if you know what I mean.' But I could tell that secretly he was overjoyed at the result, as was I.

I suggested we all go somewhere for a drink and the other two immediately agreed. Miles said he knew of a pub nearby, so we followed him there and once settled in a booth with a whiskey in our hands, we reflected on the outcome. Miles was ecstatic and quite unrestrained in his delight at the final price. He insisted on paying for the round of drinks even though it had been my idea to begin with.

'Well, that should make them bloody well sit up at Venice!'

Merryweather looked puzzled at the mention of Venice so Miles had to explain for him. He raised his eyebrows and I could see his brain calculating how much the works he owned would be worth if Katherine were to be selected. Then he fell silent and I could tell it was beginning to dawn on him how much he'd forfeited by selling his other three paintings to Kumar. I was considering how much my collection had increased in value in the last half hour, probably close to a million pounds. Merryweather started to look despondent, so much so, that Miles asked him if he was feeling alright. He drained his glass and abruptly got up, saying he had to go and catch his train to Macclesfield. When he'd left, Miles insisted on buying another round of drinks. While he was at the bar my mobile rang and I answered it.

'Hello, sir. We've just heard from our agent at the auction. Just to let you know that he was successful for you this afternoon at Christie's. The final price he paid was £90,000. Apparently there was one other serious bidder on the floor that he had to see off first. I do hope that's satisfactory to you?'

I realised who was calling me.

'Yes, that's fine. Absolutely fine,' I answered,

'Right, sir. We'll send you the dispatch details and our bill in the post. Thank you, sir. Glad we could be of help. Good day.'

Chapter 24

Whilst pregnant with their second child, Jeanne Hebuterne (1898–1920) threw herself from a third storey window two days after the death of Amedeo Modighliani from tuberculosis.

I couldn't have wished for a better resolution to the day. The only person who seemed unhappy was Merryweather but I didn't have much sympathy for him as he'd turned a small profit on the paintings Kumar had bought from him the previous year. Besides, he still had a few others whose value would increase as a result of the auction. All it did was highlight the nature of the art market and the fact that prices are governed by supply and demand, just like everything else.

Miles had wanted to carry on drinking to celebrate but after another couple of rounds I sent him home saying I was exhausted, which wasn't a lie. Now the auction was over and done with, I felt a large weight had been removed from my shoulders. The next day I got up early and went to the newsagents on the corner to pick up all the newspapers. It was one of those clear November mornings you often get in London, so with them under my arm, I headed towards the Round Pond in the park. I selected an empty bench facing the sun at the water's edge near to some preening swans, and started to search for any coverage. A dot painting by Damian Hirst had reached a new record price after we'd left, and sadly it secured the strap-lines, but most of the papers reported a 'significant debut price for a new artist, Katherine Gaunt' and she was the only other artist to get a name check.

When I got home I telephoned her in Kent but she didn't sound very pleased to hear from me.

'Oh, it's you. Hello. Yes, Miles phoned last night to tell me what had happened at the auction.' She couldn't have sounded less interested to hear from me and I could tell she was expecting an explanation as to why I hadn't phoned her the day before.

'I'm sorry I didn't call you earlier. I couldn't bring myself to admit to you that I'd let the painting go to someone else . . . ' It was, of course, a fabrication but I could hardly tell her the real truth behind the auction result.

She understood and immediately changed her tune to console me.

'Oh, you poor thing. Bless you. Don't worry. These things happen. Don't feel bad about it.'

'By the way, how are the new portraits of your mum going?' I thought to ask her while I had her on the phone.

I'd seen the sketches before she'd taken them to Berlin and had told her there was something of Leonardo about them, which she'd laughingly dismissed, but I could tell she was flattered by the remark.

'Why don't you come down for the weekend and have a look?' She said, to my surprise.

I hadn't seen much of her since she'd started to paint in Kent and when I arrived I was stunned at how pregnant she'd become. Her normal waif-like figure had ballooned and her breasts were huge. I swallowed hard at the realisation that I was responsible for her metamorphosis. She said everything was going as well as it was supposed to, according to Dr Perry, the local GP in the village, and I was glad to hear it. Her mother had accepted the fact that we weren't planning marriage to go with the child and greeted me warmly. Katherine showed me one of the portraits in progress and it was the first time I'd seen an unfinished work of hers. As I looked at the recognisable features of her mother and the way in which she was working the paint around the canvas, it reminded me of something else, but I couldn't work out what it was at that time.

The whole evening I wrestled with my memory trying to get to the bottom of it. We finished dinner and all three of us decided to get to bed early. Katherine and I were still not sleeping together when in Kent and the peace and quiet was welcome. The house was secluded and I fell asleep, immediately dreaming of being in my room in London. This time there were drawings of babies on the walls and I frantically looked for something familiar. Finally I found the three early works, the 'bike', the 'boar' and the 'gallery', and I recognised the brushwork in the unfinished portrait of her mother. I woke up abruptly and understood that the 'gallery' painting that Katherine had sent me as a present – when she'd dumped me – was unfinished.

The next day she showed me sketches for three life-size, full figure self-portraits, which came as a surprise to me.

'I wanted something to remind me what pregnancy feels like. For later on,' she explained. 'I've decided I'm going to keep them when they're finished. Do you think Miles will mind?'

I could see they would be worth a fortune as rarities and for that reason Miles wouldn't be happy, but thought it better for her to find that out herself, so I suggested,

'I'm sure he'll understand, but you really should ask him about it.'

Later on her mother wanted to go to The Chapter Arms for supper and dutifully, I telephoned and booked a table for us. Katherine wanted to invite Miles and Ann for Sunday lunch so before she changed her mind I called him. Quite surprisingly, she took the phone and persuaded them to drive Celia and Darcy down. I think she'd enjoyed showing me the work in progress and wanted to show them to him, but she also wanted to clear the idea of keeping the self-portraits for herself. When we got back to the house I had another look at the unfinished portrait before going to bed to make sure I hadn't been mistaken in what I'd deduced from my dream.

The next day Miles arrived at noon with Ann and the girls, who I hadn't seen for months, and I clowned around with them on the lawn for a while. They'd discovered tennis that summer and were eager to show me their new rackets. They wanted to have a knock around with me on the court straight away, but I told them to wait until after lunch when the sun would maybe come out. At first they both kicked up a fuss until Ann rescued me by summoning us all in for lunch. Celia and Darcy insisted on sitting either side of me and Miles carved at one end of the table, while Katherine sat at the other. After we'd eaten, the talk focused on pregnancy with Ann and Katherine's mother exchanging various stories about motherhood.

'But do tell me about the new work, Kath,' Miles probed, 'I want to know all about it. I mean, I've driven all this way, so it's hardly fair if you don't!'

We knew it was the main reason he'd been keen to come down.

'Do you want to see it? I'm more than happy to show you,' she said and seemed unusually accommodating. Ann asked if she could have a look too, and then the girls, not wanting to be left out, cried that they needed to see. She didn't mind them fussing at all, and it occurred to me that pregnancy was making her less precious about her work which couldn't be a bad thing. I volunteered to make some coffee while Katherine led them off to the studio and her mother helped me clear the table. About ten minutes later Miles reappeared.

'It's fantastic. Her best stuff yet. What do you think, Jamie?'

He'd never sought my opinion on her work before, but I showed no hesitation in agreeing with him.

'You're right, it is. Did she show you the sketches for the self-portraits?'

'Yes. Now they really are something special. What a shame she doesn't want to sell them. The very fact there's only three of them will make them collector's items, and worth a fortune. Her ladyship has agreed to allow me the privilege of displaying them, though, when they're finished. Which is something, I suppose,' he said testily.

The sun came out and I took the girls on the court to hit a few balls across the net. Katherine made some tea and we had a slice of homemade cake. Soon after that we were waving goodbye as their Volvo estate set off down the gravel driveway and out onto the road.

What Miles had said echoed around my brain into the evening so I probed Katherine.

'Did he kick up a fuss when you told him you wanted to hold on to the self-portraits?'

'Hmmm, I could tell he wasn't happy about it,' she said.

'You know, I think he's frightened of you,' I suggested.

She was quick to disagree with me.

'Don't be so ridiculous! He's a grown man, for God's sake. Why on earth should he be frightened of me?'

'Well, for one thing, he doesn't want to fall out with you. You're his biggest artist, remember?' I think this fact had slipped her mind. 'And you can be quite intimidating at times.'

I'm sure when he saw how adamant she was, he had dropped the subject for fear of an argument with her.

I stayed up late and poured myself a brandy. I'd liked what it had done to me on the Friday night, evoking the strange dream about the brushwork, and I held a vague hope that the same sort of thing might happen again. But probably because I was yearning for sleep it eluded me for hours. I tried breathing slowly and deeply without any success. I tried visualising my study and my collection of paintings but that didn't work either. Then, I'm not sure when, it started to rain and I fell asleep and dreamed instantly.

The sound of the rain striking the windows of my bedroom set the scene outside in a park somewhere at night, and I was seeking cover from the rain under an immense oak tree. I recognised the place as Kenwood in London, and I was stood at the bottom of the meadow next to the Thousand Pound Pond. Watching large fish come up to the surface, it reminded me of the pond outside Reyes' house. I started to look for his body in the water but then felt some light and heat behind me and turned to see flames curling up from the big white house at the top of the meadow. Suddenly I was standing in front of the house, peering in through the windows trying to see what was going on inside. I picked out the vague shapes of people moving through the smoke but didn't recognise any of them. There was a lot of commotion as they took down the paintings trying to save them. Then I felt a hand on my shoulder, and Miles was there pulling me away. I was following him down a corridor in a hospital and we entered a room to find Katherine in one of the beds. She was awake and seemed to be unhurt, and I thought perhaps she'd been rescued from the fire. I looked at the other beds and Reyes lay in one, and Lawrence in another, but they seemed to be asleep. A clap of thunder penetrated the walls of the hospital and I sat up, wide awake in my bed.

There was a storm going on and, instinctively, I got up and walked over to the window to take a look outside. I was less steady on my feet than I thought and slipped with a sudden cramp in my leg. I collapsed in a heap on the floor crippled with pain. Lightning flashed and lit up the bedroom while I waited for the pain to subside. There was the sudden sound of wood splitting outside. I crawled to the bedside table and reached for my unfinished brandy. My shaking fingers brushed past it, almost knocking it over. Finally I took hold of it and drained what was left, shivering with pain, fear, and the cold.

Chapter 25

Robert Fagan (1761–1816), the English painter, archeologist and art dealer, leapt from a window to his death in Rome.

At the end of November, the estate agent rang to see if I still wanted to rent the cottage over Christmas so I called Miles to check if he was still interested in joining us, as I'd suggested it to him in Kent over lunch. They were due at Ann's parents in Sussex on Christmas Day and he confirmed they could join us for Boxing Day until the New Year. Katherine and her mother were coming down too, so I rang the agent back and confirmed the rental. Miles would be leaving for Japan at the end of January as the group show had finally materialised. The sponsors had taken a special interest in Katy Lynton, what with the echoes of oriental painting surrounding her work. He was planning to stay out there for the first few days of the show and then go on to Australia, where he was meeting with public galleries in Sydney and Melbourne to arrange taking the show there later in the year.

I experienced a bit of luck concerning the paintings Reyes had bought from the National Portrait Gallery show. Miles contacted the lawyers sorting out his estate and they agreed that rather than part with another £30,000 to complete payment, they were willing to offload them to me for £30,000, which I thought, for five of Katherine's paintings, was an absolute bargain. Miles had pocketed the fifty per cent that Reyes had paid upfront and was happy for me to pay the balance and keep the work.

The new room next door was filling up rather nicely. I was busily moving the paintings around and my original study held those I was known to own, whilst the new room held my secret collection. This way I could invite anyone over and not feel I was hiding anything from them. My pitcher plants had settled in rather well, thriving in the atmosphere I was maintaining in both the rooms. But it meant I had to have flying insects constantly delivered to feed them on as they had a voracious appetite.

I left London on December 19th for the cottage to prepare for Christmas and it was a comfort to arrive there again. I picked up the keys from the local agent's office in Corsham on the way. After stopping for some groceries, it was nearly three when I pulled into the drive. I made sure there was plenty of dry wood for the open fire in the living room and went out for a long walk as dusk approached. I did a quick inventory check and found everything appeared to be in exactly the same place as when I'd left in September, although it was evident a cleaner had been in and a telephone line had been installed, it seemed to have been empty the whole time.

I started a fire in the grate, put on a CD of Phil Spector's Christmas album, and remembering the fresh water pool out in the garden, I suddenly had a desire to see it again. It was located in a secluded corner out of sight from the house, so I made sure the fire was safely alight, and armed with a torch, went out to take a look in the darkness. Fortunately the moon was up and approaching its fullest but I was glad I had taken the torch with me all the same. Even with its help I still managed to stumble a few times over loose rocks and large stones, and heard the occasional crunch of the odd snail under my feet. I struck out past a grove of small trees that I knew bordered on the pool and promptly lost my footing and found myself underwater. Luckily the torch was waterproof, and as I held my breath I was able to pinpoint the direction of the bank and scramble towards it keeping my eyes open. The pool was only about five feet deep, but in the dark it felt a lot deeper. I clawed at the bank with my free hand and feeling my head break above water, I saw the moon in the sky towards the south east. Then I lost my grip and went under the surface again. At the third attempt I managed to haul myself up onto the bank and get my breath back. The water was icy cold and I began shivering uncontrollably.

I staggered back towards the house and felt completely stupid taking off my wet clothes and showering. I imagined what Reyes had felt like when he'd fallen into his pool, but then, he had done it deliberately, I was sure now. I experienced some guilt that I hadn't been able to stop him falling from the balcony that day. It had all happened so quickly. What would I have said to the police if they'd questioned me? Thank God I'd got out of there before anyone had turned up. It didn't bare thinking about. So I made my way downstairs and poured myself a brandy and sat in front of the fire, which I stoked up to a good blaze. I thought of buying some strings of Christmas lights the next day, to drape around the pool edge. What with Celia and Darcy coming down, I didn't want the possibility of any more accidents happening.

Katherine and her mother arrived on the 22nd by train and I picked them up at Bath Station. It had a quaint feel to it and was much smaller than I'd expected for such a grand town. There were a lot of building works in progress in the area and the traffic was disrupted. When I arrived and pulled up next to the taxi rank, they were waiting outside with far too many bags for just two people. It had been a long journey for them beginning in Kent before 8am, getting the train to London then transferring across to Paddington for the Bath train, so I took them out to lunch. We exchanged bits of news and I described the cottage to them.

'I'm sure you'll like it. There's even a fresh water swimming pool fed by an underground stream. Obviously too cold to use at this time of the year.'

They were enjoying my descriptions and were especially impressed by the pool. Then they barraged me with typical women's questions.

'Have you ordered a turkey?'

'Is there enough bedding for Miles' family when they arrive?'

'What about vegetables?'

'You know the shops will be closed for a few days, so we should stock up.'

'Do you have any candles, in case there's a power cut?'

Judging by the number of suitcases and bags they'd brought along, I was surprised they could think of anything we had collectively forgotten. I was beginning to find it tiresome so I changed the subject.

'You may want to attend midnight mass in Bath Abbey. On Christmas Eve?'

I turned to her mother on saying this, and I could tell she liked the idea.

'That's splendid! Afterwards I can call Sydney and speak with my sister Joyce and her family. It'll be twelve hours later there, at noon. They'll be just sitting down to lunch,' she explained.

The thought of sitting down to a roast turkey and all the trimmings on a glorious sunny day in thirty-five degree heat was rather strange, but it appealed to my perverse sense of humour and I supposed it's all down to what one is used to.

We spent the next few days settling in, going for walks through woods of skeletal trees, dodging the frequent bouts of rain and taking it in turns to cook. We played Scrabble in the living room while the open fire kept us warm and we drifted into a semi-trance state of mind. My arrangement of Christmas lights around the pool looked very festive and we ventured out at twilight with a warming drink to watch the twinkling lights mirrored on the water's surface, and they wondered how cold the water would be.

The temperature dropped dramatically on Christmas Eve and

flakes of snow fell around the car as we drove into Bath for midnight mass. It was crowded and I couldn't understand why I'd never thought to attend one before, somewhere in London. I began to experience an absolution from the events of the past year, singing the hymns in the congregation. As I looked around at the vast number of stained glass windows in the Abbey, my mind traced the journey I'd taken from last Christmas in Lamu where I'd witnessed Lawrence's death, through the spring in London, then in Spain with Katherine, the summer at the cottage, to America and Reyes' suicide, and then the autumn in London, before I arrived back there in the Abbey. I saw that Katherine and her mother were holding hands with tears in their eyes and I gazed up at the fan, vaulting above my head and lost myself for a moment.

When the mass finished I shepherded them out through the crowds to the car. A lot of snow had fallen whilst we'd been inside and Katherine calmed her mother while I cleared the fresh snow from the windscreen and windows. I promised I'd drive home slowly and suggested they sit in the back together, and as we left the city we chatted to try to take our minds off of the thick snow blanket on the road ahead of us.

'I think *It's a Wonderful Life* is on the box tomorrow, with James Stewart. It always brings me to tears,' I said, hoping it would help. Katherine joined in.

'And we must watch the Queen's message, eh, Mum? We never used to miss it back in Aus.'

I stoked up the fire, fixed us all a hot toddy and Mrs Gaunt called her sister in Australia. It was after two thirty before we took to our beds, and Katherine and I slept together for the first time in months.

Chapter 26

Gagneraux Beningne (1756–95), the French artist, committed suicide in Florence by leaping from a window.

Christmas Day morning was clear and bright, so I suggested we venture out for a walk in the virgin snow after breakfast. The setting was spectacular and we enjoyed the fabulous views down into Bath. There wasn't a soul about and the snow lay untouched on the lanes and across the fields. Crows flew here and there, and we could see other birds sitting on electricity poles enjoying the warmth of the sunshine. It encouraged us and raised our spirits and for the rest of the day we busied ourselves preparing Christmas lunch.

We got a call from Miles as we sat down to eat, he asked how bad the snow was as he wanted to gauge how much time to allow for the drive over from Sussex. After lunch we exchanged presents and I gave Katherine a rare, early copy of Vasari's *Lives of the Artists*. For her mother, I'd found a signed John Carey first edition, as I knew he was her favorite author. Katherine gave me a fold-up bicycle and her mother, a beautiful Victorian necklace consisting of two parallel gold chains that met at the front and held a large ruby in place. It looked perfect when she put it on. Her mother gave me a box containing her husband's gold wristwatch. I was particularly taken with it as Kumar had acquired the portrait of her father from the National Portrait Gallery show in the summer, and I recognised it as the one he was wearing in the painting. She gave Katherine her father's gold fountain pen.

I craved some male company and spent Boxing Day looking forward to seeing Miles again, so I took off on a long walk after brunch through the white landscape. There were few signs of life as I threaded my way along the silent footpaths but the odd squirrel appeared looking for food. I came across a mess of pigeon feathers betraying a kill, and surprised a small buck deer that had ventured out from its hiding place. I wondered if the routine I'd experienced for the last few days with Katherine and her mother was a sample of what was to come when the baby arrived. I wondered how I was going to cope with it.

Walking along, I weighed up whether I wanted a girl or a boy, but ended up not really caring either way, just so long as it grew up tall. I picked up some local farm eggs and by the time I got back to the cottage was in a settled frame of mind. We expected Miles to be with us by six, so I volunteered to prepare a meal for them and Katherine's mum wanted to help.

Miles and Ann arrived with Celia and Darcy in tow and the sound of the two girls' sparkling, high, young voices was very welcome. Miles came in carrying a crate of champagne saying a celebration was in order. We gathered in the living room awaiting an explanation from him.

'With great pleasure I can announce that Katherine has been chosen to represent Australia at the Venice Biennale next May, with a retrospective exhibition of her work. And you . . . ' at this moment he pointed a finger at me, ' . . . will be required to supply most of the bloody work, as you no doubt must be aware!'

I went white and for a moment thought he'd found out about my secret collection, but then realised that even without it I owned a significant number, well over a dozen in fact. Miles had heard the good news from his mole at the Australian Arts Council and we drank to Katherine's health and success. I secretly thought what an amazing exhibition it could be if it included all the works in my possession.

For the rest of the evening Miles was on his best form, entertaining us with anecdotes from his various travels abroad over the years. He was looking forward to the show in Japan and then going on to Australia, and drew Mrs Gaunt into talking about Sydney and where she'd grown up on the Gold Coast. After that Miles and I got stuck into a bottle of port with some cheese by ourselves in the kitchen.

'So, ready for fatherhood, matey?' he asked with a sly smile, 'The first is the hardest. Once that's out of the way, it's a breeze,' he added, refilling his glass and mine. Then he changed the subject. 'So, how many of Kath's have you got now?'

The question threw me completely and I wished I hadn't drunk so much that evening but what with Katherine not drinking at all, I had overcompensated to keep him company.

'God, what a question,' I replied and rather than be specific, I adopted a blasé attitude to avoid being caught out.

'So many . . . I've lost count!' I offered, and we both doubled up with laughter at this.

'My God, but it must be worth a fortune, old son. That auction really did the business, huh?'

And with that we clinked our glasses of port again, drank them down in one draft and decided to finish off the bottle.

The prospect of the show in Venice filled my mind when we went to bed. I listened to Katherine lightly snoring next to me, as I carefully pictured her paintings and I tried to separate them into those that Miles knew I owned and those he didn't. But through the fog of the port it was impossible to recall distinctly, and I realised I'd have to go through all the paperwork since the first show to compile a definitive list. He would, of course, have a record of those he'd supplied me with and my list had to agree with his, otherwise his suspicions would be aroused. I turned to face my side of the bed and sleep overtook me. I was again out walking in the snow alone, uncovering blank buried canvases as I went along. I remember that I approached a small ramshackle shed and went in to find an empty, rusty old pram inside. I tripped over it and had difficulty disentangling myself.

I woke up the next morning alone in the bed, with a terrible hangover and felt sure Miles would be feeling the same way. We'd followed his champagne with red wine, and then port, all in all, a recipe for disaster. Then I heard light footsteps coming up the stairs and there was a soft tapping on the door of the bedroom. Celia came in holding a mug of coffee for me. She crept forward, holding it as if it were a peace offering.

'Morning, Uncle Jamie. Katherine says it's how you like it.'

I sat up in bed and accepted the coffee. She stood watching me as I took a sip.

'That's fine, Celia. Tastes perfect. Thank you.'

She was visibly relieved to hear this but instead of leaving, she wandered around the room, and I knew she was building up the courage to say something to me.

'Uncle Jamie?'

'Yes, Celia?'

'Can I ask you something?'

'Of course you may.'

'Mummy say's I shouldn't listen to other people talking, but what can I do when I'm in the room and I can hear what they're saying?'

I could see she had a point.

'Well, Celia, all I can say is, if that's the case, they shouldn't be saying anything they don't want you to hear.'

She grew less timid upon hearing this.

'In that case, can I ask you something else?' she said.

I nodded, wondering what she was going to reveal she'd heard.

'What does 'high maintenance' mean? I've asked Mummy and she won't tell me. She told me not to ask Daddy, so I asked Lawrence at the wedding, and he just laughed. Can you tell me please?'

I suddenly remembered the conversation I'd had with Ann

that day after lunch, over a year before, when she'd tried to warn me about Katherine. The girls were both in the room at the time and we were all watching television.

'Well, Celia, 'high maintenance' means . . . ' I started, and at this point she came and sat down next to the bed, very attentively, looking as if she were ready to start taking notes at a lecture.

'Can you imagine having a pet rabbit?' She nodded. 'And you had to feed it every day, perhaps maybe several times a day, at the same times.' She nodded again. 'And you have to make sure it has some fresh water to drink all the time? And you have to clean out its cage every day, so it stays healthy.' By this time she was continuously nodding her head at me. 'Then it needs exercise, so you've got to make sure you let it out and run around, but not get eaten by any foxes . . . '

'I see, so it only applies to things that can't look after themselves? What about those cows in Lamu? They can't look after themselves, otherwise they wouldn't be so skinny. My teacher at school says they're sacred, which means special. So why don't the people feed them, if they're special? They must be 'high maintenance' then. Can people be high maintenance?'

'Yes, they can be. Sometimes,' I said.

'So is Katherine high maintenance? That's what Mummy said to you.'

I felt put on the spot and I was just wondering what on earth I was going to say to her, when the door opened and Ann stood in the doorway.

'Celia! Come down this minute. You were only supposed to bring Jamie's coffee up, and not to disturb him! C'mon! Now, I said!' She grabbed her hand and hoisted her up from the floor. 'Sorry, Jamie,' she said, I told her not to bother you.'

And they were gone out of the door, leaving me to decide how 'high maintenance' Katherine had become.

The smell and taste of the coffee helped me recover so I showered and thought about the day ahead. The snow had almost gone and had left the ground very wet underfoot, but it meant we could get out and visit some places nearby. We opted for Wells, and after seeing the Chapter House and the marvellous Cathedral clock go through its tableau, we sat in a high street cafe and shared a few different kinds of Cornish pasty. We went up Glastonbury Tor and gazed down at the Severn Estuary across the Somerset Flats. I told Celia and Darcy about the Giant Severn Bore that appears like clockwork every summer like one of the big waves in Hawaii. They made me promise I'd bring them to see it one day. As the sun went down, a cat appeared out of nowhere from inside the tower and gave me a bit of a fright.

I could spend more time describing the last week of that year but we all secretly wanted it to end as soon as possible, apart from the two girls. In fact it was their presence that lightened the general mood and the cottage would have been a very somber place without them. All my suggestions to fill the time were welcomed by everyone and I felt in charge of some sort of holiday camp. There was an exchange between Katherine and Miles regarding the self-portraits that I was witness to. He was far from happy and said it was ludicrous to show them without a view to selling them. Katherine said in that case she was happy not to let him exhibit them at all, which created an impasse between them. This lasted until New Year's Eve, when the bleak weather returned and it rained the whole day. I decided to stay out of their disagreement and busied myself preparing supper, the last one with Miles' family before he headed back with them to London. There was a break in the rain and the two of us walked up to the local pub for a pint before supper. I took the opportunity to say something to him.

'Look, Miles, about the self-portraits. She isn't seeing things at all clearly at the moment. But I'm sure the birth of the baby will help put things in perspective for her.'

He was far from letting it go and started shaking his head at me as we walked along.

'To be perfectly honest with you, Jamie, I don't agree. It's the classic confrontation between the temperamental artist and the level-headed dealer. I'm sorry, but if I acquiesce on this I'll probably begin to see other things slip out of my control. And I'm not having it.'

Since the auction, perhaps he was beginning to realise he wasn't the only person affecting her career. But the very fact we'd talked about it helped and by the time we'd had a pint and got back, he was approaching his old self again. We sat down to eat and the girls were sad when I mentioned it was the last supper, and they cried out in melodramatic dismay throughout the meal. We laughed at their histrionics and it helped to massage the friction between Katherine and Miles. Finally midnight chimed on the grandfather clock in the hall and we stood and hugged one another, glad to be rid of the spent year. Miles and Katherine were especially tearful and made up, and as all of this was going on Ann jostled Celia and Darcy off to bed.

Chapter 27

Richard Maxfield (1927–69) was born in Seattle and was a composer of instrumental, electro-acoustic and electronic music. In a drug induced state he jumped out of a window at the age of forty-two.

A few days later, the three of us left in my car and I was quite sad to be leaving. The cottage had provided me with a makeshift family of sorts, something I had been without since my foster parents had died. I'd been able to reflect on what had been achieved over the last twelve months and on the whole, I thought my year had been pretty fruitful. The new year would see me becoming a father and no doubt that would change my perspective. For Katherine and her mother, well, I supposed they'd enjoyed being there because it had enabled them to escape from life for a while.

They preferred to get a lift into London with me, rather than take the train to Paddington, and after I'd dropped them off at Waterloo I began to think what a decent person Mrs Gaunt was. It was the longest we'd ever spent together and she'd accepted me, even though I'd made it clear I wasn't about to propose to Katherine. I secretly hoped she thought I was better suited to her precious daughter than Lawrence had been.

I was looking forward to some time alone to make up the list of Katherine's work that I'd bought legitimately as myself. I toyed with the idea of suggesting to Miles that he ask Kumar to loan some of his work for the Venice retrospective. That brought a smile to my lips as I parked up in the rain and made my way up to my flat. I checked on the paintings in both rooms and everyone seemed fine. I studied the wristwatch Katherine's father was wearing to verify it was the same one her mother had given me at Christmas. Initially, I had worn it down at the cottage to show how pleased I was with it, but not being used to wearing a watch, I had taken it off once alone in my car. He told me his father had given it to him when he was a boy and he was keen to see it again. I went to get it, so that I might hold it up against the canvas to show him. It had stopped ticking so I absentmindedly began to wind it as I re-entered the room, and he shouted over at me.

'Careful! It's fragile!'

I sat down at my desk and scribbled a note ordering some fire extinguishers. My dream about the fire at Kenwood House before Christmas was still agitating me and I wanted to prepare for the worst, even though there was insurance cover for the two collections, one policy under Kumar's name and one under mine. I spent the rest of the day opening post and unpacking, looking out periodically to see if there was a break in the rain. I was keen to try out the bicycle Katherine had given me but unfortunately the wet, empty streets stared back up at me through the fogged up windows. In the post a travel leaflet had arrived plugging the Yucatan Peninsula in Mexico, and there was the temptation to escape there from the London rain for a while. Katherine rang to say they'd arrived back safely in Kent and I could tell she was excited about something.

'I've received an invitation to New York this month, to give a talk and show the sketches. You know, the ones I took to Berlin. Would you like to come with me?'

I realised Miles was due to be in Tokyo then, otherwise she would naturally have asked him to go with her. I had a sudden impulsive thought.

'Why don't I meet up with you in New York on my way back from Mexico?'

'What? When are you going to Mexico? When did you decide that?' She sounded bewildered.

'About five minutes ago. I thought I could finish the book on succulents down there.'

Within half an hour I'd secured a last minute flight to the Yucatan and booked myself a hotel room. Hopefully I could do most of the remaining work on the new book and be Kumar at the same time, offering work to Miles for the Venice show. It would be easy enough to arrange, all I had to do was deliver the paintings to Slough where they could be picked up by whoever was to curate the show, and I guessed it would be Miles.

The next day I called him to ask when Venice would be announced and when he would need my paintings, but he was in no hurry for them.

'There'll be an announcement about it this weekend in the papers. I've just put together a press release. But the work can remain where it is for the moment. I'll have to go out there first and check out how much space they're going to give me before I know how much of your collection I'm going to nick,' he joked.

He said his plan was to exhibit Katherine's portraits of her mother in April and make the selection for Venice straight afterwards.

'I've thought about what you said regarding the self-portraits . . . You're right, you know. I totally overreacted. In fact, I'm going down to Kent at the weekend to clear it up with her before I leave for Japan.'

It was a relief to hear him saying this and I told him so.

'Thank God for that. I'm sure it's for the best. By the way, I've decided to go to Mexico for a while and finish the book on succulents I've been working on. But I had an idea, why don't you contact Kumar and ask him if he'll loan you some of his work for Venice as well?'

'How do you know about Manish Kumar?' he asked me, quick as a flash.

I was lost for words for a moment.

'Oh . . . he's emailed me a couple of times, asking me if I wanted to sell him any of her work. I said no, of course. I assumed you must have put him in touch with me.' I thought I would throw it back at him. It worked, because he replied as an accused man would.

'Not me, guv'nor, honest. These collectors, they're real buggers, I don't know how they find out the things they do. I really don't! Well, have fun in Mexico.'

I really had to be more careful about what I said to Miles in the future. He was a sharp fellow and that was twice I'd been almost caught out when in conversation with him. I'd already panicked on Boxing Day over his questions regarding the size of my collection.

Thankfully the next morning was dry, so I unpacked the folding bicycle and set off for Kensington Gardens. Within five minutes I was negotiating traffic on Bayswater Road, to cross into the park and go down Broad Walk. Checking there were no wardens or mounted police about, I made a couple of illegal circuits of the Round Pond before continuing south to Kensington High Street. Instead of exiting the park there, I turned left and followed its edge eastwards past the Royal Barracks and then parallel with Park Lane, north up to Speakers Corner. Still inside the park, I sped along past Lancaster Gate and finished my lap opposite Orme Square. The circular trip had taken me about half an hour and it was difficult to think of another present that had given such instant gratification. I cycled home to take a shower and have breakfast.

Knowing I had only a few days before leaving for Mexico, I was determined not to waste any time. It was Wednesday and my flight was on Friday. Nicola was away with her father and Jessica was visiting some relatives in Kenya. I'd had my fill of Katherine for the time being, so I ended up writing. There were no phone calls, no rings on the front door bell downstairs, no dogs barking, no children crying, and no other disturbing noises like neighbours hammering nails in walls, or any sudden drilling for no apparent reason.

After several hours working in perfect silence I began to notice the grandfather clock ticking across the hallway in the second room. The more I tried to ignore it, the louder it got and I put in some earplugs to try to get it out of my head. But the only way was with music so I put *100 Country Greats* on loud and continued working until the daylight faded. I switched on some lights and went next door to find out just how loud the clock's ticking was. Standing in the hallway, I opened the front door to the second room and remembered I didn't own a grandfather clock, I'd been thinking of the one down at the cottage.

I hadn't left much time to prepare the list to send through to Miles and I discovered he'd taken my advice and mailed Kumar, so Kumar replied saying he would be delighted to lend some work, and was 'honoured to be part of such an esteemed event as the Venice Biennale.'

That evening I had an overwhelming desire to eat a curry so I ordered a local takeaway over the phone and went to collect it on the bike. Someone was crying out next door and I went in to check everything was all right. It was Katherine. I'd neglected the fact I'd been away from her for two weeks and now I was intending to go away again, without even discussing it. She made me feel terribly guilty and I stayed in there a good hour or so making sure she understood why I was making the trip. We were, after all, going to meet up on my way back, in New York, weren't we? Then her parents told me they were finding it difficult to adjust to their new location across the hallway.

'Why on earth do we have to be in here? We don't know any of these people, apart from Katherine,' they complained.

Earlier, I'd noticed that some of those left in the first room wondered why all the disruption had been necessary, as they'd all been getting on so well up until then.

'Where's that lovely couple gone? I enjoyed talking to them,' I heard someone say, I forget who it was.

No doubt the vast empty walls of the second room were proving disconcerting to her parents so I tried to reason with them, explaining there were some new arrivals due in soon. Feeling the atmosphere calm, I left, and after sitting back down in my flat I began to feel claustrophobic. With a headache brewing, I went out for a ride to clear my head of all the voices I was hearing. I made a mental note to pick up some bicycle lights the next day, as I didn't want to cause any accidents riding around London in the dark.

It took me most of the next day to complete my list. I checked and double-checked all my invoices and had to do a lot of trawling through old emails, both mine and Kumar's. Imagine my irritation being caught up in all of this when Katherine called of all people, asking me some ludicrous questions about recipes for dishes I'd prepared at the cottage over Christmas. In exasperation I said I was far too busy to speak and that I'd ring her back later on. After I put the phone down I realised I hadn't asked her how she was feeling. But then, she'd sounded fine, and she would have said something if she wasn't, wouldn't she? Once happy with the list I mailed it over to Miles and drew my chair back from my computer, exhausted. The light was beginning to fade outside so I quickly cycled over to Queensway to pick up some bike lights and once in the shop noticed I hadn't put any shoes on, but no one seemed to care. I bought a bicycle lock in there at the same time.

The fire extinguishers arrived the next day which entailed drilling holes in the walls, in order to screw their holding brackets in place. They needed to be next to each door, but not hidden behind them, so they could be gotten hold of easily in a hurry. I felt Katherine's father watching me and muttering as I put the one up in his room, and as a result I mounted the brackets crookedly. I also put one up in the corridor and one in the hallway between the two rooms. This took up most of the afternoon and there was barely enough time to pack my bags, eat some food, and leave fresh ladybirds and water for the pitcher plants before it was midnight. I fell asleep as soon as my head hit the pillow.

In the morning I made my way to Gatwick and at the check-in desk they told me my booking had been for the day before. I felt stupid and didn't know what to say. It was the first time I'd ever missed a flight and I couldn't work out how it had come about. I tried to get on the flight that day but of course it was full and so was the waiting list. I wandered off to a row of seats to sit down and tried to work out how my plans had gone wrong. All about me people were coming and going and I felt genuinely excluded, as if I were a member of the staff working there and not involved at all in the frenzy of travel. But it was much worse than that. At least the staff had a purpose for being there, whereas I just felt out of place. The more I sat there, the more I began to feel people were staring at me. I could see one or two of them whispering, so I wouldn't notice them talking about me, then I caught them having a good laugh at my expense. After about fifteen minutes I couldn't take any more, so I gathered up my bags and trudged off to get the Gatwick Express back to Victoria. There was a delay on the line outside Reigate so the train took a lot longer than it should have done, but at that moment it all seemed to be of no consequence to me.

Chapter 28

Oskar Nedbal (1874–1930) was a Czech violinist, composer and conductor. He was born in Tabor, South Bohemia, and conducted the Czech Philharmonic Orchestra, and was a founder member of the Bohemian String Quartet. Because of mounting personal debts, he jumped out of a window on Christmas Eve.

I took the bike out for a circuit of Hyde Park. It wasn't the best weather for cycling as fine rain had been falling all morning but it made no difference to me. As I moved along it was refreshing to feel the cold mist spraying my face. The weather had kept most people indoors and apart from the occasional group of tourists and a few dog-walkers, I had the park to myself. I tried to think positively and decided to find the next possible date to get away to Mexico. I searched for a while but could find no direct flight, so I had to go via Miami, leaving Heathrow on Monday. That left two more days to fill, so I pottered around, flitting between the rooms, explaining what had happened and how stupid I'd been. One small consolation was that I was able to see Nicola that night. She was keen for me to meet her father for Sunday lunch the next day but since I wasn't in the mood, I said I'd be happier to meet him at some other time.

The journey was smooth until I got to Miami where an immigration official didn't like the look of my face. Even though I was in transit and not entering the States, I was escorted to a room for further questioning, along with about fifty other unlucky travellers who were also being detained. In one corner two Japanese girls sneezed and were immediately surrounded by officials and given face masks to wear as a precaution against

Asian bird flu. I watched as a couple of Star Trek devotees in immaculate Star Fleet uniforms were summoned up to the high desk and their details carefully checked over. I remember the man had a fine pair of gold, pointed sideburns. After an hour or so of waiting, I was allowed to continue my journey but as luck would have it, my connecting flight had already left for Mexico with my luggage on board and I was given a seat on a flight the following day. I was taken in a shuttle bus to a hotel and spent a couple of hours shopping for clothes at a vast department store a couple of blocks down the street. I was tempted to buy all manner of useful things in there: ropes, guns, knives, handcuffs, baseball bats, and a very large pair of scissors which could have come straight out of *Der Struwwelpeter*.

In Mexico I did manage to write a bit for the succulents book. I ate lobster most days and hired a bicycle to do some cycling round the island, but I was bored and lonely by the end of my stay. On the return journey, I was detained once more in Miami and I found myself back at the same hotel after missing my connecting flight to London. The man at the front desk remembered me and jovially asked if I wanted my usual room. As my plane circled over Heathrow, I looked out of the window and saw the grey morning skies welcoming me back to London and I couldn't wait to see everybody again.

As my train pulled into Paddington it occurred to me I'd forgotten to go to New York and meet up with Katherine on the way back from Mexico. It was, of course, the result of all the chaos I'd experienced. Back at home I picked up the phone to call Katherine, but realising the time in New York, I thought better of it. The last thing I wanted to do was to wake her up in the middle of the night. The flight from Miami had been very bumpy so I put my head down for a few hours sleep and thought about what I'd say when I did speak to her. She'd immediately think I hadn't turned up deliberately just to spite her, and it was going to be difficult to convince her it was a genuine mistake.

When I woke up I made some coffee and switched on the television. I deliberately hadn't picked up a newspaper the whole time I had been in Mexico, and thought catching up with some news might help me get over my jet lag. I slumped in the sofa with my coffee and focused on the screen which showed footage of a street somewhere in central London. At first I thought there had been a terrorist attack as there was debris and some smoldering timber lying around. But as I continued following the footage, I could see it was the remains of a burnt out building that looked vaguely familiar, and then I picked up the thread of what the newscaster was saying.

' . . . The gallery is known as Goodfellows2 and it's thought that the owner is away in the Far East on business. No one was injured in the fire, and foul play is not suspected . . . '

The voice moved onto another news story and the picture on the screen changed. I wasn't sure if I'd heard correctly so I switched on my computer to check the story online but it was true. I tried calling Ann at home but the line was constantly busy so I tried Jessica's mobile instead.

'Jamie! You're back. Have you heard the terrible news? It happened late last night. Thank God nobody's been hurt.' I was glad to hear she hadn't been injured at all.

'I just tried Ann at home but the number's constantly busy,' I said, 'have you spoken to her?'

'I think she's taken it off the hook to avoid any more calls. I spoke to her and she's been getting them non-stop since the news broke. Mostly the press. That was at five this morning. You should try her mobile if you want to speak to her. Miles is due back this afternoon.'

I gave Ann's mobile a call. It rang for ages and eventually she answered sounding weary.

'Hi, Jamie. It's awful, isn't it? I can't do anything as I've got both the girls at home with flu. Miles knows about it. He phoned me from Hong Kong this morning when he was changing planes. He's landing at about five tonight. You should be able to reach him after that.'

I waited ten minutes and then called Katherine's hotel in New York. It was about 8:30am there and she was awake. I apologised for my non-appearance but she already knew about the fire and for some reason she thought I'd flown straight back to London because of it, so I didn't try to change her opinion. The two events were connected in her mind and of course she focused on the fire.

'Miles is on his way back from Tokyo,' I explained, 'and until he arrives later it'll be impossible to assess what the damage is. I'll call you later when I've got more news.'

She seemed to be in a strange mood but I put it down to her having just woken up. She said she wasn't feeling great but wouldn't go into details. Throughout the afternoon I kept a check on what was emerging in news bulletins and Katherine's name began to get mentioned more and more. I realised the painting I'd loaned for New York could very well have been lost in the fire but, equally, it may have gone to Tokyo for the group show and been spared. It was insured of course, but that really offered no consolation, and I shivered at the thought of never seeing it again.

Miles called me from the airport and I agreed to meet him over at the gallery. When I arrived there was police tape cordoning off the area and he was in his office across the street talking to some fire officers. They were coming to the end of their meeting so he took me inside the, still smoldering, building. There was an awful smell everywhere. We both felt nauseous and couldn't remain inside for long. We made our way out into the street.

'What rotten bleeding luck! Apparently a back projection light on one of Katy's paintings overheated and started it off. We had them tested ages ago and they were all fine. It'll be covered by the insurance which is a consolation of sorts. It was my stupid idea to leave them on at night when the place was closed. It looked great from the street . . . '

He confirmed my painting was in Tokyo but he'd lost a substantial amount of work including several of Katy's paintings and, I was surprised to hear, some early work of Katherine's.

'I didn't know there was any early work of hers still in existence?' I probed.

'There was. I kept two canvases back for myself when she first came in to see me. I've got the slides at home somewhere.'

I thought it was inappropriate to press him any further, although I could hardly wait to see what they'd looked like, and if they bore any resemblance to the three I owned.

The fire had made the late editions of the *Evening Standard* and all the free London papers, and I began to see what a publicity coup it had been. Miles had lost work, granted, but it was insured so he'd be able to refurbish the space, and both he and the artists would be well recompensed for their losses. Katherine and Katy's names had been emblazoned across several million newspapers and I noted the fire had been covered across the world on the internet. It seems there's nothing like a good fire to create publicity and this one had been ideal in the sense that there had been no casualties, human, that is. I left Miles and went home to telephone Katherine again in New York. I suddenly remembered the dream about the fire in Kenwood House. The second half, where I'd come across Katherine in a hospital bed alongside Lawrence and Reyes, still remained unexplained.

When I got hold of Katherine I decided to tell her the real reason I hadn't made it to New York but she seemed unimpressed. Not that I thought she didn't believe me, but more that she found it difficult to be interested in anything I had to say.

'Is anything wrong?' I asked her. I knew from experience that she never chose to tell me how she felt and needed to be coaxed into revealing her emotions.

'No . . . no, I just don't feel my best,' she replied hesitantly.

'Would you like me to come over? I still might be able to get on a flight today,' I tried again.

'No, there's really no point now. I'm due to leave tomorrow anyway.'

I wondered if the problem could be anything to do with the pregnancy, which was at an advanced stage, so I told her to see a doctor in New York. Again she said there was no point. I told her I'd meet her at the airport and drive her directly down to Kent, and after taking her arrival details we said goodbye.

Her mood had worried me as she'd seemed detached and preoccupied. I knew she loved New York as the energy of the place usually filled her with excitement, so I wondered what could be behind her lack of enthusiasm. I could only think it was something to do with the baby. I slept very little that night or the next, due to my worrying about it, which rendered me unable to concentrate on anything. All I managed to do was wander in and out of the two rooms, unable to block their comments from my ears.

'It's very unlike her,' Miles said, and everyone agreed.

'She really should see a doctor as soon as she gets back,' her mother suggested.

I remembered I still hadn't unpacked and that took up the rest of the night before I retired to bed.

I woke up to a wet and dismal day, and made sure I had enough time to drive to the airport before her plane landed. To my dismay it was delayed for two hours so I had to while away the time drinking coffee and trying to pick out suspicious looking characters in the crowds. By the time she appeared my two sleepless nights and the early morning had caught up with me, together with too many cappuccinos. I was fractious and ready to take offence at any remark but nothing prepared me for the sight of her coming through the terminal hall. She looked the worst I had ever seen her and as pale as a ghost. She was staggering on her feet as if drunk, so I clutched her round the shoulders and prevented her from keeling over. I took hold of her baggage trolley with one hand and steered her towards the exit with the other. Once I'd deposited her on a bench outside, I hurried to get the car and found my hands shaking as I paid the parking ticket at the exit gate. When I pulled in, she sank back into the passenger seat, closed her eyes and promptly fell asleep. I carefully fastened her seat belt to avoid her swollen tummy. I followed signs for the M25 and began to hear deafening alarm bells in my ears. An ambulance overtook me with flashing lights and I felt sick as it sped off up the road in the driving rain. I gritted my teeth and put my foot down hard to the floor.

Chapter 29

Francesca Woodman (1958–81) was an American photographer born in Denver, Colorado who worked mainly with self-portraits and fantastical representations of the human body and the space it occupies. The five hundred photographs she created during her short life were rediscovered in the late 1980s to critical acclaim. She tragically threw herself from the window of her loft in the East Village of New York at the age of twenty-three.

It took me about ninety minutes to get Katherine down to Chartham Hatch. I stopped at a service station under the pretence of buying some fuel, just in case she woke up, and once away from the car, I called her mother to see if she could book an appointment with Dr Perry. I waited on the line and by a stroke of luck there had been a cancellation that afternoon meaning I could go straight there. Mrs Gaunt said she'd wait for us at the surgery. There was no need to bother Katherine with the news of what we'd arranged. I had no desire for an altercation with her in the car over whether or not she'd go. I was still tetchy from earlier and might have lost my temper with her which wouldn't have helped the situation.

Katherine was still asleep when we pulled up outside the surgery. Her mother and I carefully woke her up and helped her out of the car and up the pathway. We took seats in the waiting room and within half an hour Dr Perry was able to see her. I went outside to smoke a cigarette, then the door of the surgery opened and her mother was calling to me. I ran over and she said that Katherine had to go to hospital immediately and I heard myself offering to drive her there. I felt as if I was observing the whole episode from another place. We helped her into the back seat of the car and her mother sat in the front giving me directions as we drove. I must have gone through a speed camera and I thought I saw a flash as it went off, but knew I had no control over anything. I was separated from events, as if I was watching through a glass screen. I experienced numbness in my limbs, and a feeling I was accelerating towards some unavoidable conclusion.

We went straight into Casualty at the hospital. Katherine was taken away and we saw her disappearing down a white corridor on a stretcher. We said nothing but feared the worst, and wandered round the hospital invisibly connected as if we were manacled together. I bought us two teas at the cafe which kept our hands warm, and deliberately over sweetened the cups with sugar. As her mother sipped at hers, she didn't object to the taste. I found some copies of the local paper and offered one to her.

'Please call me Edith,' she said as she took it.

I'd never known what her first name was up until that moment. It hadn't even occurred to me that she had a Christian name. I suppose that because we weren't due to be related by me marrying Katherine, I never thought I'd feel close enough to her to use it. The experience we were sharing was changing that and I was glad she'd told me – Edith.

We sat in the café and it began to get dark. Visiting time came so it was busy for a while, and then after an hour or so, the cafe cleared. We were left alone sitting at a table.

Do you mind that I didn't want to marry Katherine?

The question had formed itself quite perfectly within my head, but I couldn't bring myself to say it out loud. I suddenly had a desire to know what she really thought. There was a long pause during which Edith looked across at me several times, as if she knew the question I wanted to ask her and was uncertain whether to be frank with me or not. Then as she opened her mouth to say something, a tall man in a white coat appeared and started speaking to us. His name was Dr Wingfield, and as he was trying to explain to us about the pregnancy, I heard him use the word 'miscarriage'. I remember he had a soothing voice that held much authority but very little emotion. He gave me the sense something very natural had happened, however tragic it seemed to be. Yet there was light at the end of the tunnel, he said, because Katherine was going to be all right and that was a blessing. She was going to be kept in for a few days and was now sedated and sleeping soundly. He suggested we go home and telephone the hospital first thing in the morning, that nature had its own way of dealing with these things. And I believed him.

We drove back to the house in silence and I offered to stay the night so that neither of us would be alone. Edith liked that idea and made up my usual bedroom for me. I suggested we go to The Chapter Arms to eat, for a change of scenery and because she liked it there, and I thought the fact we'd be with other people would prevent either of us from becoming too morose.

Being midweek it was quiet so we were able to dine and talk without fear of being overheard.

'I had two miscarriages before Katherine came along,' Edith began quietly, 'so her father and I were quite old when we had her. That's probably why we spoiled her so. We felt we'd been given a special piece of luck, you see. So I'm no stranger to any of this.' Then she put her hand on top of mine and added, 'I'm sorry you've lost this chance to have a child with Katherine.'

When we got back to the house this went round and round in my head . . .

You've lost this chance to have a child with Katherine.

You've lost this chance to have a child with Katherine.

The way it came out didn't change each time I said it to myself. Was it meant innocently, or did she mean it was my fault? 'You've lost' meaning 'mislaid', be it by accident or design. Language can be so infuriating at times. Then I turned it around, Katherine had lost this chance to have a child with me, too, hadn't she? I'm glad the thought hadn't occurred to me whilst we had been eating, as I may have said something I would have regretted later on.

The news of the miscarriage was sinking in. After years of thinking I wasn't going to be a father the opportunity had finally come along and I'd accepted it gladly enough. Now, due to Katherine taking this unnecessary, irresponsible trip to New York, the possibility had been snatched away from me. There definitely had been a miscarriage . . . of justice. Why on earth did I let her go to New York in the first place? It could hardly have been essential to her career. The more I thought about Katherine's reckless attitude, the angrier I became. It was as if she'd attached no importance to the birth at all, she could just carry on as usual and then, hey presto, the baby would pop out when it was ready like a piece of toast in a toaster.

My bad mood stopped me from sleeping so I got up and wandered downstairs to pour myself a brandy. The house was dark but I managed to find my way to the living room. I wanted to take a look at how Katherine's portraits of Edith were coming along as I hadn't seen anything since before Christmas and it would serve to take my mind off things. I tiptoed to her studio but the door was locked which irritated me, and I felt like forcing it but instead decided to locate the key the next day, or to quiz Edith as to where the hell it was.

Back in the living room I sank down dejectedly in one of the armchairs with my brandy. As I was sitting there in the dark, it occurred to me that the second half of my Kenwood House dream now had an explanation. The reason for her being in the hospital was, of course, because of the miscarriage, I could see that now and couldn't wait to tell the others how the rest of the dream had come true. Closing my eyes, I imagined walking down the corridor inside my flat and then opening the door. I slowly walked past them all saying hello and catching up. I left and made my way to the other room . . .

At that moment a noise disturbed my reverie and I opened my eyes to find Edith standing in the living room doorway in her dressing gown.

'Oh, Jamie, it's you. I thought I heard something. I was worried.'

I told her to go back to bed and settled back into my chair, continuing where I left off, lost in my thoughts.

In the morning we rang the hospital and were told that Katherine was recovering well, and could be visited later that day. Apparently she was awake and had asked for something to eat which they said was a good sign. When we got there she was sitting up in bed and looked a lot better than she had done the previous day at the airport. I called Miles to let him know how she was, and he said he was intending to come down the next day to see her. I went over to the bed and gave her a hug and tried to impress upon her that everything was going to be fine. Edith did the same and then left the two of us alone. There was a lot of self-reproach and apology on both sides.

'Don't worry. There'll be other opportunities to have babies. I'm sure there will,' I said.

As I held her she became tearful and I was able to re-experience the sensuality that had drawn me to her in the first place.

'You should have some moments alone with your mum,' I said before leaving the bedside, but I reassured her, 'I'm going to stay down here until you come out of hospital.'

I was reminded of the morning I'd met her at Liverpool Street, after Lawrence's death, when we were getting reacquainted. I remembered the heightened senses I'd experienced then and had a similar feeling there in the corridor, outside her room.

Dr Wingfield appeared at my side and I noticed the multitude of lines on his forehead and the fact that his earlobes didn't hang at all. He had a small plaster on his chin where he'd cut himself shaving that morning, and I saw he'd done it before as there were two similar scars close to where the new plaster was. He looked uncomfortable when he caught me staring at him, but he had a smile on his face.

'There's nothing to worry about. But I want Katherine to remain in hospital for another couple of days. We're going to run some tests that could help any future plans the two of you may have for parenthood.'

Edith came out of the room to join us and he repeated what he'd just said, for her benefit, but I knew then there were no future plans for parenthood between us.

As I drove Edith home, it seemed a balance had been restored in my life that had been missing of late. What with the circumstances of the baby's conception and the planning for its arrival, I'd quite taken my eyes from my original objective. Katherine and I had produced a child and that had led me into treating her differently for a while. I'd resigned myself to an existence with her that mixed love with disdain, and I'd accepted this fate with a child on the horizon. All that had changed dramatically in the last twenty-four hours and my mind took on a vigor it had been lacking. I was back in control of my life again and I could now see the way ahead cleared of any complications.

When we got back to the house I asked Edith if she had the key to the studio, saying Katherine had asked me to check on some things for her in there. Edith found it and unlocked the door, and asked me to return the key when I'd finished. I wasn't prepared for what I found. I suppose there were up to thirty canvases in various stages of completion, all paintings of her mother. She'd exhibited about fifty sketches in Berlin and New York, so I expected roughly half of those to be converted into paintings. She'd been working in Kent virtually uninterrupted for close to six months, but judging by the number of canvases she must have been working flat-out every day. I could see the forthcoming exhibition would be her crowning glory, showing a depth of understanding of her subject matter never seen before. The fact that they were mother and daughter had opened up fascinating new avenues of expression to her, and 'Mother/ Daughter' suggested itself as a wonderful title for the show. I made a note to suggest it to Miles when he came down.

Edith was shown in various poses and dressed in a variety of clothes and as I took time to study them all, I could see the slight nuances of mood in every one. There was a bright and flamboyant use of colour, but after losing the child I doubted she would be able to continue with this. I now knew that five or six of her paintings were unfinished. If she could be persuaded, there were probably more canvases to be painted, betraying a more somber mood with an accent on darker tones, redolent of Goya. I realised it was my job to get her to pick up her brushes again and paint out her grief. I tried to put back everything where it had been and locked the door. I found Edith in the kitchen preparing some food.

'I'm sorry I've been so long. I started to look at the canvases and forgot what the time was,' I admitted. She threw me a rueful, understanding smile.

'Not to worry, I understand. They're truly wonderful, aren't they? I've recognised things in them I'd forgotten all about. While she was away in New York, I looked in there myself several times. In a funny sort of way I can see my whole life in them. It reminded me of the past.'

She stopped what she was doing and stared down at the table. I began to feel awkward so I opened a bottle of wine, thinking we could both do with a glass. We sat down to eat and for the first time I started to see features in her face that Katherine had inherited from her. The positioning of the eyes and mouth were unmistakable, for one thing, and the high forehead, but I didn't mention this to her as I didn't want her to feel uncomfortable that I was studying her. She was, of course, nowhere near as perfect as Katherine but the basis for the beauty was there to see.

'I'm very proud of her,' she said as we ate, 'but the talent probably came from her grandfather. He used to draw and paint a lot. Landscapes. That's what he used to love. He lived most of his life on the New South Wales border, in Victoria, around Beechworth. The country up there is quite remarkable. You should let Katherine take you there when you go to Australia. The sunsets there do have a special quality.'

At the mention of sunsets I suffered a slight nervous spasm. An image of a cat being decapitated jumped back into my mind, but I shrugged it off into the recesses of the past and got up to clear the dishes from the table.

Chapter 30

Yves Klein (1928–62) was a French conceptual artist, the son of two painters in Nice, and an important figure in post-war European Art. In October 1960, he staged a photo entitled 'Saut dans le Vide' or 'Leap into the Void' on Rue Gentil Bernard, in Fontenay aux Roses, outside Paris. In the photograph Klein appears to be launching himself from a first floor parapet into the air above the street. A cyclist passes below, whilst Klein assumes the pose of a conductor in front of an orchestra.

That night I couldn't get the images of the new portraits out of my head. I hadn't been this excited since discovering the 'bike' and the 'boar' in Paris. It took all of my self control not to search for Edith's key and steal down to have another look at them, and maybe even hazard some sexual gratification in there at the same time. I knew I'd be lost if I did, but I was aroused just thinking about it so I masturbated in the bed, otherwise there was no way I'd have gotten any rest. A fitful sleep overtook me but the next morning I had no memory of any dreams.

I woke in a bad mood but after taking a shower and noticing there was some blue sky around I began to feel better. We were just about to leave for the hospital when Miles called from his train saying he wanted to be picked up from the station, so I agreed to drop Edith at the hospital and then go and collect him. I got a bit lost in the one way system in Canterbury, and by the time I arrived he was pacing up and down outside the station, clasping a bouquet of flowers and what looked like a box of chocolates.

'Blimey, you took your time!' he snorted at me as he jumped in the car. He was obviously feeling harassed with sorting out the chaos after the fire. I asked him how it was going.

'Bit of a bloody mess, to tell you the truth,' he replied, pleased to be able to share his thoughts with someone, 'The insurers are making an issue about the lights on Katy's paintings but they'll cough up sooner or later. But you've had your own things to deal with. I'm so sorry to hear about what happened to Kath. How is she?'

'She should be able to come home soon.' I tried to put a positive note in my voice.

'That's good news. I really must have the gallery refurbished in time for the new show,' he said concerned.

'I've seen some of the work and it's phenomenal,' I said, trying to lift both our spirits, 'Oh, and I thought of 'Mother/Daughter' as a title. What do you think?'

He thought for a moment, but he was obviously thinking of other things.

'Could work,' he said, 'It's worth suggesting to her.'

We drove for a while without talking, both immersed in our own problems. We pulled into the hospital car park.

'I was thinking I might take her away somewhere for a while. Just the two of us,' I said.

'Take Edith along as well,' he suggested, 'She'll be able to help out, and you never know, Kath may start some new sketches.'

He turned and winked at me after he'd said this, and we both laughed conspiratorially as we got out of the car.

She was up and sitting in a chair when we got to her room. Miles commented on how well she looked.

'Well, well, well. You look nice and bright today, my dear cherub. Must be this hospital food.'

'Dr Wingfield has said he's happy for her to leave tomorrow,' Edith told us. 'Shall we all have some tea to celebrate?'

We drank tea and the rest of Miles' visit consisted of the three of us chatting together almost as if Katherine wasn't in the room. It always happens when one visits someone incapacitated or when there's an elderly person in the room. One tries very hard to include them in the conversation but they never really take any part, and everyone is forever glancing over at them to see if they're following what's being discussed. In this case it was especially difficult, as Katherine was the centre of all of our worlds, and anything we talked about impinged or depended upon her in one way or another. It struck me then that we were all irretrievably locked in with her existence, whether we liked it or not.

I offered Miles a lift back to Canterbury and after we'd dropped him at the station I brought up the question of Katherine's convalescence with Edith.

'Why don't the three of us go away somewhere? It's bound to help her recovery.'

'That's a good idea. I'm sure the doctors will agree to it.'

'It shouldn't be anywhere too far away. But by the sea, and somewhere with some heat,' I suggested, and I had somewhere in mind.

'Yes, but not too hot,' Edith cautioned.

I thought of going back to Spain. Katherine had enjoyed it there the last time, and there was the added advantage that I knew the area well enough to make all the arrangements for us. Edith was happy with the suggestion and once we had Katherine settled back at the house, I told her about the plan. She accepted without any fuss and I gave Miles a call to tell him the news.

'That's great!' he said with obvious glee in his voice, 'Make sure she takes a bloody sketchbook with her, and loads of pencils!'

There was no reason to delay our trip and after Dr Perry had agreed to our plans, I booked some flights departing two days later. I headed back to London to pick up my passport and some things. I hadn't been home for a week and had been wearing some of Katherine's father's clothes whilst I'd been staying at Edith's. It felt a bit strange to be honest, but his underwear had come straight out of unopened cellophane packets, so all I really used was a couple of his shirts. Edith said they fitted me well when she saw me in them.

Driving back to town, I was glad to have a break from the two women. It was dark by the time I reached my flat and I'd just got in the door when Jessica rang to say she was going to drop by after work. I went to visit next door, settled back in the gallery rooms and told them about Katherine's unexpected trip to the hospital. Her father was distraught but I managed to calm him down with Edith's help.

'For crying out loud! She just doesn't take enough care of herself!' he bemoaned.

'She should never have gone to New York in the first place, being so pregnant. Why on earth did you let her?' Edith shrieked.

'You can say that again!' Jamie jumped in. 'Your precious fucking daughter, thinking she's immune to the world. Above us all!'

I had great difficulty diffusing the situation. With Lawrence's help Jamie began to see some sense, but I was far from convinced that he fully understood what was happening. Jake and Dinos were ready to lend their support to Katherine, of course, and asked if there was anything they could do. I heard someone calling from the study so I ran across the dividing hallway and back to my flat, leaving them all muttering to themselves. It was Jamie, making a fuss again, upsetting someone from the first exhibition whose name I couldn't remember. It was becoming difficult to restrain him as he'd begun to throw his weight around recently and intimidate the others. He took everything that happened as a personal attack on himself, no matter how unavoidable it was. He thought every upset was an affirmation of his low self-esteem, and I thought I may have to isolate him if his behaviour continued to be so disruptive. But I didn't know where I could put him.

Jessica was full of news about the fire and admitted she felt responsible as she'd been the one who'd put the lights on behind Katy's paintings each night. I told her not to blame herself and after a couple of drinks she felt better. She told me more about the extent of the damage. The building had been gutted and it was going to take a couple of months to restore, so as to be ready for Katherine's show. Just before she'd left work the insurers had come through, agreeing to pay Miles well over a million pounds in compensation. Not a bad pay check, I thought, for so much free publicity. Furthermore, Miles had shrewdly approached the owners of the building and got them to extend his lease for a further ten years. His argument being that they were getting a virtually new building for free, paid for out of his fire insurance. As for the artists, most of them would welcome the handout as money they could live on whilst preparing new work. Jessica got up to leave and politely asked me how Katherine's recovery was progressing. I told her I was taking her away for a while, but Katherine had never been a major topic in our conversations.

After she'd gone I found my diary. Katherine and I would be away until Easter which was coming up in three weeks time. I hoped she would be fully recovered by then and perhaps even sketching Edith for a few more portraits to add to the show. Miles said he wanted to put it on at the end of April, so by the time the Venice Biennale took place in May the reviews would be coming out. That gave her the whole of April to continue painting so we might expect another ten canvases if we were lucky. Miles and I had both started to look upon her as a workhorse, a commodity capable of making both our fortunes. We'd become partners in our golden goose, laying her golden eggs.

The next day I called to see how she was feeling and after she'd checked and double-checked the flight times, and where we were meeting at Gatwick, she was beginning to feel her old self again. I wanted to have a word with Edith to confirm a taxi had been booked and was relieved to get her off the phone. I'd recently discovered a liquid food for the pitcher plants and made sure they were catered for. Once everyone understood that I was going to be looking after Katherine, who was sick, they were sympathetic and accepted I wasn't going to be around for a while. That afternoon I went to Bloomsbury to Cornelissen's to pick up a couple of sketchbooks that I knew Katherine used, plus a selection of her favourite pencils and crayons. I thought she might get angry at my Machiavellian strategy but I felt sure in the end she'd thank me for it.

I arranged to have dinner with Nicola before going away as it seemed ages since we'd seen one another, and we arranged to meet back at Ping Pong. After we'd shared some saki and snacks, I apologised for being out of touch for so long.

'Things have been out of control just lately. I've been trying to finish a book on succulents, and a relative has just been taken ill,' I explained.

'But I thought you didn't have any relatives?' she questioned, looking suspiciously at me.

It was the first time I'd seen her look that way at me.

'I mean, a close friend,' I said but I knew she didn't believe me.

We continued eating for a while and I felt that I was trying a little too hard with her. I remembered the last time I'd seen her, she had invited me to lunch to meet her father and I hadn't gone. I thought that may be why she was being difficult with me.

'By the way, the next time your father's in town, I'd love to meet him,' I said.

She started to look serious, 'Jamie, I've met someone else.'

I was shocked and ordered more saki.

'Who is he?' I asked. She shook her head at me and looked at her food. 'Where did you meet him? Please tell me,' I persevered.

'No. Don't be so nosey,' she said,' I don't have to tell you. Besides, I don't want to.'

Later on, when I'd paid the bill and we were on the doorstep saying goodbye, I felt sad we weren't leaving together. As I walked home alone I realised we'd been seeing each other on and off for a year, making no demands on one another. That's what she'd found wrong, she'd explained it earlier over dinner.

'It's going nowhere, Jamie. I have to move on. You're always so . . . so preoccupied.'

But there had just been too many things going on for me to see it. I'd have to concentrate even harder to make sure life went the way I wanted it to.

Chapter 31

Ana Christina Cesar (1952–83) was a poet from Rio de Janiero. She admired Sylvia Plath and jumped out of a window of her parent's apartment in Rio de Janiero in 1983.

I was relieved to get away from London. On the plane Katherine and Edith were seated together on one side of the aisle and I was on the other, lost in my thoughts for the duration of the flight. We arrived in the late afternoon and the motorway towards the coast was empty as the Spanish took their lunch. The central reservation was filled with lilac oleander bushes coming into flower, and field upon field of sunflowers stretched away on either side of the road, pointing their heads towards the bright sun, looking like legions of green shower heads. Majestic umbrella pines followed as we neared the coast and I took the 381 across country to avoid the early evening build-up of traffic outside Cadiz. We skirted Medina Sidonia, rounded a bend, and austere Vejer peered down at us from its hilltop throne, before we were on the slip road heading towards the Atlantic.

I made the two women sit in the back as if I were driving a taxi, since I wanted to enjoy the scenery and have more uninterrupted time to myself, plus it gave them the opportunity to talk to each other. Periodically I would try to listen in, but all I could catch was the odd word or two so I had no real idea of what they were talking about. But as the drive continued I became convinced they were talking about me and I strained my ears to try to hear what they were saying. The more I tried to eavesdrop, the more frustrating it became, and by the time we'd reached our hostel I was mentally exhausted.

I unloaded the car and parked up behind. The accommodation was different from that which Katherine and I had stayed in the year before, and I much preferred it. The atmosphere was more hospitable and it was run by a group of sisters with their widowed mother in charge of the superb kitchen. Nothing was too much trouble for them and it had a cool, bright, dining room at the front which you could happily sit in all day. I had done this many times before on previous trips. Local people would come and go, saying 'hello' and having a quick coffee or drink, visitors would take lunch, and even the local police made a habit of eating there but they always sat inside, rather than with the public out front. There was a nice selection of homemade traditional cakes on offer that I thought Edith may like to taste with her tea. I'd booked two rooms on the only floor that overlooked the ocean and both had twin beds which suited me, but when Her Royal Highness saw them she wasn't at all pleased. She said that at night she needed to be hugged and suggested we push the beds together. After she'd made me struggle on all fours, tying the legs together with some string she'd produced from God knows where, she finally seemed happy. In fact, we ended up with a bed far bigger than a normal double, which I welcomed as I need my own space, especially with Katherine. I don't like being clung to very much and she was a clinger. I left her to rest for a while and tapped on Edith's door, suggesting we take an early supper downstairs after Katherine had taken a nap. I said I was going out for a walk to stretch my legs and she asked if she could come along.

The retreating tide had exposed sand with a beautiful pink tinge to it and we ambled along, occasionally stopping to take a closer look at something washed up in the surf. Edith found something quite remarkable, a roughly spherical, flat shell about the size of a pound coin. One side had the impression of what looked like an ear carved on it in orange-brown and the other was smooth and pearly white, and had a spiral curling into the center. It looked rather like an eye and we started to notice more of them. When the eye was faced up it reminded me of Reyes' cat, watching me from the balcony in Texas.

'Do you mind me asking?' I said, 'How long did you sit for the sketches on average?'

I hoped I could get an idea of the rate at which Katherine worked.

'I didn't sit for any of them. I offered to, but she said it wasn't necessary,' she replied.

That meant Katherine had drawn them totally from memory, something I'd never heard the like of before and I told her so.

'I'd like to see her start again soon,' I added, 'Maybe while we're down here. Don't tell her, but I brought some sketchbooks along, just in case. It would suggest she was returning to normal, don't you think?'

'I can't tell what's normal any more, as far as my daughter is concerned.'

I wasn't quite sure what she meant by this. It could have been a veiled reference to an opinion of me, but I decided to let it go and not press her for more of an explanation.

The next day I took the car into the nearest town and found an internet café. I'd managed to finish the first draft of the succulents book before leaving and had dropped it off at my publishers, so I was eager to get some feedback from them. I also wanted to find out something about the strange shells we'd seen on the beach. I'd noticed that the waitress in the restaurant was wearing one as a pendant and she told me they were called Shiva's Eyes. I Google'd the term and discovered that they were the trap door for a mollusc known as the Blue Turban. Apparently when the animal dies the trap door is released into the ocean, and it was comforting to learn that the death of an animal leads to the creation of something so beautiful. They are regarded as good luck charms and in Sri Lanka they can grow to the size of a small plate, meaning the shell they had originated from would have been almost a yard across. My online session ran out and the computer screen went blank, so I pumped in half a euro and checked my emails, then I checked Kumar's account.

Miles and Kumar had been exchanging emails to decide which paintings would go to Venice and it promised to be a stunning show. Kumar had agreed to lend the major work from the National Portrait Gallery comprising Katherine's father, Lawrence, Jake and Dinos, and Miles himself. I still hadn't brought the subject up with them back in the rooms as they'd told me they hated travelling and I knew they'd detest all that dirty, smelly water you get in the summer in the Venice canals.

Katherine began to venture out with us on walks along the beach and she developed a healthy glow. She'd been demanding in bed but I'd endured it with the shutters down, making believe I was with Jessica or Nicola in the pitch dark. One morning she seemed bored with her reading and was pacing around our bedroom whilst I was getting dressed. I judged this to be the right moment to reveal the sketchbooks I'd brought, so I said I had a surprise for her and she perked up.

'Now be a good girl and just sit down on the bed,' I instructed her and she meekly did so. I went over to my suitcase and began rifling around.

'Now close your eyes.'

I could feel her anticipation rising by the second.

'And hold out your hands too!' I exclaimed trying to prolong the excitement.

I placed the sketchbooks and the pencil cases on the palms of her open hands.

'Now you can open your eyes!' I said.

I could immediately tell she wasn't at all pleased at what she saw. She cast them onto the bed, got up and went to sulk by the window.

'God, you're so manipulative! I hate you,' she shouted.

'Now that's not very nice. I thought I was being helpful. I think you should grow up, Katherine. And get on with what you're good at!'

I decided to play it rough with her and pretended to be cross, so I grabbed the car keys and stormed out of the room. I drove up to Cadiz, following the road up past Plaza de Espana and past the Candelaria. I parked in an underground car park next to the docks and wandered round the old town aimlessly. I stopped off for a coffee in the Genovese gardens for a while and had a look at the succulent beds there. Tiny stray cats peered out at me from within the foliage of the cypress trees. Why was my life being spent plagued by cats, I wondered? I headed towards the Cathedral and turned off to look in the Plaza de Las Flores which always smells strongly of magnolia blossoms, but that just served to remind me of Louisiana again. I looked around the temporary market that had been constructed above the rebuilding of the old one, and could hear the construction work going on below my feet. Then I felt hungry and decided to take a ferry across to Puerto de Santa Maria and go for some shellfish at Romerijo's, before wandering around there for a while.

I returned to the hostel at about six o'clock and found Katherine sitting with her back to me in the restaurant, busying herself with one of the sketchbooks. I decided not to disturb her and went outside to where Edith was sitting reading in the sunshine. I asked her if she fancied a walk along the beach and she raised her eyes from her book and winked at me.

Things began to settle into a rhythm. I took a wake up dip in the chilly ocean before breakfast, and this was followed by Katherine drawing for a couple of hours, then all of us took a walk before lunch. After that Edith and I would make ourselves scarce so as not to distract Katherine from working. Her mood began to stabilise and it was obvious the sketching was helping her get over the loss of the baby. The quality of the air and the seafood worked wonders, and none of us touched alcohol for most of the three weeks we spent there. On one of the last evenings Katherine showed me her latest sketches.

'I want to turn the best ones into paintings,' she said and I could tell she was proud of them.

'They're wonderful,' I declared as I looked through.

'I want to say thank you for bringing the sketchbooks along. It was very thoughtful of you. I'm sorry I was so mean when you got them out.'

She gave me a hug with tearful eyes as we sat on the bed, and it took all my strength to prise her arms loose and get her to compose herself ready for supper, as Edith was waiting for us downstairs.

I lost my mobile phone somewhere. I'd been checking my emails regularly in the nearest town and discovered it was missing on the drive back one day. I knew I'd had it with me earlier as always, just in case either Katherine or Edith needed me. So, I went back to the internet café and asked if it had been handed in. The owner couldn't help me so I retraced my steps, but I still couldn't find it. Over lunch I explained what had happened and Katherine offered to lend me hers as Edith still had one if needed, and I accepted it gratefully. The next day I had it sitting on the passenger seat while I was driving. I heard the bleep of an incoming message, so without thinking I pulled over to read it.

> GLAD YOURE FEELING
> BETTER NOW . . . WE CAN
> ALWAYS TRY AGAIN
> NEXT TIME YOURE IN
> AUS! KISSES TO YOU
> ALISTAIR XXX

I read it again. And again. I checked who the sender was but there was no name, just the number's prefix +61, which I knew to be Australia, and its significance began to dawn on me. I carried on driving and went to the café for a while but I couldn't concentrate, so I walked around the corner to sit in the quiet shade of a plaza. I had passed through it many times, going to and from the cafe from the car, and it had always had a pleasant, friendly atmosphere. There were nearly always children playing football, making noise and injecting it with life. On this day, however, it was empty and as I sat there thinking about the text message, I noticed it metamorphosing into the setting for a de Chirico painting, a place of isolation and foreboding, full of darkened doorways and hidden meaning.

Katherine claimed she'd told me she was pregnant after returning from Australia in the summer. But it was possible she'd come off the pill before going there, slept with this Alistair and conceived, then decided to tell me I was the father. But perhaps it was just an old friend showing support for her and I was misinterpreting the message. But maybe I wasn't. In the end I didn't know what to think. Perhaps that's why she was so keen to contact me when she was away. She'd wanted to confess that she'd slept with someone else and felt terribly guilty about it. If that was the case, why hadn't she told me when she'd got back? Second thoughts, perhaps? Or lack of certainty? I'd never found out why she was looking for me so desperately. I was away in America visiting Reyes at the time and had never asked her about it. The thought that Katherine had duped me into accepting the child was mine gained credibility inside my head, and my feelings of hatred towards her instinctively welled up, as they'd done when she'd rejected me for Lawrence.

That night as I lay in bed with my eyes open, I went over and over the things that had to be done before the Venice Biennale. Katherine hadn't shown much enthusiasm for going but Miles and I agreed it was essential that she attend. We'd look pretty foolish without our golden goose in tow. Apparently the refurbishment of Goodfellows2 was on schedule and invitations for Katherine's show were already being sent out for the re-opening on April 30th. It looked like there were going to be forty canvases, at a minimum price of £50,000, making a gross of at least £2,000,000 when sold. Miles had allowed me to reserve five of what I considered to be the best works at the knockdown price of £150,000. Together with what Kumar had secured, I'd be taking possession of a massive quarter of the paintings. I was already thinking of putting a couple of her earlier works into a Christie's New York auction scheduled for that autumn, with a reserve in the region of £90,000 each, and the proceeds from this would go towards financing the purchase of the new work.

I decided to start hunting in Venice for the perfect hotel for us to stay at. I drifted off to sleep with Katherine's gentle snoring behind me and the roar of the ocean coming in through the open window.

Chapter 32

Elise Cowen (1933–62) was an American poet of the Beat generation. A life-long depressive, she jumped through a locked living room window at her parent's home and fell seven stories to her death.

I never thought I'd be thankful for losing a mobile phone because I'd never have found out about Alistair in Australia, otherwise. To think that she'd fooled me into accepting the child was mine. None of them could believe it when I got back to London.

'It doesn't fuckin' surprise me at all!' Lawrence said, shouting out of his frame.

'Well, she was two-timing me in Paris. That's why I dumped her. She told you something different, of course,' Didier added.

Then Miles piped in, 'You never can be too sure about a girl that devastatingly beautiful. You're just asking for trouble, chum.'

Her father defended her saying she wasn't capable of doing such a thing, but soon got shouted down. Lawrence was in favour of getting rid of her straight away.

'Why not? We don't need her anymore, do we? Besides, there's no room for anyone else in here,' Miles agreed.

But it wasn't as simple as that. I explained why they had to go to Venice and they could help me by not kicking up such a fuss about it. I put on *Jezebel* for them and locked the door to get back to some peace and quiet in my own flat across the hall.

I called Miles the next day and told him about Katherine drawing Edith completely from memory, and he was as surprised to hear about it as I was. He told me that Leonardo was the only artist he'd heard of who was capable of the same thing. Apparently if he spotted a face that interested him, he would follow the person the whole day until he had an impression so well formed in his mind that he could manufacture a likeness on paper.

Miles had already finalised the catalogue at the printers using the title I suggested of 'Mother/Daughter'. Neither of us had cleared it with Katherine but we felt sure she'd approve of it if she knew. I told him there would probably be ten more canvases to add to the show and he was more than pleased. It meant the new work would have to be an addendum to the catalogue but he wasn't concerned.

'Not to worry. The extra canvases will add some excitement. Unseen work and all that. By the way, brownie points to you for getting her back to work again. Well done, matey.'

I was pleased he'd acknowledged me as having played some role and I wanted to ask his advice.

'How are we going to persuade her to go to Venice? You know she's not keen. We've got to get her to change her mind.'

'Well, old son, I suppose a proposal is out of the question? You know she can't manage life without you these days. It's bleeding obvious she adores you. And it could be sort of a honeymoon, don't you think . . . ?' he suggested it half jokingly, but I knew he was being deadly serious.

After what I'd discovered recently there was no way I wanted to marry her, but how many marriages are for the right reasons? And what are the right reasons anyway? It would definitely help to convince her to go, he was right about that. I decided to consider it as a last resort, if all else failed.

I had some meetings in town over the next few days and my car was being serviced, so I used the Underground to get about. It always seemed to be the rush hour and I began to think I was recognising people in the bustling crowds passing me by. Familiar faces would leap out at me from the hordes and I'd search my memory for some name to call out. Most of the time I gave up, but occasionally a name popped into my head and I'd shout it out, only to have a blank face turned towards me. After my last meeting I was waiting for a train home at Oxford Circus Station. It was five thirty and seriously packed, and I found myself near the front of the platform next to the rails. The roar in the tunnel increased as a train approached and as the front of it shot into the station, a man dressed in a grey suit pushed past me and threw himself onto the line. The train was so noisy I couldn't tell if anyone screamed and it was as if the whole thing was happening in silence. No one around me moved a muscle and I suppose everyone, like me, couldn't believe what they'd witnessed, but for some reason a smile came onto my face and I began to laugh hysterically. Instead of admonishing me for my inappropriate behaviour, people started to console me, perhaps thinking that I knew the man. A woman put her arm around my shoulders.

'There, there, you poor thing. Come and sit down. Over here.'

She guided me through the crowds towards a bench and I heard someone telling the people sitting there:

'Make room for him. Make room! He's a friend of the victim!'

They sat me down like an invalid and the woman pushed a handkerchief into my hands, which I used to blow my nose. A young transport policeman in a bright yellow vest crouched down next to me and asked who I was. I said I didn't know the victim but it had all been just too much for me. The woman who'd been standing behind me when it happened corroborated the fact that I was an innocent bystander. The policeman took a few particulars from me and an announcement blared out:

'ALTERNATIVE TRAVEL ARRANGEMENTS SHOULD BE MADE BY ALL PASSENGERS . . . THIS PLATFORM IS CLOSED . . . THIS PLATFORM IS CLOSED'

People drifted off in different directions and the woman asked if I was all right. I told her I was fine and thanked her, and she smiled and disappeared into the crowds. Shakily, I made my way up to street level and hailed a taxi on Oxford Street. I was sitting in the back approaching the top of Gloucester Terrace, when I noticed a familiar smell in the cab and looked down to see that I was still clutching the handkerchief the woman had given me. Bringing it up to my nose, I was aware of a scent that had become very familiar to me over the past year and a half, it was the same one Katherine used.

The smell of the perfume did as much to unsettle me as the accident had. I couldn't remember what the woman looked like. Surely it wasn't Katherine? I would have recognised her, wouldn't I? I began to wonder what on earth had driven the man to commit suicide. He may have felt he'd lost control of his life, and whatever he did made no difference one way or the other. Others were in charge of events that engulfed him. If this happens occasionally one can deal with it but if it happened all the time, well, it would be too much to bear. That was probably the root of his sad desperation. By committing suicide, I suppose he was at last in control.

I sat down with some tea and thought again about the lost baby and Katherine's attempt to pin the identity of the father on me. How on earth did she think she could get away with it? It was pathetic. And she'd provided me with the ultimate means to uncover the truth by lending me her own phone, with Alistair's message on it! I pitied her, amazed at how passively I'd accepted her claim and without any suspicion she was screwing somebody else behind my back. She may well have been seeing other men during the time we'd got back together, as well as Alistair . . .

At that moment just the thought of her made me want to laugh. It was always such a relief to be rid of her whenever we parted. I'm sure she'd noticed it. I kept finding her troublesome, long, curly blonde hairs everywhere; in the bathroom, on the bed sheets, in the kitchen, even in my food, and at times it would infuriate me. In Spain I'd started to see them when they weren't even there.

That night I woke up struggling to breathe. In my dream I'd swallowed some hair. I was in La Capaninna's, sitting at a table with her ladyship and Miles and Ann. None of them realised what was wrong with me as I sat there choking. I tried to explain but nobody understood what I was saying which made me even more desperate, and I coughed all the more.

When I woke up it took me a while to recover and I had to drink a couple of glasses of water because my mouth felt so dry. I saw it was four thirty in the morning. I didn't feeling like staying in bed any longer, so I made myself some hot chocolate thinking it would help me get back to sleep. I wandered about my flat listlessly and tried looking at a few magazines. They knew I was awake. I could hear them calling out at me through the walls. At that moment the last thing I needed was to have to deal with their incessant bickering and parsimony. I started to hear the incessant tick-tock of the grandfather clock from the other room, but knew I was imagining it. I continued drinking the hot chocolate and the sound of the clock grew deafening in my ears.

I needed to occupy myself, to get some fresh air, so I unfolded my bike. I'd fixed the new lights on but the sun was just coming up, and when I pulled off from the curb it looked like it was going to be a dry, clear morning. I headed eastwards across London's deserted streets and after about forty-five minutes I found myself in Farringdon, heading towards Miles' gallery. I pulled up outside Goodfellows2 and found it was covered in scaffolding and had a couple of skips outside. I tried to look through the windows and from what I could see the refurbishment looked close to being complete. I guessed it would be ready in about two weeks, right on schedule and in time for Katherine's show. The interior had been updated and was barely recognisable. There seemed to be much more wall space and the stairwell had been moved away from the center to create a wide atrium. Swathes of daylight shone down onto the dark, polished, wooden floors through new skylights that had been fitted in the roof. By now the sun was blazing down so I turned the bike round and started for home. A café was just opening on the corner of Paul Street. I stopped for a coffee, and as I sat down outside at a table in the sunshine, I became conscious of the fact that I was still dressed in my pyjamas.

Chapter 33

*Gilles Deleuze (1925–95) was a French philosopher. From the
early 1960s until his death, he wrote many influential books
on philosophy, literature, film and fine art. A heavy smoker,
he suffered from lung cancer and had a lung removed. He had
a tracheotomy and lost the power of speech. In 1995 he threw
himself from the window of his apartment.*

My proposal of marriage took Katherine completely by surprise.
I decided to ask her on the way back from my bike ride that
morning.

'Wow! I accept, of course. But when?' she asked.

'What about the beginning of May?' I suggested. 'We could
go to Venice straight afterwards and stay there a few days. Then
maybe go somewhere more exotic for a honeymoon.'

At first she wasn't keen on going, but I told her she was crazy
not to attend. Besides, I'd discovered a great place for us to stay
and it wasn't a fabrication. Although Venice was getting booked
up I'd found the perfect place, the Hotel Al Ponte Dei Sospiri. It
only had eight rooms, all suites, and looked wonderful. It had
Murano glass chandeliers and full Venetian décor, including
gold wardrobes, draped curtains and Juliette balconies. I'd bull-
dozed my way through all the penciled bookings, and taken the
whole hotel from the eve of the Biennale for five days. The hotel
had salivated at my request and agreed to hold all eight rooms
for me for just seventy-two hours and the deadline was midnight
that night. All I had to do was get Katherine to agree to go and I
could confirm the booking. Once I'd described the hotel to
her – two minutes walk from St Mark's Square, and the balcony
of our room overlooking the Bridge of Sighs – she caved in and
agreed to come. Secretly, I was more relieved at this fact than

her having agreed to marry me. I couldn't wait to get off the phone and ring the hotel immediately to confirm. She found my enthusiasm infectious and wanted to tell Edith the news straight away. We agreed on a quiet service at a registry office, perhaps Kensington Town Hall, with just a few guests invited.

I took a pen and paper and made a list of the people I wanted to invite to stay with us at the hotel:

Room 1: Jamie & Katherine (double)
Room 2: Miles & Ann (double)
Room 3: Celia and Darcy (sharing a twin)
Room 4: Edith (a single)
Room 5: Jake (single)
Room 6: Dinos (single)

If all the people accepted it would leave two rooms free that I could offer to Miles if he wanted to invite anyone special along. I had half a mind to suggest he invited Jessica. The idea of having her there to pounce on at some point during our stay excited me. I got on the phone to tell Miles the good news and that I'd booked the hotel. He was delighted to join us although it meant cancelling his own booking at the lavish Cipriani across the Lido, but he said he'd much prefer to stay with us than to spend a fortune there. Of course he'd be bringing Ann and the girls along. He told me he was going to leave Jessica back in London to hold the fort at the gallery. I got hold of Jake and Dinos who said they'd be delighted to come and if necessary share a room. They asked what we'd like as a wedding present but I had no idea what to tell them. A sculpture would do but I had no idea where we'd put it.

By the time I'd confirmed the hotel and got back to Katherine, I was enjoying myself and wondered why on earth I hadn't thought of this marriage idea before. She was keen for me to go down to Kent and see her, but I was beginning to feel exhausted from my lack of sleep so said I'd make it down at the weekend instead. I asked her how her work was progressing and she told me even though she'd only been back a week, she had already made a start on all ten of the planned additional canvases.

For the rest of the week I packed up the work that Kumar had arranged to lend to Miles and took it out to the Slough office for collection. Then I attended to the other art that I'd agreed to lend for the show. The two rooms felt quite empty now but I could live with that even though I'd got so used to having them around. We'd had our disagreements, granted, but now the family was being broken up, I would miss the bickering and social politics that had become the fabric of my daily routine. One by one they disappeared, whimpering beneath the bubble wrap and I was a little fearful as to how I'd cope without them.

My sleep patterns had changed drastically and I began waking up in the middle of the night as if with jet lag, unsure where I was and feeling desperately lonely. By the time Saturday came I was glad to break the pattern and head down to Kent. We dined at the Chapter Arms and I drank far too much. I ended up leaving my car there and getting a taxi for the three of us, back to Edith's house. My drunken state necessitated my sleeping in my own room but since I'd proposed, Katherine wasn't putting any pressure on me to make love to her.

I woke up late the next morning and joined Katherine and Edith downstairs, expecting to be in the doghouse, of course. The remarkable thing was that they weren't put out in the slightest by my behaviour. It was as if by proposing to Katherine I'd waved a magic wand and put them both under a spell. I gingerly asked if there was any coffee and a fresh pot appeared in front of me. They made me some buttered toast and squeezed a glass of fresh orange juice. As my teeth crunched loudly on the toast, I felt awkward disturbing the silence of the kitchen. The calm was unsettling and I didn't know what to do, so I decided to pay no attention to either of them and picked up the *Sunday Telegraph* from the kitchen table and browsed through it.

'Why don't you go through to the sitting room? It'll be much more comfortable for you in there,' Edith suggested with a genuine smile.

Why not, I thought? I took my coffee and paper, sat down in one of the armchairs and promptly dozed off, waking up to hear them setting the table for lunch. It was close to two o'clock and I couldn't remember when I'd last had such a relaxing Sunday. I could smell a roast chicken they were preparing and five minutes later, half asleep, I was standing above the cooked bird holding a large carving knife and fork. They both looked up at me, waiting patiently for me to carve meat onto their plates like two, hungry, little birds in a nest. I had an enormous appetite and began tucking into my heaped plate to avoid any conversation. Feeling less conspicuous once I'd eaten, I began to tell them more about the hotel in Venice. Neither of them had ever been before and it was obvious they were looking forward to the trip.

'Where do you want to go, once the five days are over? For a honeymoon, I mean,' Katherine asked me.

To tell the truth I hadn't thought that far ahead.

'Oh, I don't know. Why don't you decide.'

'We'll have to think about who to invite to the ceremony, apart from close family, of course.' She was excited and looked at Edith when she said this, who silently nodded her approval. They had obviously been discussing it.

'I can organise all that for you,' Edith offered, 'I'd be happy to.'

I felt that I was only there to fulfill my role as the initiator of this whole thing, which I was of course, but it was evident they were taking control, making sure it all went the way they wanted it to.

We decided on an early night but my insomnia surfaced again. The comfort of the day had reminded me how lonely my flat in London had become and I wondered how I'd manage – for however long it turned out to be – without my paintings. Then Edith and Katherine encroached upon my thoughts. Mother and daughter; how close they were. I envied their silent understanding and contentment. How easy it would be to get up, go down to the kitchen, take a knife out from one of the drawers and put an end to them both while they slept so peacefully in their beds. It would be so much easier than having to go through with this grotesque pantomime I'd written for myself.

I opened my eyes and found myself standing naked in Edith's bedroom. Looking down, I saw I was holding the carving knife from lunch in my right hand. In a panic I dropped the knife and watched it falling silently onto the carpet in slow motion. I picked it up and went downstairs to the kitchen where I suddenly felt hungry. I cut some meat off the chicken carcass in the fridge and stuffed it into my mouth. I found a cold beer and drank it down greedily in a couple of gulps. I started to shiver and hurried back upstairs to bury myself under the warm blankets of my bed. It took a good half hour to stop shivering and restore some warmth to my body, and eventually I slipped off to sleep.

The next two weeks rushed by like breaking waves reaching the shore and my insomnia continued. At times I found myself totally submerged in the waves, losing equilibrium for a while, coming up and gasping for air. At other times they would unexpectedly knock me off my feet as I misjudged their strength. Sometimes one would ripple gently past me.

All of a sudden it was time for Katherine's show, and she insisted I arrive with her as her fiancée. She'd been staying at her flat in Olympia to attend to the hanging of her work, and picked me up in a cab on the way to the gallery in one of her impeccable Von Furstenburg dresses. I had on a sober Paul Smith lounge suit, I remember. As we drove down Park Lane, I was convinced we were on our way to the wedding ceremony.

'This is the wrong way to get to the Kings Road, excuse me . . . ' I started to tap on the window to get the driver's attention. But Katherine grabbed my arm.

'We're picking Mother up from Waterloo Station, darling. Remember? On the way to the gallery? What are you talking about?'

She took my hand and started squeezing it frantically.

Miles was keen for them to arrive together, as 'Mother/Daughter' was the title of the show, thanks to me. We got to the gallery soon after seven, and it was packed. Miles had managed to convince Dom Perignon to sponsor the opening and waitresses in black dresses passed amongst the guests refilling their glasses. I must say the show looked terrific and I noted that my purchases were marked with a red dot, so the first thing I did was to make sure Kumar's had also been similarly marked. I wandered around looking at the works, particularly the newer ones I was less familiar with. I saw with surprise and irritation that several of these featured Katherine as the subject. So, she'd quietly spirited herself into the work and, in effect, they had become self-portraits. This revelation I wasn't prepared for. Now I understood why she'd been so reticent to let me view the post-Spain portraits when I'd asked her in Kent. I noticed they had also been marked with red dots and I immediately looked for Miles to take issue with him about it.

'Didn't you know?' he said to me, dumbfounded.

'Katherine and Edith wanted them. I'm surprised they haven't told you.'

I'd interrupted a conversation he was having, and to show his irritation he made some joke at my expense and I got that same feeling of loneliness and exclusion I'd felt so many times before in relation to all things Katherine. I couldn't concentrate on what he was saying to me, so I wandered off dejected.

I desperately wanted to be alone. I found a quiet corner under the stairs to sulk in private. Here I was, about to marry Katherine, and she was making me feel unworthy of her again. This time she was recruiting her mother to help her. They both deserved the same fate and I regretted not taking the opportunity a fortnight earlier in Kent. I grabbed a few canapés as the trays passed by and got my glass refilled several times, so I was quite drunk by the time people started to leave. I noticed Miles had neglected to come over and speak to me as he normally would do at his shows. I supposed he was just too busy attending to more important guests there than me. Lost in my thoughts I heard a familiar voice.

'Hello, stranger. What's up with you?' And I turned to find Jessica standing next to me.

'Come on. Come with me,' she coaxed.

I obediently followed her up the stairs and across the empty mezzanine floor. In a far corner out of direct light, there was a door. She opened it with a key and I went in after her. She locked it behind us and started to unbutton my fly. I impulsively worked on loosening her top as I kissed her neck, and soon I was entering her feverishly. She moaned as I thrust at her and we both climaxed in a rush. As I relaxed with my chin on her shoulder and her hair in my eyes, I opened them fully. We appeared to be in a storeroom and my gaze settled on one of the self-portraits Katherine had found time to paint whilst she'd been pregnant. Her cold, green eyes were staring accusingly back at me and boring into mine.

Chapter 34

Vsevolod Garshin (1855–88) was a Russian short story writer. His father committed suicide in his presence when he was seven and despite literary success, he was plagued with mental illness. At the age of thirty-three, he jumped from the fifth floor of his apartment block.

My insomnia became worse after the opening, and the wedding service at Kensington Town Hall seemed inconsequential to me. I was surprised to see photographers outside snapping our picture when we emerged from the building, but I couldn't see what there was of interest to the outside world. It was only Katherine and I getting married. As we walked down the steps to a waiting taxi Miles, Ann, Edith, Celia and Darcy all threw confetti and rice over us and some of it went in my eye.

Katherine had booked flights from Venice, via Rome, to Manila in the Philippines, somewhere she said she'd always wanted to go. She'd found an idyllic island for us to spend two weeks in a beach hut, and it sounded quite nice.

The reviews of the show were ecstatic and set-up Venice perfectly for Miles. The remains of my collection back at home looked pretty sorry for themselves and I began to regret Kumar contributing any of his work at all, but I suppose I wouldn't have secured so many new canvases if he'd refused.

After the ceremony we went to the Electric in Portobello Road for an informal dinner in a private room. Miles had organised it all, and people dropped by to congratulate us. After an hour or so, Edith wanted to get to Waterloo to catch a train back to Kent and others took this as their cue to leave. Soon everyone had left, apart from Miles, and the three of us proceeded to get very drunk. It was mainly fueled by my enthusiasm, as it was the only way I could guarantee sleep for myself later on. Something had been constantly bugging me since the opening.

'By the way, what happened to those three self-portraits you wanted to paint at Christmas, of you being pregnant? Are you still going to do them?'

Miles turned to Katherine in his drunken stupor, as if to reinforce my question with his own curiosity, but of course he already knew what the answer was as I'd seen them in his storeroom when I was with Jessica.

'Of course I finished them. And this fucking little cunt has still got them stashed away,' she replied, and Miles raised his glass to her with a cunning smile. I was relieved she'd finally admitted their existence to me. 'And he better have some decent insurance this time, 'life' as well as 'contents', because his won't be worth living if anything happens to them. I fucking promise you that,' she added aggressively, and the tone of her voice scared me. I'd never got this drunk with her before and what Lawrence had told me back on Lamu came to mind.

Miles seemed to perk up and I could see that he was indeed scared of her. 'Pet, listen to me. They're as safe as houses. Don't you worry about that, my little cherub. But do let me suggest something. Why don't we each keep one? It's a triptych, n'est-ce pas? A trio?' With this question he turned to her, and after a moment she nodded her head drunkenly. 'To the triptych,' he declared, 'Miles . . . Katherine . . . and Jamie!' and he clinked glasses with us both as he said our names. We all chorused it together a second time.

From then until Venice, I was in a state of uncertainty about anything. My lack of sleep was beginning to take its toll and I was finding it difficult to make any sort of decision. I fully intended to ask her why she'd been trying to get hold of me whilst she was in Australia but the right moment never presented itself. It sat at the back of my mind, in a dark and dangerous corner, and part of me didn't want to go there.

Katherine stayed with me in my flat for those last few days and without her help I don't think I'd have had the enthusiasm to pack my things, let alone make it to the airport. She was constantly on the phone with Edith or Miles, discussing domestic or business matters and my diminishing energy levels seemed to be matched by an increase in hers. I started to confuse who she was talking to on the phone, and began, at one stage, to think it was Lawrence. She made sure we got to the airport on time to meet up with Edith and then checked us all in. During the flight I began to doze off and I dreamed I was back with Jessica in the storeroom. This time Katherine caught us and knocked me to the ground with clenched fists. She threw canvases on top of me in a scary rage. Every canvas put me into further darkness and panic, and I punched my hands through them with a sense of finding freedom with each one I destroyed, but I grew progressively weaker every time. A stewardess woke me and offered a food tray. I was sweating profusely and Katherine asked if I was all right and felt my temples, but I just said that I'd had a strange dream.

We came through Italian immigration, picked up our bags and made our way to the hotel where a waiter met us by the water's edge, carrying three glasses of Prosecco. We stepped out of our gondola on to the jetty and our bags magically disappeared from view. The three of us checked in and Katherine and I took Room 101, the Ducal Suite. I must say it was magnificent. It had marble floors throughout and the living room had a wrought iron balcony overlooking the Bridge of Sighs. There was a bottle of chilled Prosecco with two glasses outside on a glass table. The phone rang and it was Miles welcoming us to Venice and asking us to be ready downstairs by seven o'clock for the opening reception. We decided to take a nap and Katherine wanted some affection but my exhaustion and unfamiliarity with the setting overtook me, and I shrunk bewildered in her hands. This made me feel even less important. I mumbled an apology saying I had no idea what was wrong with me, and heard her sighing. We rolled over to face our respective sides of the bed and I tried to sleep, but the complexity of my thoughts wouldn't allow me any rest. Pretty soon I heard Katherine's gentle snoring behind me and I got up to look around the suite. It was just as I had hoped for. There were marble floors and tall, floor to ceiling windows in the living room that led onto the balcony with the canal directly below, and I could smell it was starting to take on its characteristic stink for the summer. I looked at my watch and saw it was approaching five, so I went back to the bedroom and woke Katherine up as it was time for us to get ready.

We gathered in the hotel reception and Miles was already waiting with two gondolas. Due to my lack of sleep, together with all the Prosecco I'd drunk, I found the movements of the gondola very upsetting and felt like throwing up into the canal, but I managed to keep down whatever there was inside me. We travelled for about fifteen minutes through choppy water and approached a mooring where I saw a lot of lights crisscrossing in the sky above, as if it were a giant outdoor disco. Miles led us along a red carpet and up some steps into what seemed to be a palace full of smartly dressed dignitaries. Within a few minutes I was being introduced to lots of people, all of whose names I immediately forgot. I vaguely remember there were the organisers of the Biennale, the Venice town council, representatives of the Australian Arts Council, some of the Italian Royal family, and then other people Miles seemed to know. We were introduced to the British contingent and artists filed past, some of whose names were vaguely familiar to me, and most of them looked very old. Someone put a glass of champagne in my hand and Katherine became the center of attention, so I faded into insignificance.

She was like one of those elephantiasis victims on Lamu. I'd become her embarrassing appendage, something that followed pathetically wherever she went. The people we were introduced to had no idea who I was, they just grinned inanely in my direction, just to let me know they were acknowledging my existence as her grotesque swollen limb. I emptied my glass and it was refilled, and I couldn't wait for the whole thing to end.

We were taken into an immense dining room and I was sat next to Her Royal Highness, everybody was fawning over her so much it was disgusting. I tried to eat something but only managed to pick at the dishes that were put in front of me. I remember Miles speaking to me across Katherine, but I had no idea what he was talking about. I couldn't concentrate on what he or anyone else was saying to me. I do remember Katherine asking me if I was feeling alright so I just nodded back and gave her a weak smile. I started to think I was being completely ignored by everyone at the table and I felt invisible from then on. I continued to sip at the champagne in my glass. At least the circulating waiters passing behind me could see that I existed, as they kept filling up my glass at every opportunity. The noise of the conversations around me got louder and louder and it became a deafening row. I found a paper napkin in my pocket and desperately tore two pieces from it to make earplugs that would keep the painful voices out of my brain. I couldn't work out what they had to talk about, was there really that much to say about art? I recollected whenever I'd been at the opening of an exhibition it was as if the walls were blank for the amount of attention was paid to what was on them. All of these thoughts served to make me feel more isolated than I was already feeling. I felt like jumping on the table and screaming at the top of my lungs for them to shut up and stop their incessant chattering. But I knew if I did that, they wouldn't even notice. Perhaps they would stop for a few seconds and then carry on as if nothing had happened, like when a stranger enters the bar of a country pub.

At last everything was cleared away and pots of coffee were brought in with the accompanying cups, saucers and spoons. But this led to a different, equally irritating din of cups hitting saucers, and spoons hitting cups, and spoons falling and hitting saucers. Then the chatter started up again and brandy glasses were brought together over and over again. I held my fingers in my ears to see if that would help to keep it all away. Katherine asked me again if I was all right and I heard a voice inside me saying: I've got a slight headache, nothing more.

She asked me if I wanted to go and the voice said: I'm fine for a while.

She told me to tell her if it became too much and I wanted to leave. At last I saw that some people were getting up from the table and I looked at my watch. The time was only ten thirty, when I thought it had been way past midnight. Then all of the diners started to get up and move away from the table like one large, black centipede. I followed along behind Miles and the rest as they headed towards the front of the building where we'd arrived, what seemed like a lifetime ago. It was exactly the same as when the crowd exits a play in the West End. First there's the queue for the cloakroom and then the interminable wait for transport to arrive. While we were waiting in line for our various coats, I thought I spotted Manish Kumar putting on a heavy topcoat behind us, near some restrooms and I was surprised that he hadn't told me he'd changed his mind about attending. I watched as he pulled a scarf and some gloves from his pockets, and realised he must have been finding the chill air of Venice quite a change from what he was used to back in India. It was then my turn to retrieve my coat, and after I did so I looked back, but he'd disappeared.

About fifteen minutes later, Miles managed to get two gondolas for us. I almost capsized one of them as I drunkenly lost my footing whilst trying to get on board. Finally we were all seated and heading back to the hotel. Miles and Katherine were keen to have a drink at the bar with Jake and Dinos, but Edith wanted to turn in and Ann had to check on Celia and Darcy. I left too and went up to our room. I took off my shoes and socks and splashed some cold water over my face before lying down on the bed. I couldn't get the image of Kumar out of my mind, standing there pulling on his gloves. What was he doing there? I distinctly remembered him telling me he couldn't attend.

I must have fallen asleep and was woken up by the sound of Katherine hammering loudly on the door. I got up to let her in and she waltzed straight past me, commenting on the full moon that was up in the sky outside. She went onto the balcony and told me to come out and take a look at it with her. I winced to hear the imperious tone that always accompanied her heavy drinking and I despised her yet again for bossing me around. Now I knew how her paintings had felt, being manipulated the whole time. I wanted to break free from Katherine. I saw her silhouette framed by the moonlight outside and knew it was the moment I'd been waiting for. I moved towards her with my hands stretched out and broke into a run, but the carpet beneath my feet slid forward on the slippery marble floor. I closed my eyes and felt cold air streaming over my face. I thought I heard the claxon of a train sounding as it passed, but realised it was my name being called out.

'JAAA . . . MIEEEEE!'

The sound faded away, and I opened my eyes in time to see my portrait rapidly approaching me in the deafening silence of a dream.

Chapter 35

James Thornberry (1964–2007) an established and successful British botanical writer, drowned within yards of the Bridge of Sighs on the opening night of the Venice Biennale. He was attending the event with his wife, the internationally known portrait painter, Katherine Gaunt, who was representing Australia there. They had been married only several days. He fell from his room at the Hotel Al Ponte Dei Sospiri, and for a while the authorities suspected his wife of pushing him from the balcony, thus murdering him. She was arrested but later released for lack of a motive or any evidence. Her first husband, Lawrence Hardwicke, a celebrated British sculptor, had also died in a drowning accident, on the island of Lamu eighteen months previously, but she had not been present. Coincidentally, James Thornberry had been an eye witness to her first husband's death. Friends and relatives all attested to his increasing depression and isolation in the months leading up to his death and it was suspected he had taken his own life. He was an avid collector of his wife's work. His body was found in the canal with no shoes or socks on.